Praise for the Crochet Mysteries

"A gentle and charming novel that will warm the reader like a favorite afghan. Its quirky and likable characters are appealing and real."
—Earlene Fowler, national bestselling author of *The Road to Cardinal Valley*

"[A] charming mystery. Who can resist a sleuth named Pink, a slew of interesting minor characters, and a fun fringe-of-Hollywood setting?"
—Monica Ferris, *USA Today* bestselling author of *Knit Your Own Murder*

"Crochet fans will love the patterns in the back, and others will enjoy unraveling the knots leading to the killer."
—*Publishers Weekly*

"[These] characters are so unique that they are not easily forgotten! They are witty and charming, a perfect group of crafters to have an armchair adventure with. . . . Absolutely stunning."
—Open Book Society

"Betty Hechtman does it all so well: writing, plotting, and character development."
—Cozy Library

"[An] enjoyable series with likable characters."
—The Mystery Reader

"Crocheters couldn't ask for a more rollicking read."
—*Crochet Today!*

"Betty Hechtman has written an enjoyable amateur sleuth featuring a likable lead protagonist who has reinvented herself one stitch at a time."
—Genre Go Round Reviews

"Combining a little suspense, a little romance, and a little hooking, Betty Hechtman's charming crochet mystery series is clever and lively."
—Fresh Fiction

Hooking for Trouble

BETTY HECHTMAN

BERKLEY PRIME CRIME
New York

BERKLEY PRIME CRIME
Published by Berkley
An imprint of Penguin Random House LLC
375 Hudson Street, New York, New York 10014

Copyright © 2016 by Betty Hechtman
Excerpt from *Yarn to Go* by Betty Hechtman copyright © 2013 by Betty Hechtman
Penguin Random House supports copyright. Copyright fuels creativity, encourages
diverse voices, promotes free speech, and creates a vibrant culture. Thank you for buying
an authorized edition of this book and for complying with copyright laws by not
reproducing, scanning, or distributing any part of it in any form without permission.
You are supporting writers and allowing Penguin Random House to continue to
publish books for every reader.

BERKLEY is a registered trademark and BERKLEY PRIME CRIME and the B colophon
are trademarks of Penguin Random House LLC.

ISBN: 9780425279458

First Edition: November 2016

Printed in the United States of America
1   3   5   7   9   10   8   6   4   2

Cover art by Cathy Gendron
Cover design by Rita Frangie
Book design by Kristin del Rosario

In Memory of Linda Hopkins

Acknowledgements

It was a pleasure working with Julie Mianecki on this manuscript. As always, Jessica Faust helped me keep on top of things. I feel like the Berkley art department peeked into my imagination for the wonderful cover they designed.

Once again Linda Hopkins was a wonderful help with the pattern and so much else. It makes me sad to know that she won't see this thank you.

Thanks to Roberta and Dominic Martia for all the support and encouragement.

My knit and crochet group have offered friendship, yarn help, life advice and some laughs. Thank you Rene Biedermann, Alice Chiredjian, Terry Cohen, Tricia Culkin, Clara Feeney, Sonia Flaum, Lily Gillis, Winnie Hineson, Linda Hopkins, Reva Mallon, Elayne Moschin, Anna Thomsen and Paula Tesler.

Burl, Max and Samantha, you will always be the best!

CHAPTER 1

"THAT YARN IS GOING TO CHOKE ME," ELISE BEL-mont said, trying to pull the pink fibers off her tongue. More of them floated on the air, tickling the noses and sticking to the clothes of everyone in the vicinity of Adele Abrams.

"I don't know what you're fussing about," Adele said, holding up the piece on her long crochet hook. The move made more of the mohairlike fibers come loose, and they floated my way. Before I could swipe them from the air, they'd landed on my black sweater.

"I hope you're not using that yarn to teach the class," Mrs. Shedd told Adele. As an afterthought, she added, "You didn't buy it here, did you?" She looked at the rows of cubbies holding yarn in the back part of the bookstore.

Adele was befuddled by everyone attacking her yarn. "No, I'm not using it for the class, and no, I didn't get it here. It's just the perfect color for my honeymoon shrug," she said. She held it out to display the color, and the whole group of Tarzana Hookers tried to shield their faces from the onslaught of loose fibers. Adele looked at the label on the skein of yarn. "It's just a mixture of mohair and some other stuff. I might have bought it at Bargain Circus," she said offhandedly.

We were at one of what our crochet group, the Tarzana Hookers, called our happy hour get-togethers. Some people have a cocktail to release the tensions of the day—our group used crochet.

The conversation and friendship probably helped, too. The Tarzana part of our name referred to the San Fernando Valley community, where Shedd & Royal Books and More was located. The bookstore where we met had a lot of space and had recently added a yarn department, which I was in charge of, along with my other duties as event coordinator and assistant manager.

Adele Abrams worked at the bookstore as well. She was in charge of the children's department. It hadn't been her choice. Really, Adele had wanted the position I'd gotten when I was first hired: event coordinator. She'd been given the children's department as a consolation prize.

Adele made an immediate segue from the honeymoon shrug to her upcoming wedding.

"Have I shown you the photos of the venue?" she asked. The group nodded while trying to hide that they were rolling their eyes. Adele produced the pictures on her phone anyway and showed them around.

"That's the lake, where you can have your ceremony on a barge." She waited until everyone acknowledged that they'd seen it. She flipped through the rest of them and showed off the rose garden with a gazebo for a ceremony, a small chapel, and several small outside areas. "That's the one Cutchykins and I are using," she said when she got to the last one. It featured an outdoor seating area on a slope that looked over the lake. I only hoped there wasn't going to be a barge wedding happening at the same time. Adele was busy pointing out the gazebo, which would be decorated with the bride's colors of choice. The reception was to be in a small cottage that was completely devoted to Adele's event.

I nudged my friend Dinah Lyons. "Why don't you reserve one of those spots? The barge might be nice." She knew I was joking and made a face at the ridiculousness of it.

"That kind of place isn't for Commander and me. I'm too old for that kind of showy stuff," she said. Dinah was somewhere in her fifties. She kept the exact number quiet, even from me. Commander was in the same age range—she was divorced and he was widowed. She'd been okay with keeping their relationship uncommitted, but he'd wanted it all to be proper and legitimate, so she'd finally agreed to become Mrs. Blaine.

"Hmm, two upcoming weddings," Rhoda Klein said, looking up from the doll she was making. "You do know they always say things go in threes."

When I looked up, the whole table was staring at me. "No way," I said. "I'm fine with things the way they are, and so is Mason." There was so much baggage that came with middle-aged dating. His kids, my kids. My late husband, his ex-wife. It was enough that we had decided to belong to each other, though I'm not even sure either of us knew what exactly that meant. I thought it was an adult version of going steady.

I brought up the schedule, glad to be able to change the subject. "Adele, it's time for your class."

Adele pursed her lips at me, no doubt annoyed that I'd

spoken first. "Okay, put away your projects and make room for our new students." Adele began patrolling the table to make sure everyone did as she'd ordered.

We had tried putting on what we called Yarn University at the bookstore and it had been a tremendous success. Mrs. Shedd was always looking for new revenue streams, so had urged me to keep offering classes. Part of my duties as event coordinator slash head of the yarn department slash assistant manager was to run the classes. It made sense, since they were events at the bookstore.

The plan was to offer a new group of classes each month. The class about to begin was in Tunisian crochet. The technique produced stitches that had a different texture than regular crochet and almost resembled knitting. Adele began to lay out a selection of long hooks and hooks with cables attached as people began to come in.

My job was to be the greeter, so I stood at the entrance of the yarn department and checked people off as they arrived. There were going to be five of the Hookers and five outside students. CeeCee Collins came sailing across the bookstore first.

"Sorry I missed happy hour, dear," she said, giving me a hug. CeeCee was our resident celebrity. Her career had spanned decades and, until recently, she'd always been referred to as a veteran actress, which really meant old and on the back burner. But then CeeCee had gotten a supporting lead in *Caught by a Kiss*, a movie about a vampire who crocheted, and her new position was cemented when she was nominated for an Academy Award. CeeCee was self-absorbed, but at the same time she had an incredibly generous spirit.

She took an empty seat and folded her hands on the table like a polite student.

Our next arrival seemed a little prickly. When I asked her name, she leaned over and pointed to it on my clipboard with several rapid taps. "Susan Dryer," she said. She glanced over at the table with obvious disdain before asking where the instructor would be. When Adele waved her hand, Susan took the seat adjacent.

"Lauren Plimpton," the next arrival said. "My sister was going to come, too, but she flaked." I glanced up at her. She was dressed in comfortable jeans and a fuzzy gray hoodie. My immediate impression of her was that she was quiet and would be no trouble, which was good, since I'd already given the trouble spot to Susan. When Lauren was asked to tell us about herself, she hesitated before saying she was divorced with two kids and she'd learned how to crochet when she had to do a lot of waiting around, but gave no more details.

Susan didn't need an invitation to give us her bio. She assured us that she was a very experienced crocheter who could have taught herself Tunisian crochet, but she decided it would be interesting learning from a qualified instructor. "You are qualified?" Susan said, peering over her glasses at Adele.

Adele took the comment as a reproach, and I hastily stepped in. "I can assure you that Adele is an excellent instructor whose love of crochet is legendary." Susan made a noise like she wasn't completely satisfied with my answer.

"Well, then, let's get started," Susan said in a sharp voice. "And what's with all this pink fuzz?" She tried to brush some fibers off the sleeve of her dark green jacket.

"We're still waiting for a couple more students," I said. "Sorry about the fibers." I tried to brush them off the table, but they floated up into the air.

I sighed. On top of dealing with the annoying fibers

and surly students, today was my birthday, and nobody had remembered other than my best friend. I had been trying to hide my disappointment, but Dinah picked up on the slight pout my mouth had slipped into. "We'll celebrate after class," she assured me. "Le Grande Fromage, my treat."

"I can't believe everybody forgot," I said, glancing over the group. It wasn't like it was just any birthday. It was the big five-oh. "Well, Mason sent me flowers and a sweet note apologizing again for having to be out of town. And my parents called from Santa Fe."

Adele gave me a sharp look and spoke under her breath. "What's your problem, Pink? You seem out of sorts. We don't want you bringing everybody down."

Having her call me by my last name used to bother me—she'd started doing it to annoy me because I'd gotten the event coordinator position over her so long ago. But by now I was sure it was just habit and she didn't even remember why she did it. "You want to know why I seem upset?" I started, all set to tell the truth. I was shocked when Dinah just about physically pushed me out of the way and spoke for me.

"Molly is just bummed out about the huge house going up behind hers. The yard isn't even finished, but somebody has already moved in," Dinah said. I didn't know why she'd stopped me from mentioning my birthday, but I let it go, because just then two more students arrived.

They came in together, and I understood their situation right away. They were actually touching arms as they got to the table. It didn't matter that they introduced themselves separately as Terri and Melody—they were like one unit. Naturally, they chose seats next to each other.

The last arrival was a lone woman with a small dog in one of those dog strollers. Her name was Fanny and the dog's name was Oscar. Susan looked at both of them. "Oh, puleeze," she said with an annoyed roll of her eyes. "Can we get started now?" Susan asked in an even sharper voice. Adele nodded and began her spiel.

The first class was really just an introduction and a chance for everyone to learn the basic afghan stitch and get their supplies. I spent most of it helping everyone get their specialized hooks and yarn. When the class broke up, we had all made several swatches and were comfortable with the new technique.

"Who would have expected Adele to be such a good teacher?" Dinah said as we went down the street to the French bistro. It was a beautiful day out—the April weather in Southern California could be all over the place, but usually most of the rain was over for the year and the temperatures were milder.

"As long as she's only dealing with crochet," I countered. The Tarzana Hookers all thought crochet was the superior yarn craft, but Adele took it to an extreme. That's why I ended up in charge of the yarn department and Yarn University. Mrs. Shedd insisted that we include knitting supplies and classes, and Adele simply couldn't handle that.

I appreciated Dinah's attempt at celebrating my birthday, and I suppose I should have been grateful the counter guy didn't stick a candle in my croissant and sing "Happy Birthday," but it was still pretty depressing. The place was about to close, and we were the only customers.

Dinah offered to come home with me, but I said I'd be fine. I was already planning to make a bowl of caramel corn and watch a double feature from my collection of favorite comedies.

I knew there was something wrong as soon as I went through my back gate. The dogs were loose in the yard and Cosmo, Felix and Blondie all ran up to me. I turned on the floodlights that illuminated the yard, from the garage. When I got close to the back door, I saw it was ajar. It was dark inside, but my house wasn't supposed to be dark—I had timers set to turn on the lights.

I pulled out my phone, considering calling 911, but what was I going to say? Still, I hesitated about going inside. Finally, I stepped close to the open door and listened, but heard nothing. I decided to call my son Samuel's cell phone and tell him the situation.

"Sorry, Mom," he said, "I must have forgotten to lock the door and the dogs must have opened it." Samuel was in his twenties and lived with me. I was going to say something about responsibility and bring up the lights being off, but before I could he had hung up.

I let out a sigh and went inside. I was feeling the wall for the kitchen light when something touched my hand. I automatically recoiled and made a move toward the back door, but the lights came on and there was a burst of noise.

"Surprise!" a chorus of voices said. I was sprinkled with confetti and streamers and saw that a bunch of Mylar balloons that said "Happy Birthday" were stuck to the ceiling.

Samuel came out of the crowd with a grin. "Fooled you, didn't we?" Mason Fields was just behind him. He gave me a big hug and handed me a glass of champagne.

I was mumbling something about his flowers and his being out of town. I was more than a little stunned. Dinah came in through the back door.

"Now you understand why I shushed you when you were going to grumble about your birthday," she said.

"Thank you for keeping me from making a fool of myself," I said, seeing that Adele and her fiancé were part of the crowd.

My mother pushed through. She started to wish me a happy fiftieth, but stopped herself. "If you're that old, what will people think I am?"

The Hookers were there, along with Mrs. Shedd and her partner, Mr. Royal. My older son, Peter, was in the group, too, giving his usual look of disapproval.

Mason and Samuel high-fived each other as they told me they'd planned the whole thing, then led me into the dining room. The table was laden with deli platters, and there was a triple berry cake from my favorite bakery. It was all a bit of a blur as I greeted everybody and accepted their good wishes.

Boy, did I ever feel guilty for all my bad thoughts that everyone had forgotten my birthday.

My mother pulled me aside in the kitchen, her armload of silver bracelets jangling. "I have another surprise for you," she said. "Your father and I have decided to move back to the Valley. Samuel said we could stay here tonight, and then tomorrow we'll move into a furnished place until we find something permanent. This way the girls and I can rehearse more easily before we go on tour again. And there are more opportunities here."

I was only half listening, thinking back to my mother's last visit, when she'd turned my living room into a rehearsal hall for her singing group. I never would have guessed that my mother would have a resurgence of her career at this time of her life. She and the girls, aka Bunny and Lana, had a group called the She La Las. They had basically one hit, "My Guy Bill," which turned out to have become a classic of sorts. They were back touring, doing nostalgia shows, and since they were in better shape than some of their contemporaries, they were doing other groups' hits as well.

I saw her looking around the kitchen. "You're not planning to use my living room again, are you?" I asked.

"No, we're going to get a real place this time. I was just looking out your kitchen window. What are those lights coming through the trees? I don't remember those from before."

I had been doing my best to ignore what was going on in the yard behind mine, but now that she'd brought it up, I gave her the lowdown.

Previously there had been a small house at the front of the property, with enough trees and bushes around it that it was invisible and my yard was completely private. There had never been any reason to put coverings on the large kitchen windows, the French doors in the dining room, or the row of windows in the den, all of which looked out on my backyard.

Recently, though, the small house had sold and a developer had knocked it down. A gigantic two-story house had been built in its place. The way the property was situated, the side of that yard ran along the back of mine. Even worse, the developer had raised the whole yard up so that the house sat on a small hill, making it loom even larger over mine. All that was between us were the redwood trees in my yard and the ancient chain-link fence with some ivy growing on it.

"Lately, I noticed there were lights on in the house and the building noises seemed to have stopped, which makes me believe somebody moved in, even though it doesn't seem quite finished."

"There goes my plan for nude sunbathing," my mother said with a laugh.

"Time for presents," Mason announced as he swept me toward the dining room.

"Presents?" I said, amazed there could be more. The Hookers had all made me something. Elise presented me with a black-and-white beanie with red trim, explaining it was made from her latest vampire style kit. We all knew that Elise was obsessed with Anthony, the vampire from *Caught by a Kiss*, who crocheted to control his blood lust. Everything she made was what she called vampire style which meant that she used half double crochet stitches, which resembled fangs, and made everything in black, white and red. The black was for Anthony's color choice for clothes, white for his pale skin and red—well, that was obvious.

Rhoda was heavily into felting now and had made me a crossbody bag. The felting process made the crochet stitches disappear into a solid-looking fabric. Sheila gave me the project from the class she'd taught. It was called a hug and was done in hazy blues. Our one male member, Eduardo, presented me with a lacy scarf done in his specialty—Irish crochet. Adele's present was a surprise. She had crocheted a black tote bag that had samples of all the different crochet stitches in bright colors attached to the front. Dinah's gift was a long skinny scarf like the ones she wore, done in rainbow colors.

Samuel had written me a song, which he performed with my mother. Then Peter handed me his gift. I wasn't sure what to expect from him, since mostly what he seemed to want was for me to keep a low profile and not do anything to embarrass him. He was an uptight and very ambitious television agent. I think he was still angry at me about his name. Honestly, when he was born, I never thought about initials. I just thought of Peter the Great, not Peter Pink. I would have named him something else if I'd realized his initials would be *PP*.

I shook the box, trying to figure out what it was. I assumed it would be something practical, something to remind me how old I was. A heating pad, perhaps?

"Oh," I said, surprised when I saw the words "Junior Detective Game" on the box.

Peter chuckled. "I know how you like to get involved in mysteries. I thought this game would keep you away from the real thing."

Of course—a present with a message. I began to go through the contents. There did seem to be some kind of game, but along with it was a whole slew of equipment. I put on the Sherlock Holmes–style deerslayer hat and continued to look through everything.

"Wow," I said, holding up a container of fingerprint powder and a brush. There were tweezers, containers for evidence, a booklet on fingerprints, an ink pad and some paper. I found a booklet on forensics, along with a pair of binoculars and a magnifying glass. "What's this?" I said, picking up a bottle and reading the label. "It says it's used for finding traces of blood. This is quite a set," I said to Peter. "Thank you."

"This is the real stuff," Mason said, sorting through the supplies. Mason was an attorney whose clients were mostly naughty celebrities who no doubt had a lot of knowledge about evidence-gathering.

When I looked over to Peter, his smile had faded. "Really?" he said, sounding surprised. "I had no idea. Why don't I get you something else?" He had started gathering up all the jars and things, but I stopped him and insisted it was the perfect present.

The party ended early since it was a weeknight and everyone had an early day tomorrow. In the end, Mason and I were the only ones left. I put on the deerslayer hat and looked through the detective set again. I flipped through the pages on fingerprints and then looked at the booklet on forensics. I read a section about people always leaving something behind at a crime scene and taking something with them. "I certainly took something from the Hookers gathering." I plucked some of the pink fibers off my sweater and put them into a plastic bag from the set.

Mason chuckled and took a photo of me with the hat on. "I'm making that the background of my phone," he said, and fiddled with his phone before showing me the screen. There I was, wearing the hat and holding the bag of "evidence."

"Your son looked horrified when you started playing with the set."

"I'm sure he meant it as a joke gift, but it's great. Now all I need is a crime to solve," I said with a grin. I looked around guiltily. "Good, no one heard me."

"Let me help you clean up," Mason said, standing up and starting to gather the plates sitting on the table.

"You did enough putting on the party. I'll clear up." Mason had told me he had to go out of town and that was why he wasn't going to be there on my birthday. I had a feeling there was some truth in what he'd said, like the way people used their real initials when they gave a fake name. "And I'm betting you are really going out of town, probably tomorrow and very early."

"You got me," he said, putting up his hands in capitulation. "You're right on all counts, including a six a.m.

flight." He went on to give me the rest of the details. One of his bad-boy clients who kept having scrapes with the law was having a movie release party for himself in New York and had commanded Mason's presence. Mason put his arm around me affectionately. "That kid is my retirement fund. He gets in trouble like other people get a paper cut. He's just too young with too much money and too much fame and no sense." Mason still wanted to stay behind and help clean up, but I insisted he leave and get at least a little bit of sleep before he had to go.

"Thank you for the best birthday surprise ever," I said.

"There will be more celebrating when I get back," he said as I walked him to his car. Mason chuckled. "I think the biggest surprise was for Peter when he saw what was in the game he got for you." He put his arms around me and I moved into the hug.

"I don't suppose you want to come home with me," he said when neither of us made a move to break the embrace. He couldn't see it, but my eyes went skyward. With both his daughter, who didn't like me, and his ex-wife living at his place right now, there was no way I was going there.

He read my thoughts. "Brooklyn is going to be there for a while," he said, referring to his daughter, who had decided to follow in his footsteps and go to law school. "But Jaimee's days are numbered."

"What?" I said. "That sounds like you really have plans to get rid of her permanently."

He laughed at my comment. "No, I haven't put out a hit on her—I'm trying to match her up with somebody. Somebody who will marry her, and then I won't have to feel responsible for her anymore."

"Good luck with that," I said.

"I could stay here," he said, looking back to my place.

"Not going to work." I told him about my parents staying over and that Samuel had already put their things in my room. "I'll be sleeping in the tiny spare room on a single bed with a bunch of dogs and cats." I stopped. "Oh no, the cats." I hadn't seen them since I'd been home.

"They're okay," Mason said. "Samuel put them in your crochet room to keep them out of trouble."

"Keep them out of trouble? How about put them in a room with nothing but trouble," I said, picturing two cats in a room full of yarn. "I better go inspect the damage."

Mason rocked his head. "So many complications in a relationship. All the family baggage and animal baggage. Remember when the biggest issue was what movie to see?"

We both laughed, and then, after a long, sweet kiss, he got in his car. I stood in the driveway until he pulled away.

When I got back inside, Samuel was on his way out the front door. He waved and wished me another happy birthday. He added that he was going to catch up with some musician friends at a bar. My parents had retired to my room. I bypassed everything and went to let the cats out. My son had brought them with him on one of his moves back home. I suppose they were technically his, but I felt responsible for them. The big black-and-white male was named Holstein because of his coloring, but somehow that had morphed into Mr. Kitty because of his affectionate nature. The calico came with the name Cat Woman, but it had been shortened to just Cat.

They scampered out as soon as I cracked the door. I was afraid to look in the room, but found just one ball of yarn unraveled. I followed them into the kitchen, expecting they'd want some cat food, but Mr. Kitty was already at the back door, which I realized I'd forgotten to lock. Before I could cross the room, he had used his claws to pull open the door and the two of them had taken off into the dark yard.

The spots of darkness reminded me that several of the floodlights had burned out. When it was daytime, I forgot, and when it was dark I didn't want to get up on a ladder to change them. I wasn't even counting the two-bulb fixture attached to the top of the garage. Changing those would require me to get on the top step of the ladder, which I didn't want to do even in the daylight.

The cats seemed to have disappeared. The binoculars from the detective set were still around my neck, and I lifted them to see if they would help me locate the errant felines. Too bad they weren't night vision scopes. I laughed, thinking of what Peter's face would have looked like if there'd been one of those included in the set. It was a lot more sophisticated than I would have expected, but then again, I'd noted earlier that it had been put together by a university's forensics department.

I went to the back of the yard. It was wider than it was deep and stretched along almost the whole side of the property behind mine. The developer had stripped the ivy off their side of the old fence when they'd first started working on the property. I'd heard the plan was to put up a white vinyl fence, but so far the only barrier between the yards was the old chain-link. I was certainly grateful now that we'd planted the redwoods along the back of the yard. They at least blocked part of the view.

As I searched for the cats, I had to trample through the ivy that grew along the ground below the trees. It was springy and crunched under my feet. A long vine almost tripped me as I tried to get through it. Cat made a brief appearance and seemed to be chasing something. I didn't want to know what and hoped it would get away. Mr. Kitty was nowhere to be seen. I pressed through the vines and trees and got right up next to the fence. I saw a flash of something moving and realized the worst had happened. He'd gone over the fence into the other house's yard.

I had found an ancient gate in the fence a while back and realized this was the time to make use of the entrance. It hadn't been used in years, and dead vines ran through the openings. I finally managed to push it open just enough so I could squeeze through.

I started whispering Mr. Kitty's name. I could barely see the yard, except to note that it was all just piles of dirt. He must have heard me, because I saw he'd stopped in the middle of the yard. I whispered his name a few more times, hoping he'd run toward me. He was usually so good at coming when he was called that we referred to him as a cat-dog. Not tonight. He seemed to have remembered he was all feline, and if anything, he started to move in the opposite direction. I was considering sneaking across the open space to grab him when I heard voices. I froze and slipped back into the shadows. I glanced around, looking for the source of the sound, struggling to come up with a good reason for being in their yard.

It turned out not to matter. When I followed the sounds and saw that there were two figures on the second-floor balcony that was tacked on to the back of the house, they didn't seem concerned with what was going on in the yard.

I'd had a few conversations with the contractor regarding my concern about the drainage of the yard. Mostly I was worried that with the hill they'd created, the water and maybe the house would come pouring down into my yard when it rained. The contractor had blown me off, telling me it was all under control. He had offered a computer image of what the house was going to look like. The style was pseudo Cape Cod. He'd included images of the interior, too, so I knew the balcony came off an upstairs den.

If these were the owners, they certainly weren't a happy couple. They were moving oddly around the balcony, and it seemed as if they were struggling. I stayed hidden, hoping they'd go back inside so I could grab the cat.

I couldn't make out any words, but their tones sounded angry. Then I heard scuffling as they neared the edge of the balcony. One of them leaned over the railing and seemed about to fall. I took out the binoculars and got a better view of what was going on. The light from inside illuminated them enough for me to see it was a woman and a man. Was he trying to push her off the balcony? She seemed to be fighting him, and their voices rose. They moved away from the edge and then back again. Suddenly, the woman fell against the railing and leaned back so far, I was sure she was going to fall backward over it. The man seemed to be very close to her. Was he pushing her or trying to save her? I was about to cry out, but there was more scuffling. The man got ahold of the woman and seemed to be dragging her. I heard the distinct sound of a slap and crying as they headed inside.

I was stunned by what I'd just witnessed and was trying to figure out what to do. I could still hear them yelling. Apparently all the racket had scared Mr. Kitty, since he ran past me and got over the fence before I could squeeze through the gate. I saw that Cat was already back in the kitchen when I got there, and thankfully there was nothing with her. What should I do? I took out my cell phone and looked at it. The 911 I had punched in before the party was still there.

But what was I going to say, that I'd been creeping

around my neighbor's yard and heard them fighting? But what if I did nothing and he killed her?

There was one person I could call. We had been broken up for a long time and I hadn't seen him in months, but his number was still listed under my favorites. I hit the call button and the phone began to ring.

CHAPTER 2

"GREENBERG," HE ANSWERED IN A TERSE VOICE. Barry Greenberg was a homicide cop and my ex. I always hesitated over what to say after *ex* though. I refused to say *ex-boyfriend*, since he was in his fifties and it sounded stupid.

Since we'd been broken up for months, it didn't really matter anyway, but there was still a tie that bound us: Cosmo, the black mutt, was technically Barry and his son's dog, though he lived with me. Jeffrey came over every week or so to play with Cosmo and brush his long fur. He had a key, so my presence wasn't necessary.

I ignored the twinge of emotion at hearing Barry's voice and got right down to it. "I think one of my neighbors is trying to kill his wife."

"Molly?" Barry said since I hadn't identified myself. I heard just the slightest break in his cop voice. So I wasn't the only one who still felt a reaction. It seemed the question in his voice had been purely rhetorical, though, since he went right into asking me for details.

I quickly told him what I'd seen. "He was going to push her off the balcony and then he was dragging her inside when he hit her."

"Okay, I'll get a cruiser and check it out." I told him the location and urged him to hurry.

I waited to hear the whine of sirens, but there was only silence. I couldn't help pacing up and down near my front door, wondering if I should go out into the yard and see what was going on. I was about to head for the kitchen door when there was a soft knock at my front door.

Though it was quiet, Cosmo and Felix awakened instantly and rushed to the door to do watchdog duty. Of course, Blondie the Greta Garbo of dogs had not joined them. As soon as I opened the door a crack, Barry slipped in. Felix continued to bark, but Cosmo recognized Barry and made a play for attention.

"Well?" I said impatient to hear the details as Barry gave the black mutt a hello pet. Felix stood his ground until Barry crouched down and held his hand out. The gray terrier mix approached him hesitantly, but seemed to take a hint from Cosmo and decide Barry was okay. After a sniff, he let Barry ruffle his fur.

"Well?" I said again. "Are you going to tell me what happened?"

Barry blew out his breath and looked directly at me. "Where exactly were you when you saw what you thought you saw?"

I led him into the kitchen and pointed out the large windows that looked out onto the yard. "I was back there," I said.

"Could you be more specific?" he asked.

"Okay," I said. "I used an old gate and went into their yard." I quickly added that it was because of the cats. Barry shook his head with dismay.

"Molly, that's trespassing."

"It was a cat emergency," I countered. "Anyway, I could have seen the same thing from my yard." To prove it, I took him outside and we went to the back of the yard. True, we had to squeeze in next to a tree and hang on to the gate, but I was able to point out the back balcony on the house. "What is it?" I said. "Did he kill her and you need me to be a witness?"

Barry's cop face broke, and he smiled. "No. How about you completely misread what was going on," he said. "I'm just glad I had the good sense not to come with sirens and flashing lights."

When we were back inside, he finally gave me the details. "What they said was that they were practicing the tango for some television dancing show and what you saw as abuse was simply drama."

"What?" I said, incredulous. "I'm telling you, I heard a slap, and the woman sounded like she was crying." I paused a moment as what he said sunk in a little more. "Did you see them both?" I asked. "Did you check her for bruises?"

"Molly, they were very cordial and didn't seem to be hiding anything."

"Did you look around?" I asked.

"Yes. They showed us that their kids were asleep. Apparently it was the live-in nanny's night off, because she came home while we were there." He looked at me. "And no, she didn't have any bruises, either."

"Did you tell them who sent you over?"

"Don't worry. I just said a concerned neighbor called

us, but not which one." He appeared tired, but then that was his natural state. He'd been a detective so long that he'd learned how to survive on little sleep. There were shadows under his dark eyes and stubble was starting to show on his chin. He kept his dark hair cut short so that it never really looked mussed. He clothes still looked neat. He'd never divulged his secret, but I had a feeling he'd somehow found clothes that never wrinkled. He gave me that look, the one that was somewhere between scolding and teasing. "You do realize you have crime on your mind all the time."

He suddenly seemed to notice the confetti that was still on the floor and the balloons stuck to the ceiling. "It's your birthday," he said. He glanced at his watch and, seeing that it was after midnight, said, "It *was* your birthday. I'm sorry. I forgot."

"You're not under any obligation now that we're . . ." I searched for a title. ". . . just sharing custody of a dog," I said finally.

It seemed to register that it was a big birthday for me. "Even so, I should have remembered your birthday." He hesitated. "Particularly since it is an important one." He said the last part gingerly, as if he was testing the waters to see if I was going to be one of those people who claimed to stay forty-nine for life.

"It's okay. I can handle being fifty. I heard it's the new thirty, anyway," I said with a smile. Maybe it was bothering me a little, but I wasn't going to show it. "There's all kinds of food left," I said. "And cake." I led him to the dining room. "Are you hungry?" I asked.

"That's okay," he said. I noticed that he seemed to be avoiding even looking at the array of food.

"C'mon. Whatever you eat I won't have to worry about putting away."

"When you put it that way, it sounds like I'd be doing you a favor." He looked over the plates of cold cuts and side dishes hungrily. I knew only too well how Barry operated. He had trained himself to get by on little sleep and long hours without food. It was as if he was able to turn off his hunger, but once there was food available, it roared back to life. He was Mr. Self-control. I encouraged him to take lots of food and even take a plate home for Jeffrey. He made himself a roast beef sandwich on a brioche bun and then added some chopped Italian salad, roasted potatoes, truffle macaroni and cheese and some green salad. He pulled out a chair and began to eat with gusto while I cleared up the wrapping paper.

"You said my neighbors were practicing for a television dance show. Who are they?"

Barry put down his fork and flipped out his notebook and opened it. "Her name is Cheyenne Chambers. Or that's what she goes by. I suppose it is really Cheyenne Chambers Mackenzie. His name is Garrett Mackenzie, and he's her manager as well as her husband."

I saw that my mother had come across the house and was hanging in the shadows near the entrance to the dining room. Barry stopped to take a bite of the sandwich he'd made as she sailed into the room. "Cheyenne Chambers lives over there?" She turned to me. "You must know who she is. She and her sisters are the group ChIlLa." She pronounced it *Shyla*. "They had that hit that became a classic." My mother began to sing it. Not just sing it, but belt it out and do some footwork along with it. I remembered it. It was one of those songs that was supposed to give you hope that the next day would bring something better. My mother stopped after a few bars. "And now she's a judge on that program *Show Me Your Tune*." When I didn't seem to place it, my mother explained more. It was another one of those popular talent competition shows, but it was all about show tunes and production numbers.

"She really knows how to keep herself out there," my mother said. "Maybe I should take a lesson from her. I'll have to talk to Peter and see if he can help." I didn't say anything, but I was thinking, Good luck on that one. If Peter was concerned about me embarrassing him, I could just imagine his reaction to his grandmother wanting him to get her on a reality show. She was talking to me, but I noticed her throw Barry a dirty look. Not that he saw it. All his attention seemed to be on his impromptu meal. She'd never been a fan of us as a couple. The next dirty look was for me, and without a word I knew she was wondering what was he doing there and hoping I wasn't going to mess things up with Mason. She was a big fan of Mason's.

To keep the peace, I hustled my mother out of there and into the kitchen, where she gave me the mini lecture I'd expected. I let her think he'd just dropped by to wish me a happy birthday rather than explaining the real reason. I could only imagine what she would say if she knew that I had sent the cops to check on Cheyenne. I waited until she got mugs of herbal tea for herself and my father and retreated to my bedroom before I went back into the dining room.

I went to pick up the detective set Peter had given me, but Barry saw it first. "What's this?" he asked, reading the cover. He flipped open the box and smiled when he saw the deerslayer hat and the magnifying glass. Then he noticed the binoculars still around my neck. He tried to give me a stern look. "What were you doing out there—playing detective?"

I repeated that I had just been looking for the cats. Barry poked through the rest of it. "This is real stuff." He looked at the fingerprint powder and the bottle marked "Blood Detector." I explained that it was designed by the forensic department of some university and showed off the fingerprints I had collected from my guests.

"I suppose Mason gave it to you," he said. I corrected him and told him it was Peter.

Then I explained that Peter had gotten it as a joke and had thought it was just a board game.

I cut Barry a piece of cake and suggested he take some home to Jeffrey. "I feel bad not doing something for your birthday," he said. "I know you probably don't want another bottle of perfume, but how about this? I'll do a repair of your choice."

I should explain that Barry could fix anything—except maybe our relationship. Anyway, when we'd been together, literally everything in my house was in tip-top shape. Since then, well, there were quite a few things that needed attention. I thanked him and said I'd take him up on it, though I really didn't intend to.

There was an awkward moment at the door. I didn't know what else to do, so I patted his arm. "So that's what we do now," he said, giving my arm a mechanical pat. His lips curled into a half smile. Then he told me to stay out of trouble and thanked me for the food.

I shut the door behind him. And then I had a troubling thought: If Cheyenne and her husband had been practicing the tango, where was the music?

CHAPTER 3

MY MOTHER WAS IN THE KITCHEN WHEN I GOT UP the next morning. Something in the oven smelled good and I heard the whir of the blender. I could tell by the green color in the blender carafe that my mother was making her famous morning drink. It resembled pond scum, and the only way to drink it was by not looking at it.

She was pouring me a glass before I could get to the coffeepot. "This will wake you right up," she said, pushing it on me. I closed my eyes and started to hold my nose as well, but then the flavor hit me. It had a mild green taste, mixed with raspberry.

I was waiting for her to ask what Barry had been doing here last night, but she said nothing, and I took that to mean she didn't really want to know. She poured the rest of the drink in two glasses. "Your father lives by my green drink," she said.

"What's in the oven?" I asked, taking in the delicious scent.

"Granola. We like the homemade version so much more." She started to rattle off the ingredients and then said she'd leave me some.

"We're just going to stay in this furnished apartment for a month or so, until we find a place." She came over and gave me a squeeze. "It's going to be such fun to be so close to you. Maybe I'll join that crochet group of yours. It would be a great thing to do when I'm hanging around, waiting to go onstage." My mother smiled at me. "Isn't it fun how we're both in the midst of new chapters in our lives."

There was one little difference, though: Hers was by choice; mine was by necessity. When my husband died a little over three years ago, everything had changed. I had helped him in his public relations business, but wasn't in a position to take it over. I'd been suddenly adrift, with a lot of time on my hands, and lonely. The job at the bookstore had been a new beginning for me and had led me into the crochet group.

Thinking of my life now, it was hard to imagine how desolate I had felt right after Charlie died. My life now was full of yarn, people and pets. And Mrs. Shedd kept giving me more responsibilities at the bookstore.

The thought of those responsibilities whipped me back to the present. "I'm late," I said, putting the glass down.

"You should finish it," my mother said. "Look at all the energy I have." She did a little dance to prove it.

I laughed, then went to my room to grab some clothes and came back across the house to use the small bathroom to shower and get dressed. My mother was just taking the granola out of the oven when I zipped through the kitchen to the back door. The dogs and cats had figured out I was leaving, even though my pattern was different. They knew the drill and were sitting by the door.

I doled out a treat to each of them. My original plan had been to use the treats to keep them busy when I went out the door. I'd hoped they'd associate my leaving with something good. It didn't work. They expected the treats now, and they still stayed by the glass door looking sad as I walked across the yard.

I was just giving out the last treat when Mr. Kitty slipped out the door. I managed to get outside and shut it before the rest of them escaped, but he scampered across the yard before I could stop him. I ran after him, which only made him run faster. I caught up with him just as he got to the back fence.

"At least you didn't go over the fence this time." Going into the neighbor's yard under the cover of darkness was one thing, but with the sun out, no way. But as long as I was standing at the fence, why not have a look? Maybe if I looked in there now, it would all seem different. The house did look finished, but the rest of the place certainly didn't. I shuddered when I looked at the yard. It looked like a danger zone. I remembered hearing music playing there before and seeing workmen moving around in the yard. Now I realized that had been a while ago, and it seemed work had stopped.

It appeared a hole had been dug for a pool and some kind of framework had been put up on the sides. I gathered that the plan was to put in a patio below the balcony where all the action had taken place. But for now there were just boxes of pavers lying around the area. A tall shovel was stuck in the dirt, and a wheelbarrow rested on its side.

I remembered that Barry had mentioned kids and a

nanny. Seeing the condition of the yard, I guessed it must be off-limits to them. It was certainly no place to play.

I was relieved I'd managed to grab Mr. Kitty before he got into the neighboring yard. Now that I knew who was living there and it was light out, I didn't want to go past the fence.

I deposited the black-and-white cat inside and gathered up my belongings. Enough time had gone by that I had to give out another round of good-bye treats. This time I made sure no one slipped out the door with me.

I threw my stuff in the greenmobile, as I called my vintage blue green Mercedes. Frankly, with the way cars were these days, it was a relief to just put the key in to start it. Shedd & Royal was barely a five-minute drive away. In no time, I had pulled into the parking lot and was walking around the corner to the front door.

Since it was still fairly early, I wasn't expecting the commotion that greeted me. Mrs. Shedd was standing with someone and seemed to be fluttering around a woman. Mr. Royal was with a number of people carrying cameras. Rayaad, our cashier, was watching it all from her post at the front of the store.

"What's going on?" I asked. Better to be forewarned before I walked into something.

"Some local famous person brought her kids for story time. There were a bunch of photographers following her outside. Mrs. Shedd said they could come inside."

"Do you know the woman's name?" I asked.

Rayaad shrugged. "I didn't quite get it. I heard the guys with the cameras saying something about a show she was on. It had *Show* in the title."

I stopped in my tracks. It seemed almost too coincidental.

"Is it called *Show Me Your Tune*?" I asked. Rayaad nodded. "Her name isn't Cheyenne, is it?"

Rayaad's face brightened in recognition. "Yes, that's it."

I slipped to the side of the store and went into the café. Bob, our barista, was behind the counter putting together a bunch of drinks, but for the moment the place was empty. "What's going on?" I asked as he pushed another cup into one of the holders.

"A bunch of paparazzi were hanging out front when some celebrity showed up with her kids. I got to watch it all from here. She looked like she was all upset that they were waiting for her. Then Mrs. Shedd decided to let them in. I'd bet anyting she's making sure they get the bookstore name in their shots."

I asked Bob for a red eye. My mother's green drink might pep her up, but I still needed caffeine. The coffee with a shot of espresso added was just what I needed. Bob poured the coffee and got ready to make the espresso. Two men with cameras came into the café and stood behind me.

"What an actress," one of them said. "The fuss she made about us being out front." He laughed. "Right. The tip we got that she was going to be here was really anonymous."

The other man shook his head at the absurdity. "More like it was her husband."

"Nice of the bookstore gal to invite us in."

"I'm sure Cheyenne or her husband-slash-manager suggested it. Anything to get some publicity shots doing regular sorts of things." His associate nodded. I was glad that it was taking Bob a long time to make my drink, as I was curious about what they had to say. "Someone is always tipping us off on where she's going to be." Then they started to discuss the Internet and the constant need for content and how all the entertainment shows were looking for filler, too.

"It's kind of make it or break it for her group," the one with shaggy brown hair said. "How long has it been since they were hot? Their first album was a monster, and the second faded fast. If the one coming out next month tanks, they're over."

The other one, who was wearing a gray fedora, spoke up. "The word on the street is there's a track on it that will hit a nerve, like the monster hit they had on their first album. You know, one of those songs that everybody plays on Sunday night when they feel like their life is going under."

"Speak for yourself," his friend responded. "I don't need a song to pep me up. I just do this paparazzi stuff to support my real work. My real passion is photographing insects."

"Anyway, she's the one doing all the heavy lifting for the group," the guy with the gray fedora said. "She keeps getting herself on reality shows and talk shows. Ilona Chambers doesn't have to do anything. Being married to a successful country singer keeps her in the limelight and pays for everything."

Bob gave me a funny look since my drink was sitting on the counter waiting for me, but I hadn't taken it.

One of the photographers leaned around me and motioned toward Bob. "What do you have to do around here to get waited on?"

I took my coffee and went back into the bookstore. All the action was right around the information desk. Cheyenne was posing for a photograph with Mrs. Shedd. Then

Adele came over to the group in her Dorothy costume—they must have been reading *The Wizard of Oz* today—and began posing with Cheyenne, a blond woman I didn't know and the kids. There was a man hanging off to the side of the group. I hadn't gotten much of a view of him in the dark, but I was guessing it was Garrett Mackenzie, Cheyenne's husband. For all of Cheyenne's flash, he was pretty nondescript. Just this side of six feet, I guessed, with dark hair cut in a short style. He wore jeans and a graphic T-shirt with a leather jacket thrown on top. He walked over to adjust one of the little girls' jackets so that the "I love the ChIlLas" clearly showed. He had the kind of walk that was all shoulders and said, *I'm important.*

I deliberately clung to the side of the bookstore and made my way to the yarn department. I didn't want to get caught up in the middle of everything, even though there was no reason for me to keep a low profile. There was no way Cheyenne knew I'd sent the cops.

"There you are," Mrs. Shedd said as I finished crocheting the last row of a pot holder. "Cheyenne was asking for you." Mrs. Shedd had a singsongy cadence to her speech, like she was being overly accommodating.

"Oh no." I dropped my crochet hook and it hit the table with a loud ping. I was wrong. Cheyenne knew it was me. I wanted to slide under the table and disappear. I could tell my boss was trying to make a good impression on Cheyenne.

I tried to pull Mrs. Shedd aside. "A funny thing happened after you all left my birthday party," I began. But it was too late to say more. I stood up and prepared for the onslaught as Cheyenne stepped up to the table.

What she did next totally surprised me. She didn't even look at me, but instead at the pot holder I'd been working on. "Crochet saved my life," she said, picking up my hook. Then she turned to me. "I understand that you have a crochet group and classes."

I stumbled over my words now that I realized she didn't know who I was or what I'd done. "Yes, we love crochet here." I indicated the big selection of crochet hooks.

I had a list of the classes in a plastic sheet and showed it to her. While she read it over, I got a better look at her. There was something gushy about her. Like she was trying too hard to be a regular person. I confirmed what Barry said. She had no visible bruises. I wanted so badly to ask her about her tango dance number, but I didn't want to take the chance that it would connect me to the previous night. She had a soft shape I could identify with. In other words, she was built like a normal person instead of a size zero model. She was dressed comfortably in black leggings and a long red sweater.

"This one is definitely for me," she said, pointing at the Tunisian class. Adele had joined us by now and quickly announced that she was the teacher.

"We've already started, but I'd be happy to give you a catch-up class," she said.

Cheyenne touched the puffed sleeves of Adele's blue-and-white-checked dress. "You look like somebody I can relate to. We considered using a photograph of us all dressing up as Alice in Wonderland for our upcoming album cover. We still have the outfits," she said with a smile before turning to me. "Sign me up for that, please." I told her when the next meeting was and then Adele spirited her away for the catch-up lesson.

Mrs. Shedd watched them go and, when they were out of earshot, turned to me. "You know I love having CeeCee in your group. She's certainly well-known. But Cheyenne has such a big personality, she's going to bring attention to the bookstore. Please don't do anything to mess this up, and make sure Adele doesn't either."

"What happened to her kids?" I asked, looking around the big space. I could see into the children's department, and it was empty except for Cheyenne and Adele.

"You know how it is with celebrities—they all have nannies for their kids. You must have seen her. A pretty girl with blond hair. She took the kids home already."

As she finished explaining, Mr. Royal came up to us, holding a frame. He handed it to Mrs. Shedd, and she smiled with pleasure.

She held it up for me to see, and I understood why she was smiling. It was a photograph of her with Cheyenne. It was meant to be a candid shot and showed the two of them talking while the nanny helped the two little girls put on their jackets.

As my two bosses admired the photograph, I thought how funny it was that they tried to give off the impression that they were merely partners in the bookstore. We all knew there was more going on. Pamela Shedd and Joshua Royal were a definite example of how opposites made a good team. She worried incessantly about the success of the bookstore, which, considering the current state of bookstores, seemed warranted. But to counteract all the online shopping, Mrs. Shedd had turned the bookstore into a cornucopia of attractions. We had all the usual bookstore activities, like author events and writers' groups, and of course, the Hookers met here, which had led to adding a yarn department. The crochet parties and Yarn University had grown out of the new addition.

Mr. Royal was always optimistic and seemed confident that everything would work out. Pamela—I never could bring myself to call her that out loud—looked her sixty-something age, though there wasn't a strand of gray in her honey blond hair and it still had a silky texture. Mr. Royal had a boyish quality due to the agile way he moved and his enthusiastic expression. His shaggy hair was getting more shot through with gray, but it just seemed to add an interesting dimension to the color.

For the moment, he was staying put, but in the past he'd taken off frequently to travel the world, doing all sorts of things. When I'd first started at the bookstore and Mrs. Shedd had mentioned her partner, he was nowhere to be seen and I'd thought he didn't exist. She was very patient about letting him take time off when he itched for an adventure. And all the traveling had left him with lots of skills.

"I was thinking we could start our own gallery," Mr. Royal said. "All the stores around here have photographs with their celebrity clients, so it's time we did, too." He suggested a prominent place near the cash register that would be hard to miss. He went off to get a hammer while Mrs. Shedd let out a satisfied sigh. Then she looked to me.

"Molly, you started to tell me something about last night."

CHAPTER 4

WHEN I FINALLY GOT HOME THAT NIGHT, ALL signs of my parents' visit were gone. I moved my slippers and such back to my bedroom, glad to have my space again. "It's going to be great having them here," Samuel said when I came into the kitchen. He gestured to a canister on the counter. "She left some of her famous granola, and there's a green drink in the fridge. She said I ought to make sure you drink it." He winced as he looked at me, knowing that was an impossible task to have been given. I knew it didn't taste bad, but I just couldn't get past the pond-scum look.

He was making himself a grilled cheese and tomato sandwich and offered to add one for me.

"A much better offer than the drink," I said, and he went to put together another sandwich while I took out a container of tomato bisque soup and poured it into a saucepan.

Samuel saw me looking at the living room. "Don't worry. They won't be rehearsing here. They're going to get a real rehearsal hall before they go on tour again, and in the meantime, they can use the rec room at the place they're staying."

I was glad to see my younger son seeming so cheerful. He loved his grandmother, and he loved that he was the musical director for her group.

We ate our soup and sandwiches together, and then he was off for an open mic night at a pizza place.

The house seemed very quiet after the previous night. Mason called to let me know he'd arrived and missed me. Dinah called as well. She and Commander were discussing their wedding plans, and it was making her anxious. To help, he'd offered to take it all over so that all she'd have to do was show up. I think he'd figured it was a good way to keep her from getting cold feet. She thought it didn't seem fair for him to do it all, and they'd agreed to work on it together, but he was taking the lead.

I told her about the episode after the party. She was more interested in hearing about Barry than about my neighbors' dancing routine. "I wondered about inviting him to the party," she said. "But I was afraid it might seem awkward. But it seems like fate took care of it."

In the background, I heard Commander calling Dinah to look at a menu for their wedding breakfast, so I let her go.

I think there's some kind of saying about idle hands getting in trouble. It was certainly true for me. I tried crocheting for a while, but I felt restless. The detective set was just sitting there, waiting for me to play with it.

I unpacked everything and then looked at the game portion, which was all my son Peter had noticed. But I wasn't much interested in games after being part of the real thing. I picked up the binoculars and looked out through the French doors at my yard. It was only dimly lit, thanks to the burned-out bulbs. But bright enough to see a flash of black-and-white run across the yard.

I got up and went to the kitchen, where I saw the door was ajar. Samuel must have just gone out it without locking it behind him, again. Mr. Kitty was an escape artist, and Cat had made use of the open door. I saw her on the prowl. They were both headed right to the back fence.

I felt pretty comfortable going to the back there since my yard was so dimly lit, and after seeing the condition of the neighbors' yard the day before, I was pretty sure no one was going to be out there.

I couldn't grab both of them at once. I went for Cat first, since she was more the hunter of the two. She'd left me a number of "gifts" in her time, and I really didn't want another one. Once I'd deposited her inside, I went back to get Mr. Kitty. I was relieved that he hadn't jumped the fence again, instead seeming content to rummage around in the ivy. I glanced up at the house in the next yard. There was nothing wrong with having a look, I figured. From this spot, I could see into the first-floor windows. I used the binoculars for a better view. It seemed a lot more peaceful than the other night. I recognized the nanny's long blond hair as she sat strumming a guitar for the little girls. A man walked in, and I knew he wasn't Cheyenne's husband, Garrett. This man seemed shorter, with a much slighter build, and he was wearing a cowboy hat with the sides rolled up. Of course, it had to be Ilona's husband.

I had gotten the 411 on the singing group from my mother. Cheyenne was the leader of the group, and her sister Ilona did some acting and was married to a country singer. My mother didn't say much about the third sister other than that she wasn't at all like the other two. I struggled to remember the country singer's name. Matt Meadowbrook. I don't know what it was exactly about his body language, but I could tell he was watching the nanny with interest. I heard someone walking in the yard and slipped back into the shadows just as I recognized the distinctive gait of Garrett Mackenzie. He stopped outside the window and looked in. What was that about? Was he spying on his own family? Was I imaging something sinister in his body language, like he wasn't happy with what he was seeing? Maybe Barry was right, that I did have crime on the brain and saw everything through that filter.

But anybody who knew anything about show business divorces lately knew that it had become a cliché for the husband to get involved with the nanny. Was it something like that? Matt Meadowbrook seemed to be eyeing her, too. Was Garrett jealous? I don't know why these celebrity women hired such pretty young women. Personally, I would have been looking for somebody who looked like Mrs. Doubtfire.

Garrett must have heard Mr. Kitty rustling in the ivy, because he turned in our direction, and I was glad I hadn't changed the bulbs—I was invisible to his gaze. He muttered something and went around to the front. I heard a door shut.

"Enough detective work for one night," I said to Mr. Kitty when I finally snagged him.

The cat turned around and looked at me with his big greenish eyes. Was he on to me? Did he know that his escapes had become an excuse for me to spy on the neighbors?

CHAPTER 5

"WE HAVE A NEW STUDENT," I SAID TO THE GATHERING of the Tunisian crochet class. Adele shot me an unhappy look, no doubt thinking I was stepping on her territory as teacher. But since I was in charge of the whole Yarn University, I was really like the dean, so I thought it fair that I handle introductions.

It was the second meeting of the class, and Rhoda, CeeCee, Elise, and Dinah had shown up from the Hookers. Terri and Melody, the two women who seemed like one unit, as well as Lauren and Susan, were also present. Fanny wheeled Oscar in as I was speaking, inspiring Susan to let out another "Oh, puleeze." The dog jumped out of the stroller and into CeeCee's lap, which delighted her. Since it was right after the happy hour gathering of the Hookers, Sheila and Eduardo had moved to the end of the table and were just observing the class.

"I think you all will recognize her," I said, turning to see if she'd made an appearance yet. Cheyenne was just coming through the bookstore. She had a tote bag with the ChILLa logo and was wearing high-fashion jeans and a loose-fitting royal blue top under a jean jacket with the collar turned up. She'd thrown on a multicolored scarf, which completed the "perfect pop star doing everyday life" look.

"Sorry I'm late," she said when she reached the table. Everyone was nodding, so I was pretty sure the group knew who she was. Even so, I said her name and mentioned ChILLa and her position as a judge on *Show Me Your Tune*. "And is there something else?" I prompted, to see if she would mention whatever the supposed dance number was for. She looked at me blankly. "No, that's it for now. Of course, with our new album coming out, we'll be making the rounds of talk shows."

Rhoda asked where she'd learned to crochet, and Cheyenne seemed to stumble. "It was a while ago. I was staying somewhere and it was an activity." She quickly changed the topic to the class. "I've always wanted to learn how to do Tunisian crochet. Adele gave me a demo, but I can't wait to try it for myself. Tell me what I need to get started." She looked to me. I had already put together a kit with a hook attached to a cable and the assorted yarns for the project Adele had designed for the class.

Susan watched as I handed the supplies to Cheyenne. "Aren't you forgetting something?" she said in a pointed tone. "Doesn't she have to pay for her supplies, or do celebrity types get special treatment?"

"I can assure you, Cheyenne paid for her supplies just like the rest of you. I simply added it on to the price of the class for her."

Cheyenne simply ignored Susan and walked around the table. "Do you mind if I sit next to my sister?"

"Sister?" a bunch of us said together. Cheyenne seemed mystified. Then she chuckled. "Lauren, you're doing it again?" She turned back to the rest of us. "I bet she introduced herself as Lauren Plimpton and said she had two kids and nothing more." Cheyenne gave her sister a disparaging look. "I keep telling her she needs to have a persona even when she isn't onstage. My other sister, Ilona, certainly does. And look where it's got her. She's an actress and everybody knows who she is when she walks some red carpet event with her husband, Matt Meadowbrook. I'm sure you all recognize his name." She waited while everyone but Susan nodded in acknowledgment. Susan merely appeared annoyed.

Cheyenne gave Lauren a disparaging shake of her head before she continued. "You'd never guess that she was the same—just a minute," she said, interrupting herself, and then went across the bookstore to the music and video department. She came back a moment later holding a CD. "You wouldn't recognize her as the person sitting across the table," she said with a laugh, and then passed the CD around. I got the first look. Cheyenne was certainly right. On the cover of the CD, Lauren was sporting a rainbow-colored wig with a chopped-off, asymmetrical style. She was wearing a skirt about the length most figure skaters wore, which she'd paired with white thigh-high hose held in place by garters and chunky high-heeled shoes. She did not resemble the plain-looking thirtysomething mom across the table who seem baffled at being the center of attention.

I noticed that Mrs. Shedd was hanging at the edge of the yarn department, watching what was going on. Cheyenne gestured toward her while she spoke to her sister. "You ought to get them to hang a photo of you up by the front, like they did of me. We'll get Ilona to come in, and they can add her photo, too."

"Cheyenne, geez, I just came here to crochet."

Out of the corner of my eye, I saw CeeCee's eyes flash as she turned to look across the bookstore. "When did you start hanging up photos of your celebrity customers?" There was just a touch of anger in her usually cheery-sounding voice. The dog reacted to it and jumped off her lap and went back into his stroller. I could see CeeCee's point. She'd been a customer and head of the Hookers for a long time, and she was certainly a celebrity. She'd had a long career, and was currently having a whole new one, thanks to her role in *Caught by a Kiss*. She was recognized all the time, and customers often asked to snap selfies with her, even when she was in the midst of working with the crochet group.

Mrs. Shedd quickly realized her error and joined the group. "CeeCee, we'd be honored to have a photo of you. And you, too," she said, turning to Lauren.

"There you go," Cheyenne said, patting her sister on the back. Cheyenne seemed to have a naturally big personality, and it seemed natural for her to project it. Clearly, Lauren wasn't the same. "Wait until the new album comes out and everyone hears the song you wrote." Cheyenne addressed all of us. "It's really kick-ass, and I can't wait for you to hear it." She pulled her sister up. "We could sing a few bars for them."

"Not now," Lauren said, pulling free and sitting back down.

"You should talk to Molly about setting up something at the bookstore around the time of its release," Mrs. Shedd suggested. "You could sign CDs and maybe sing a number or two."

"Why wait? We could do something for this album."
She held out the CD she brought to show us. "Maybe we
could do something in two weeks." Cheyenne pulled out
her phone and began to check her calendar. I was stunned
at how fast she reacted. She certainly knew the meaning
of *seize the moment*.

"Molly," Mrs. Shedd prodded when I didn't react.

"Right," I said, backing away to get the calendar from
the information booth. When I returned, Susan was looking really steamed and beginning to tap her crochet hook
on the table in a most annoying manner. She shot us all a
disgusted look, put down the hook, and got up from the
table. "I'm not here for all this celebrity nonsense. I'm
going to the restroom, and when I come back this class
better start, or I want a refund."

We all watched her go, a little surprised by the sharp-
ness of her tone. We were even more surprised when Lauren spoke up. "And make that refund in cash," she said in
a perfect mimic of Susan's nasally voice.

ONCE WE GOT STARTED THE CLASS WENT ALMOST
smoothly. Adele had us all start our scarves, and she
helped Cheyenne catch up. Lauren's yarn choice caused
Adele to get flustered. She was the only one who had chosen different yarn from what was recommended. Adele
was convinced that the fuzzy nature of some of the skeins
was going to cause Lauren problems. She urged her to
reconsider, but Lauren was resolute.

Much to Susan's chagrin, we had treats. CeeCee brought
in some brownies her housekeeper had made. I was clean-
ing up and noticed a chocolate smudge on a plastic bag.
"Wow," I said to Dinah, "it's a fingerprint. I'm taking this

for my set." I put the whole bag into a paper sack and marked it with the date. Then I tried to re-create who was sitting where to determine whose fingerprint it was.

"Why are you bothering with all that?" Dinah said.

"You're right. I'm getting a little too carried away with collecting evidence—evidence of what?" I said with a laugh. Even so, I put it aside, planning to add it to my collection when I got home.

With the class over, I could have ended my workday, but Mason was still out of town and my son said he would feed the animals. "I don't know how you manage dealing with all the divas around here," Dinah said. She'd gotten a drink from the café and was sitting at the yarn department table, working on another pot holder. They were her go-to projects to carry around and work on when she didn't want to have to concentrate too hard.

"Thank heavens I worked out the date for Cheyenne before Susan came back and started a mutiny," I said. "It's a good thing we have Terri, Melody and Fanny to balance things off. I suppose I should include Lauren, too. I say if she wants to keep a low profile, it's okay with me, particularly regarding the class."

Dinah seemed to be in no hurry to leave, either. "Commander has a bunch of things for me to look over for our wedding. I don't get it. It's just going to be a simple ceremony at City Hall and then a brunch. How much planning do you have to do?"

"I think it's sweet it means so much to him," I said, and she softened.

"I guess it is. I'm sure everything will be fine once it's over with." She let out a sigh. "He wants to talk about where we're going to live."

Her mention of housing made me think of the monster

mansion behind me and all that had gone on there. I filled
Dinah in. "I'm sure glad that Cheyenne doesn't know I'm
the person who sent the cops over." I picked up some loose
strands of yarn and threw them away. "She's really big on
promoting herself. Don't you think if she was doing some
dance number on a TV show she would have mentioned it?"

Dinah looked up from her work. "I agree. She outdid
Adele in the center-of-attention department."

"If there's no dance routine, that would mean I was right
and there was some kind of altercation going on."

Dinah laughed at my word choice. "You're starting to
sound like a cop. *Altercation?* How about a family feud?"

I was getting ready to call it a night when Adele rushed
across the bookstore and back into the yarn department.
She threw her arms around me so hard I almost fell on the
table.

"Emergency, Pink, emergency!" She stopped only long
enough to swallow a sob. "I just saw on the news on my
phone that our wedding venue went bankrupt and they've
shut the doors permanently." She let go of me and flopped
into one of the chairs. "What am I going to do?"

CHAPTER 6

IT WAS THE NEXT NIGHT, AND I COULD HEAR THE landline ringing from across my dark backyard. I rushed to open the door and get to it before it went to voice mail.

"I was about to give up," Mason said after I managed a breathy hello. "I tried your cell and sent you a text." He sounded exasperated.

"Sorry," I said. I was behind the times. My phone was usually in my purse, where I might or might not hear it ring. I had turned off all the dings and dongs to signal texts and e-mails, too. The rest of the world might be staring at the screens on their phones, but I was more interested in what was going on where I was. "I was just going to check my messages and e-mails when I got home."

"I can't wait to get back," Mason said. "Miss me?"

"Of course," I said. We had talked every night since he'd been gone, but often only for a few minutes due to the time difference. Mason was in the dark about what had gone on in the house behind me. Really all we'd done was check in with each other. I would tell him about everything when he got back.

Samuel might have taken care of the animals, but he hadn't turned on the outside lights. While I talked to Mason, I flipped on the floodlights in the backyard. The number of them burned out seemed to have grown.

I said something about the lights being burned out and he suggested I get Samuel to change them.

I mumbled an agreement, knowing that the problem was remembering that the bulbs were burned out during the day when my son was there.

"I've got another call," he grumbled. "I'm sure it's my client." Mason sighed. "He couldn't even get through his movie release without getting into trouble. I have to go. He's a basket case. I hope we can settle everything tomorrow." I heard his voice brighten. "And then I can come home." I heard him chuckle. "If Samuel hasn't changed your light-bulbs by then, I will." Then after his usual "Love you," he was gone.

I looked out the kitchen window at my dingy yard and decided I wasn't waiting for anyone or even daylight. I would just do it and be done with it.

I dragged the ladder up to a fixture with its bulb out. I'd left the lights on so I wouldn't be working in the dark, but the downside was that unless I was very careful I could get an electric shock. It was dicey getting the big floodlight bulb out and settled on the ladder and then getting ahold of the new one. I was super careful to touch only the glass portion as I fit it into the receptacle. I turned it, and then suddenly there was light.

I checked the yard to see how much more was illumi-nated. Actually, I checked out the whole area. It always amazed me how much more I could see from a ladder. Now that I could easily see over the fence, I saw the lighted pool of my next door neighbor. I turned toward the back of my yard and saw that the light shone through a break in the trees into Cheyenne's yard and dimly lit the area at the base of the balcony. Light from their windows illuminated the area even more. As I looked closer, I saw that there seemed to be something on the ground.

Ignore it, I told myself. As if that was going to happen. I got down from the ladder carefully and walked to the back of my yard. I got right up next to the sagging chain-link fence and looked over it. There was definitely something long on the ground. There was just enough light to get a hint of the color blue. I strained to get a better view, and then I almost chocked on my breath. It wasn't something; it was someone.

I had to get help, so I sprinted across the yard. I rushed inside and reached for the landline, but I totally blanked out on what number to call. When I found my cell phone, it was easy—just hit the icon and the phone did the remembering. I heard the phone begin to ring on the other end. Barry got it by the third one. Before he'd gotten out his usual "Greenberg," I interrupted.

"You have to come. Right away," I said.

"Molly?" he said, his voice losing its professional cool. "What's going on?"

The words tumbled out. "They weren't dancing on the balcony the night of my party. It was just a cover story," I said, the words tumbling into each other. "And now someone is lying on the ground."

"What were you doing in that yard?" Barry said, suddenly going back to his cop persona.

"I wasn't in the yard," I said, feeling defensive. "I only

went in there before because Mr. Kitty got in there." I felt the need to make sure Barry understood, so I explained how I had been changing the burned-out floodlight.

"In the dark? Are you crazy? You could have fallen off the ladder."

"I wasn't in the dark. I left the lights on while I changed the bulb," I said.

That only seemed to make him more concerned that I could have electrocuted myself.

"*Electrocute* is a little strong," I countered. "I got a shock doing that once, and it's more like just a buzz." I glanced out the window at the yard, realizing we were wasting time. "It doesn't matter. There's someone on the ground, right below the balcony. You need to come and bring your troops. Paramedics, the whole crowd. And hurry."

"Let's not rush to any action just yet. The last time you were sure that couple was fighting, and when I checked it out, everything was fine. I still think it was probably true that they were doing what they said, practicing some dance number."

"There are so many reasons I don't buy that," I argued. "But I don't want to waste time explaining it now."

"Molly, if I go there again and it turns out to be nothing, they're going to think we're harassing them, or that someone is playing pranks on them by calling in reports on supposed emergencies. We've had a fair share of things like that with celebrities."

"I'm telling you, someone is on the ground. I don't know if they're injured or worse. If you're not going to get some of your people over here, I'll just have to go into the yard and see to them myself."

"No, Molly," Barry warned. "Don't even go back into your own yard. I'll check it out."

"Hurry," I said.

"Sure," he replied. But he didn't sound like he meant it.

I left the kitchen and went to the entrance hall and began to pace near the front door. Shortly, I heard the wail of sirens growing louder until they stopped nearby, and I let out a breath of relief. Then there was more waiting and pacing. I knew Barry would come to give me a report eventually. I wondered if he would apologize for not believing me at first.

I jumped at the knock on the door. I pulled it open before he had time to retract his hand. As soon as he saw me, he began shaking his head slowly.

"The person is dead," I said, feeling somehow that I'd failed to get someone there fast enough to save them. For the first time, I considered who the body might be. "I should have done something more."

"Stop," he said, putting up his hand to reinforce what he'd said. He came inside and shut the door behind him. "No one is dead. There's no one there." He looked at me sternly. He let out his breath and glanced toward the living room. "Could we sit down and talk about this?"

I led the way into the adjacent room and sat on the couch. He took a chair opposite me. "Are you going to tell me what's going on?" I said.

"Nothing's going on," he said. "I went there and brought the *troops*, as you called them. Cheyenne and her husband weren't even home. The babysitter—I mean nanny—answered the door. The poor girl seemed pretty shaken to see us. But who could blame her, having a bunch of cops and paramedics pounding on the door."

"But I'm telling you I saw something in the yard. I know it was a person."

Barry let out a heavy sigh. "The nanny's name is

Jennifer Clarkson. When I told her a neighbor had reported seeing someone lying in the yard, she let us look around."

"And?" I prompted impatiently.

"And we found a cushion from a chaise longue on the ground. She said the kids had been playing on the balcony since they couldn't go in the yard and had thrown one of the cushions over the side. She showed us the balcony, and sure enough, there was a yellow cushion on one of the chaises and nothing on the other one. Everyone is accounted for. The Mackenzies were at a taping of the program she's a judge on. I couldn't speak to her because they were actively taping, but I talked to him. The kids were sound asleep." He shook his head disparagingly. "And now I have to explain to my superior why we were there again."

I started to protest, but he stopped me. "You've got to stop seeing crime wherever you look." He took something out of his pocket and held out a plastic bag. It was one of the plastic specimen bags from my detective kit. "When we went out in the yard, Jennifer found this on the ground. I talked her into giving it to me. The last thing I wanted was for them to see something of yours in their yard."

I was confused until I remembered that I'd written my name and the date on the tab. "There are just some dog hairs in there from when I was practicing collecting specimens. I must have dropped it when I went in there looking for Mr. Kitty." I glanced up at him. "Thank you. You're right. I wouldn't want something with my name on it found in their yard." He dropped it on the coffee table.

"I should really confiscate that kit," he said cracking a smile. "And you're welcome. Your identity is safe." He got up and I, along with my menagerie of pets, walked him to the door.

I told him I was sorry for the trouble, and he softened.

"I know you meant well." He gave my shoulder an affectionate squeeze and then left.

I went back to the kitchen and looked out. I know I should have stayed inside and minded my own business, but I had to have another look in that yard. I tried to stay in the shadows as I went to the back fence, stood next to one of the trees in my yard, and looked over. Sure enough, the light was hitting something long and yellow. But what I'd seen was blue.

CHAPTER 7

I WAITED UNTIL IT WAS VERY LATE AND THE lights had gone off in the Chambers-Mackenzie house. Barry would have had a fit if he knew what I was doing, but I knew I'd never sleep unless I got a better look at the cushion. I turned off my floodlights so that both yards were in the dark. I didn't dare use a flashlight, either.

The old gate opened more easily this time and I slipped into the yard. I darted to the area below the balcony, which wasn't that easy, since the ground was rough and there were tools and supplies that had been left by the workmen. Sure enough, there was a yellow chaise cushion on the ground. I lifted it, and underneath there was the stone laid for the patio. I ran my hand along the cool, irregular slab and felt something gritty. When I smelled my fingers, I noted a faint scent of salt.

I remembered something I'd read in one of the booklets that came along with the detective set about salt being used to remove blood stains. I slipped back across the yard to my place and found the small bottle in the box. I had to do a little mixing before slipping back to the yellow cushion. I lifted it and sprayed the contents of the small bottle on the ground. It only took a moment for the bits of blue glow to appear. I felt my breath suck in as I realized what it meant. The label on the bottle of Blood Detector said it reacted with any traces of blood, making this eerie glow. The salt hadn't removed it all and there was residue left behind. I jerked my fist in a triumphant movement. I was right. Blood didn't come from cushions. Someone had been lying there.

As I went back inside, I considered calling Barry and telling him what I'd found, but I decided I needed more to tell him first, like who the somebody was.

ALL THESE LATE NIGHTS WERE GETTING TO ME, and I was dragging when I left for the bookstore the next morning. But not dragging so much that I didn't have a look into Cheyenne's yard on my way to the car. I didn't want to be seen, so I stood behind one of my redwood trees and peeked out. The cushion was gone and the workmen had reappeared. I saw that they were working on the slabs of stone being laid for the patio. One of them had a pressurized hose and was washing everything down. So much for showing Barry what I'd found.

Mrs. Shedd was waiting when I arrived at work. "Joshua loves the idea of us having an event connected to the music and video department. It's his baby and he's been looking for a way to get our customers to notice the department. He's quite musical, you know. On one of his adventures he played the harmonica in a blues band in New Orleans." I thought it quite funny that she almost swooned when she described his band days.

We both looked toward the small department in an alcove near the café. "Joshua needs to know what sort of equipment we'll need. Should we do it in the regular event area? And since it is so soon, we need to get some signage up." She sighed. "Thank you for handling this. I want it to be a big success so Joshua will be pleased."

I said I'd get right on it after I got a coffee in the café. "Before I forget, Cheyenne—well, her husband—called and said they'd be stopping by this morning to have a look at things." The bookstore owner seemed a little nervous. "Molly, I really want this event to work out. We think it could add a whole new dimension to the bookstore."

She didn't say it exactly, but I got her meaning. I wasn't to let this slip through the cracks.

I gave her a reassuring touch on the arm and told her not to worry. Yeah, as long as Cheyenne and her husband didn't know we were neighbors and that I knew something was going on there. I had barely started work on designing the sign when I heard voices at the front of the store. One seemed to carry above the others, and I knew it was Cheyenne's. Even if I hadn't heard her I would have noticed her first. There was just something about her that drew my, and the public's, eye to her. I think that is what they call charisma.

Garrett was with her. He was glancing around with a displeased expression, and I felt my stomach clench. I had a feeling I'd just encountered obstacle number one. He wasn't as enthused about the proposed event as his wife was.

He put a protective arm around Cheyenne as they walked farther into the store. I recognized the tall, thin blond woman as being the third sister in the group, Ilona. She didn't seem as animated as Cheyenne. She seemed somehow languid and maybe a little sultry compared to Cheyenne's boisterousness.

I dropped what I was doing and went to greet the group. Cheyenne was all big gestures, and when she saw me, she broke free of her husband and threw her arms around me. "This is Molly," she said to her husband and sister. "She runs everything around here, including the crochet class I'm taking." As she said it, I noticed that she was wearing a beautiful cowl in shades of aqua. I complimented her on it. "I didn't realize you were such an accomplished crocheter," I said.

Cheyenne took a mock bow. "I had lots of time to perfect my skills. I was just telling my husband that I thought I might join your regular group." She turned back to him. "They have such a fun name—the Tarzana Hookers. Isn't that a hoot?" He smiled in a noncommittal manner and nodded before she continued. "You could capture some video stuff and we could put it on the website."

I said she was welcome to join us, and then extended the invitation to Ilona.

"My two sisters are the handicrafters," Ilona said. "I just wear what others make." She held out her hands and showed off a pair of pale blue fingerless gloves made in a lacy cotton.

While I was making all this friendly talk, I was thinking about the previous night and what I'd seen. What did they know about it? Barry had said they weren't even home. I thought about the episode on the balcony and tried to study Garrett without being obvious. He'd folded his arms, and I got the feeling he was unimpressed.

"See, honey, it's a perfect little spot," Cheyenne said to her husband. "I was thinking we could video it. Something simple, with just a phone, and put it up on social media." She turned to me. "These days everything is video."

He seemed to be considering it. "I don't know if the

possible value is worth the trouble. We don't want it to look like you're singing on street corners," he said.

Ilona had separated herself from the group and was looking at a fashion magazine she'd picked up as they were coming through. Cheyenne's face turned stormy. "So what if it does? We could say we're going to the fans. It would make us look generous." Her lips formed a slight pout. "I want the group to do it."

Garrett seemed about to say something, but I had the feeling he was considering that they had an audience— me—and reconsidered. "I suppose it won't do any harm, and we could put it on the website." He turned to me. "Where exactly are you going to set it up?"

As I led the way to the event area, I heard some low conversation going on behind me. Cheyenne seemed to be fussing with Garrett, and I strained my ear to hear.

"I don't know why you're being difficult about this," she said.

"Your judgment isn't always the best," he said. "It's my job to keep everything together."

"I'm the one who keeps putting herself out there."

"That's fine when it's something like hosting a talk show or a reality show that brings in some money," he muttered.

I turned back toward them when we reached the event area, and they both quickly put on smiles. Ilona looked up from the magazine. "Where's the stage?"

Mrs. Shedd joined us just then, bubbling with excitement when she realized who was there. "It's so wonderful to see you," she gushed to Cheyenne. "And you must be Ilona." Mrs. Shedd put out her hand and introduced herself. My boss had figured out the real one to please and turned on the charm when she greeted Garrett. "I think you will be very happy with the event. Molly will take care of everything."

"Now that we're living in Tarzana, it seems like a neighborly thing to do," Cheyenne said, giving her husband a sidelong glance.

Ilona glanced around and smiled. "It'll be fun. Like the old days." She turned to me. "My sister was relentless. Back then, she practically had us singing on street corners. Once we entertained at the opening of a butcher shop."

"What about Lauren? Is she okay with the plan?" Mrs. Shedd asked. Ilona started to speak, but Cheyenne stepped in.

"She's fine with it."

Garrett finally cracked a smile. "I know when I'm beat. If that's what you all want to do, I'm behind it."

Mr. Royal joined us and they discussed what equipment they would need, which turned out to be very little.

"If that's settled, we really should go," Garrett said, giving Cheyenne a nod. "We have things to take care of." His tone made it clear that she knew what he was talking about.

"It'll be all right," Cheyenne said with a little shake of her head. "We had a bit of a family trauma last night. We were on our way home from the taping of my show and we got a call from the kids' nanny. She had some kind of family emergency and had to leave. I suppose I should be grateful, because she called the service we got her from, and they sent over a temporary replacement."

"How terrible," Ilona said, suddenly zoning in on the conversation. "It's such a chore dealing with help."

"If that wasn't enough, we have some crazy neighbor who keeps sending the cops to the house. I don't know what it was about this time, but some detective called

Garrett to check if we were both okay." Cheyenne put her hands up as if to say *What next?*

What? The nanny left? Did it have anything to do with the traces of blood I found in the yard? I had to bite my tongue to keep from asking questions.

"Molly, there you are," my mother said, coming across the bookstore. "I wanted to have a look at this place where you're working." She joined our group, her bangle bracelets jangling, and it registered who I was standing with.

"Cheyenne Chambers!" my mother said with an excited squeal. "And your sister, Ilona." She surveyed the area. "Is your other sister here?" She didn't wait for an answer but continued to enthuse. "I love ChIlLa. Your last album was brilliant." She stopped long enough to see both sisters' faces light up at the praise. "Liza Aronson, lead singer of the She La Las," she said holding out her hand as she continued. "I like to think that we would have gone on to be just like you, but it was a different time. You can manage being in a group and having a family today. In my day, you had to choose one or the other, and the She La Las broke up when we all got married."

Cheyenne gave my mother a spontaneous hug and air kiss. "The She La Las! You guys did 'My Guy Bill,' right? That's a classic."

It was an opening for my mother to mention how her group was back together and touring again. For a few minutes they talked music and the road, and then Cheyenne mentioned that they were going to do a few songs and sign CDs at the bookstore.

My mother looked at Mrs. Shedd. "The girls and I could do the same thing." She led us over to the music department and found several copies of a compilation CD with their hit and other groups' hits from the era. "We're lucky to be up and kicking with our voices intact," my mother said.

"Wait, I have something to show you," Mr. Royal said. He cut open a box on the floor and pulled out several holders with record albums. "We're going to have some record players for sale, too. There's nothing like a vinyl record," he said, looking to Garrett. He was busy with his phone, only half paying attention, and responded with a nod. Cheyenne and my mother were much more excited, particularly when Mr. Royal found vinyl versions of both of their albums.

"We're always the last to know. I can't wait to tell the girls," my mother squealed. "We could sign the CDs and the records."

"What do you think, Joshua?" Mrs. Shedd said.

"I think having the She La Las perform here is a splendid idea. Why don't we do it all on the same night?" Garrett appeared hesitant, but Cheyenne was all for it.

"It will be like then and now," she said. Before she had time to realize what she'd said was kind of hurtful, my mother jumped in.

"Really it's more like now and always," she said. All the details were worked out, and my mother said she'd get in touch with the "girls" right away. Then she went on about how nice it was to be back living in the Valley after Santa Fe. "I was so surprised to find out that you're Molly's—"

Oh no, she was about to say *neighbor*. I faked a coughing fit to cover the word. It worked and successfully ended the conversation, since my mother did her motherly duty and went off to get me a drink of water.

When it was just me and Mrs. Shedd, she pulled me aside. "It was almost like you were trying to cover something up with that coughing. Is there something you're not telling me?"

I'm afraid my boss knew me too well. I debated telling her that Cheyenne lived in the big house behind me, but then she'd know I was the crazy neighbor Cheyenne had talked about. I decided it was better to leave her in the dark and just told her I'd had a sudden tickle in my throat.

"Whatever you say, Molly." Her voice sounded disbelieving. "But we don't want to give Cheyenne or her husband any reason to cancel the event. I haven't seen Joshua so excited about anything since his last adventure."

I groaned internally. I was definitely ready for the happy hour gathering of the Hookers. Too bad it was only 11 a.m.

LATER THAT AFTERNOON, RHODA CAME INTO THE yarn department and pulled out a chair. She was the kind of person you'd want to have as a neighbor. She'd be the one to bring you soup when you had the sniffles and get rid of all your used tissues for you before giving your covers a good tucking-in. She let out a sigh as she pulled out her project and got right to work. "I need to get this done," she said, glancing down at the long piece done in exotic yarn. I knew that it was the back of a long vest she was making for a customer. She was developing a local crocheting business, all based on word of mouth and people seeing the beautiful things she made. Rhoda put the piece away and looked at the bin I'd put in the middle of the table. We'd decided that our happy hour gatherings should just be about making things for others in need. We'd done caps for people going through chemo, blankets for shelters, scarves for soldiers. I'd come up with the current project: We were making cuddle toys for children in trauma.

Something soft for them to hold on to in trying times. Rhoda took out the bear she was working on.

Sheila came in next. She was the youngest in the group, still single and trying to find her way in the world. She was prone to anxiety attacks, though they seemed to be getting more manageable. I knew crocheting was her drug of choice to deal with her nerves.

She worked practically next door, so it was easy for her to get there quickly. She had developed a business selling her work as well. She had a lapghan folded up in her bag. She took it out and showed it to the group. We always showed off a project when it was finished so the group could ooh and aah about it. The positive feedback always felt good, because we were all our own worst critics. I couldn't imagine that Sheila had made any mistakes in the small blanket. It was done in shades of green with some purple thrown in and had the hazy color effect, sort of like an Impressionist painting, that was her trademark.

It was interesting to see the toy she was working on. She'd finished a bear in a toasty brown and then added a dress in a mixture of blues. She was making a bow in the same colors to add to the bear's head.

I was making a doll patterned after a knitted boy doll that Samuel had had as a kid. I still had the rather battered-looking Zoomer, as he'd named him, and I was using it as a model to re-create it in crochet.

The peace of our crocheting was shattered when Adele arrived. I hadn't seen her all day and had assumed she'd had the day off. "What am I going to do?" she said, throwing herself into a chair at the head of the table. "I can't even concentrate on my teaching responsibilities."

"What's the matter, dear?" CeeCee said, coming in next. She always appeared picture-perfect because she never knew when someone was going to snap a photo with her and stick it online. She looked at the seat Adele had chosen and made a face. They were still at odds about who was the leader of our group. CeeCee looked skyward for a moment in exasperation and chose a chair to the side of the table.

"What's the matter?' Adele repeated, as if it were an absurd question. "Just that my whole wedding has crumbled. All my plans are in the Dumpster, all the money I paid for it gone. All I have are invitations to a place that isn't there anymore."

"My, I am out of the loop," CeeCee said. "There must be someplace else you can hold it."

"What did I just walk into?" Elise said in her chirpy voice. She was a fragile-looking woman with a bubble of wispy light brown hair, but looks definitely deceived. She had an iron core that could keep her up in a hurricane. Her husband was with her. Logan Belmont had the strangest hairline—it made him look like he was wearing a cap. He was in real estate and specialized in Tarzana. He gave his wife an affectionate squeeze and greeted the rest of us before announcing that he'd be looking around and then in the café if anyone needed him.

Rhoda brought Elise up to speed on Adele's problem.

"I haven't told Cutchykins yet," Adele moaned. "I don't want his mother to know there are any problems." We all nodded knowingly. Cutchykins was the nickname that Adele and Eric Humphries called each other, and his mother had never been a fan of their match—and was probably even less of a fan now that she was living with her son.

Dinah pulled out a chair and surveyed the group. "What's going on? You people look so dour. Who died?"

"My wedding venue," Adele said.

"Just do something simple, like Dinah," Rhoda suggested. "Cut your guest list way down and you could have the ceremony at City Hall and then go out for breakfast at a coffee shop." Rhoda was always practical and a little blunt, but we all flinched at her suggestion. The concept of Adele doing anything low-key was ridiculous. All you had to do was see what she was wearing. The long crocheted vest in sparkly red was eye-catching over the black leggings and black turtleneck. To finish the look, she wore a headband made out of the same red yarn, with a huge flower attached to one side.

"Ladies," Eduardo said as he came up to the table. The energy changed with his arrival. The former romance novel cover model laid his leather bag under the table and reached into the bin. His bear was hulkier than the rest of ours. It almost looked like it had biceps. He was planning to dress it in black pants and a white shirt, much like he'd often worn in his cover model days. I wondered if he was going to give it flowing black hair like his.

He'd been absent from our early-evening gatherings for a while and had no idea of what he'd walked into. He went right into talking about the Tunisian crochet class, apologizing for not being able to sign up for it.

Eduardo had left his modeling days behind him a while ago and now owned a high-end drugstore called the Apothecary. Drugs were really just a minor part of the place. It featured everything from old-time penny candy and a soda fountain to fancy sundries like silver-plated hairbrushes and imported skin care products.

Adele was too wrapped up in her drama to join in. Elise rushed into the conversation and starting commenting about the other students. When she mentioned Cheyenne,

I froze, remembering that she'd intimated she might drop in to one of our happy hour sessions. I took a quick glance to the front and was relieved not to see her.

CeeCee made a face. "I don't understand why Mrs. Shedd made such a fuss about her coming into the store." She waved her arm toward the wall near the front. Mrs. Shedd had plastered the place with pictures of Cheyenne with her kids, Cheyenne with her sister, Cheyenne with Mrs. Shedd. CeeCee flashed her eyes. "On the scale of things, I think being Academy Award–nominated puts me on at least the same level as her. I ask you, where are all the photos of me?"

Adele recovered long enough to add, "And where is the picture of me with Cheyenne? I *am* the teacher of the Tunisian class that she's taking."

Rhoda turned to me. "Molly, aren't you upset they didn't take a photo of you with her?"

I laughed it off and then told CeeCee I was sure Mr. Royal would give her a special spot once they had some photos of her to put up.

"We could take some pictures right now," she said giving her brown hair a little primp. I had to break the bad news that Mr. Royal had left for the evening, and she wilted.

"There's something I have to tell you all," I said, moving on. "Cheyenne mentioned that she might join one of our happy hour gatherings." There was instant grumbling from Adele and CeeCee that no one had brought it up to them.

"I didn't mention it because it just came up today." I hesitated on how much to explain. "Do you remember that big white house you can see so clearly from my backyard?"

They all nodded, except Eduardo, who hadn't made it to my surprise party. "That's Cheyenne's house." I paused to try to collect my thoughts before continuing. "I might have seen some suspicious activity going on in there and called the police—well, Barry Greenberg—a couple of times."

"And?" Rhoda said, leaning forward with interest.

"It turned out to be nothing, or at least that's what Barry said. He didn't tell Cheyenne who called, so she just thinks it was a crazy neighbor."

"What did you see going on?" Elise said.

"We'll get to that," I said. "The point is, it's important that Cheyenne keeps not knowing that I'm her neighbor." I dropped my voice in case Mrs. Shedd was in the area, and then explained the event and how much it meant to Mrs. Shedd. "Cheyenne's husband isn't really in favor of it. I'm the one putting together the event. If they find out I'm the crazy neighbor . . ." I let my voice trail off.

"Got it," Rhoda said. "I won't mention a thing." The rest of them agreed, though Adele protested being left out of the event planning.

"I'm the one who made the initial connection with her when she brought her kids in to story time," she said.

"Dear, you have enough on your plate with your wedding woes," CeeCee said. "And I'm sure you wouldn't want to cause any problems with your boss by spilling who lives near where Molly lives."

Adele let out a very heavy sigh. "You're right. I have to think about Cutchykins now, and how to tell him what happened."

I think Adele expected to stay the center of attention, but Elise asked again about what I'd seen. I decided to play it down. If I told them everything, there was no way they'd be able to keep quiet about it if Cheyenne came to the group or the next meeting of the Tunisian class.

I simply told them Barry's version. They laughed when they heard that I'd thought people were fighting, but were actually practicing a dramatic dance routine, and that when I thought I saw a body, it was really a chaise cushion lying on the ground.

Dinah remained silent during my explanation, but when I got to the part about the chaise cushion, her eyes popped. She'd heard about the supposed dance routine, but I hadn't had time to tell her about what had happened the previous night. Under her breath, she said, "You can fill me in later."

"I can see why you don't want Cheyenne to know you're her neighbor," Rhoda said. "Sending the cops there twice." She looked at the others. "We'll keep your secret, won't we?" They all nodded, and the subject was dropped as we all began to concentrate on our crocheting.

The group broke up when the hour ended, but Dinah stayed at the table. She looked around to make sure there were no ears listening. "You saw a chaise cushion that you thought was a body?"

"I'm sorry I didn't tell you about it before," I began. I got up from the table and started to clear up the stray bits of yarn. Technically, my workday had ended, but that didn't mean I would just leave. My attitude was to take care of what needed to be done, whether I was on the clock or not.

"I know we've all been busy. It doesn't matter why you didn't tell me before. I want the details now." She had taken out a yellow pot holder she was close to finishing, but looked up at me to make direct eye contact. "Was it a cushion or a body?"

"You know me too well. I went light on the details with

the group. I figured keeping it simple would make it more likely they wouldn't mention anything when Cheyenne was around. How about we play the Sherlock Holmes game? I'll tell you what happened and we can put our heads together from there and see what we can deduce."

"Oh, goody," Dinah said, her face lighting up. She set down her crocheting and gave me her full attention. With the Sherlock Holmes game, as we called it, all the information had to be out there, so I began by explaining changing the floodlight bulb.

"When the light came on, I saw that it shone into the yard behind me. That's when I noticed something on the ground." I relived the moment in my mind. "It was long and it appeared blue in the dim light. My immediate thought was that it was a person and the person wasn't moving."

"You know," Dinah said, "there's something in human nature where we put together random things and see faces and people. There always seems to be someone claiming to see some religious figure in the bark on a tree."

"I know, but this wasn't like that. I can't say why, but it looked like a person."

"And then you called Barry?" Dinah asked.

"Yes, but it took a lot of doing to get him to come check it out after what happened the first time I got him to go there." I laughed to myself. "You know how the group was saying things go in threes when they were talking about your and Adele's weddings? Well, I don't think there is a chance in the world that Barry would go there a third time no matter what I claim to have seen."

"But what happened when Barry went over there that time?" Dinah asked.

"Nothing. He said the nanny, Jennifer, was there, and that Cheyenne and her husband were at a taping. He spoke to them—no, he said he spoke to Garrett on the phone because Cheyenne was in the middle of taping that show she's a judge on." I thought for a moment. "He said he had a look around the place and everything seemed fine. The kids were asleep."

"Where did the chaise cushion come in?" Dinah asked.

"I guess Barry said a neighbor reported seeing someone lying in the yard, and she showed him the balcony and the empty chaise longue. That must have been when she said the kids were fooling around and had thrown the chaise cushion off the balcony. I know he said he had a look around the yard and saw the cushion on the ground." I told her how he'd rescued my evidence bag.

"That was sweet," she said. "He was trying to protect you."

I shrugged it off. I wasn't sure if it had been a gallant act, or if he had been worried I might go back in the yard searching for it. "So, that's what Barry saw. But there's more," I said, pausing before I got to the important part. "I went out there after Barry left and checked. There was a yellow chaise cushion on the ground, but when I lifted it up, I found traces of blood."

"You really found traces of blood?" Dinah sounded incredulous. "How did you do it?"

As I explained using the Blood Detector that came in the set my son had given me, she chuckled. "Peter must be so upset he gave you that set."

"There's an understatement. He was upset when I started taking fingerprints at the party. I can only imagine how he would react if he knew it included a bottle of liquid that makes blood glow blue in the dark."

"Did you tell Barry about that?" Dinah asked.

"Are you kidding? I would have had to tell him I snuck

into the yard when he specifically told me not to, and I can just imagine what he'd say if I explained the stuff I used from the kit."

"Too bad, because he could have his people see if they could find traces of blood," Dinah offered.

"It's all gone now." I explained about the workmen being back in the yard. "Not only could I not tell where the cushion had been but they'd been washing the whole area down."

"What do you think happened to the cushion?" Dinah asked.

"I didn't consider that. It's probably back on the chaise up on the balcony."

Dinah looked at me hopefully. "I think Sherlock would deduce that if there were traces of blood under the cushion, there are probably some on the bottom of the cushion as well."

"So all I have to do is somehow get on the balcony and spritz stuff on the bottom of all the cushions and see what happens. And then tell Barry." We both laughed at the chances of any of that happening.

"If it's any consolation, I believe you saw a body. But I'm going to have to hang up my deerslayer hat for now." Dinah was looking toward the front of the store. Commander had just walked in and waved at her. He practically glowed when she waved back. She sighed as she pushed back her chair. "It's crazy that it's so hard for me to get used to someone being so happy to see me." She gave me a hug. "I know you want to prove to Barry that you're right about what you saw, but I think you might have to give up on this one. How can you find a body when you don't even know who you're looking for? Even Sherlock Holmes would have a hard time with that."

CHAPTER 8

"Good, you're still here," Joshua Royal said, coming into the yarn department. He was holding several of the vinyl records. "I think we should use the album covers in the signs we put up." He held one out for me to see. The artwork showed up much better on the large cardboard squares than it did on a small CD case. It was ChILLa's latest. It was funny looking at the picture now that I'd met them. The background was a bluff overlooking the ocean. Cheyenne was in the middle, a step ahead of her sisters. They were all dressed in different styles. Cheyenne wore a long, conservative dress, Ilona had a hippie look going, and Lauren was all wild child, with a short dress and kooky wig. The album was titled *Next Step*.

"It's too bad it didn't sell like their first one," Mr. Royal said.

"I didn't realize you were so into music," I said. I'd barely said it when I realized how ridiculous a statement it was.

The music department was his baby, so of course he'd be knowledgeable about what was going on in the business.

"They've got one more chance with their next album. If it flops, they'll be filed away as one-hit wonders." He didn't say anything when he held out the next album. It was the compilation of hits that the She La Las were on. It seemed like most of the groups had only had a couple hits at most. The cover was a collage of photos from the sixties. The artwork was so small on the CD case that if I squinted I could make out my mother's group, but on the full-size album, I could actually see the three women in their white boots and short dresses.

"It was another time when the She La Las' song came out. It was mostly about singles and whether or not it was good to dance to," Joshua said with a smile. "It must be strange to see your mother as a pop star."

"That's the truth. She's a real force of nature. But I'm happy that she is having a second chance at her career. And thank you for letting her perform here."

"You have no idea how I'm looking forward to our musical evening," he said. He showed me some copy he'd written and a drawing of how he thought we should lay out the poster.

We discussed where to put the signs to get the most attention. Then he looked at his watch. "Didn't you clock out a long time ago?" he said.

"Yes, actually I did."

"I'll take care of bringing everything to the printer. You go on home. Both Pamela and I know you put in far more hours than we pay you for. We all need some R and R if we're going to keep this place going."

It only took me a minute to grab my things and wish him a good night, and then I was out the door.

Now that it was April, the days had gotten longer, but it still always seemed to be dark when I left work. The sidewalk was shrouded in shadow as I started down the street. I didn't see the man step out from behind one of the olive trees that grew along the street until he had grabbed my arm. I felt a sudden rush of adrenaline as I started to resist and gathered my breath up to scream.

"Sunshine, it's me," Mason said as I was about to jab him with my elbow.

"What?" I squealed, feeling all shaky from the flood of fight-or-flight hormones. He was illuminated by the streetlight and I registered who he was—or, more correctly, that he wasn't a threat—and relaxed my arms. "What are you doing here?"

Mason chuckled. "You don't sound very happy to see me."

"It would help if I hadn't thought you were a mugger," I said.

"I finished up a day early and dashed to the airport. I got the last seat on the next flight out. I tried to call you." He didn't have to say more. I was getting better, but I still missed more calls and texts than I answered. "I thought I'd just come here and surprise you." He grinned and put his arm around my shoulder. "I didn't realize how dangerous it would be."

We started to walk down to the corner. "I hope you don't have some big plans for tonight," he said. "I thought we could stop by my place. I'll drop off my bag, check on everything, and change clothes. Then we could grab some dinner. How does that sound?"

"Great. I have so much to tell you," I said. He knew nothing about what had gone on at Cheyenne's. I hadn't even brought up the first time I sent the cops there. Between the way it had turned out and Barry making a late-night visit to my house, it had seemed better to let it go. But now everything had changed.

"All good, I hope," he said in a cheery voice. "You're not going to tell me someone died, are you?" He said it in a joking tone, but even so, I swallowed hard, since he had touched on the truth.

"So you're a mind reader now," I joked, trying to keep the mood light.

Mason turned toward me with a start. "What? Somebody really did die?"

"It's a little more complicated than that," I said. We had reached the corner and turned onto a side street to walk toward the parking lot that ran along the back of the stores that faced Ventura Boulevard.

"Well?" he said, urging me to continue.

"This is the kind of story where we need to be situated somewhere before I start." There was just no way I could explain the whole thing in a few sentences.

Mason started to walk faster. "I can't wait to hear."

We decided to leave my car in the parking lot, and we both climbed into his black Mercedes SUV. He tried to get me to start talking during the drive to his house, but I held out. I wanted to tell him everything without being interrupted.

Mason's dark wood ranch-style house was on a street north of Ventura Boulevard in Encino. Most of the large houses that lined the street were hidden behind tall fences. His was on a corner and had only a short fence marking off the beautifully landscaped front yard. Spotlights illuminated the trees that sat atop the slopes on either side of the walkway. "We'll go in the front door," he said, leading the way. He didn't have to explain. He didn't want to start a panic by coming in through the yard. Before we got to the door, there was the yippy sound of barking.

"Spike already knows you're here," I said.

"He recognizes the sound of the car," Mason said, sounding pleased as he took out his keys. I took it as a high compliment that Mason had come to see me before stopping to see the toy fox terrier. Mason adored the little dog, and I knew he had worried about leaving him home with his ex and daughter.

Mason had no sooner opened the door than the black-and-white dog literally jumped for joy, and when Mason leaned down to greet him, Spike popped into his arms.

I heard voices coming from the den and let out a little groan that expressed my dread at meeting up with who they belonged to.

"You wanted to meet my family," he reminded me. "I was perfectly happy keeping them separate from my social life." It was true I had pushed to meet them—well, his daughters, anyway.

I must have made another face when he said *social life*, because he rushed to explain that the phrase referred to the women before me. He realized his mistake at saying *women* and then shook his head with regret. "Whatever I say is coming out wrong. You do know that I feel completely differently about you."

"Yes," I said. Neither of us wanted a commitment like marriage, but we had realized we didn't just want to be friends with benefits, either. The term we'd come up with was *belong to each other*.

We had waited too long to make a move directly to his room and the women came out of the den. "Oh, you're back, Dad," Brooklyn said. "Good. I wanted to talk to you." Her glance moved to me, and there was a subtle downturn to her mouth.

No doubt whatever she wanted to talk about had something to do with her law school classes. She had dropped her previous career as a media buyer and decided to follow in Mason's footsteps and become a lawyer. He was so pleased about her plan that I hadn't said a word when she'd wanted to stay at his place while she went to school. Not that it was really my business anyway.

Having his ex-wife living there as well was a whole other issue, though not really my affair, either. Jaimee stood next to her daughter and looked at us.

"I hope you appreciate what a chore it was taking care of your dog. All he did was whine while you were gone," Jaimee said. It was no secret that she didn't like Spike, and the feeling was mutual.

Jaimee's reason for continuing to stay at the house was pretty ridiculous. She was on a reality show called *The Housewives of Mulholland Drive*, even though she wasn't really a housewife and she wasn't living on Mulholland Drive anymore. She was convinced that the key to her staying on the show was the drama involved with living with her ex.

I wasn't happy with her being there, but I also respected that Mason felt a sense of responsibility toward her. And I accepted that Jamiee still knew how to push his buttons.

Neither of them made any pretense of being glad to see me. What they did was simply pretend I wasn't there.

"We'll talk later," Mason said to Brooklyn. "And thanks for taking good care of Spike," he said to his ex, while steering me toward the long hall off to the side that ended in the master suite. "I can't wait to get out of these clothes."

I cringed, realizing how that sounded. I didn't want to look back and see their expressions.

Mason went on ahead into the large suite of rooms, with Spike at his heels. "I'll just get changed and we can go."

I hung in the doorway to wait. The large bedroom had a masculine feel to it—maybe it was the color choices of a lot of browns and earth tones. A sliding glass door led to a small private patio.

He rejoined me a few minutes later, slipping a leather jacket on over his Hawaiian shirt and jeans.

"Sorry, boy," he said to Spike when we got to the front door. "I'll be home later." Mason glanced at me hopefully. "Or maybe not."

It was a relief to get back in the SUV. "And now you can tell me your story," Mason said, starting up the engine. When I suggested waiting until we got to the restaurant, he said there would be plenty of time until we got there.

I knew he was right when he said he had a place at the beach in mind. He headed for the 101, and soon we'd blended into the traffic heading west.

"I'm not sure how to begin," I said, glancing out the window at the expanse of lights in the western San Fernando Valley. "Okay, here goes." I began by reminding him about the huge house going up in the yard behind mine. I explained how the back of my yard really stretched along the side of that yard. Since it might be connected, I told him about the argument I'd observed and how it had seemed that one of them was about to go over the side of the second-floor balcony.

Mason made appropriate noises to show he was listening. I took a deep breath and mentioned the first call to Barry. I could tell Mason wasn't happy about it, and was even less happy when I mentioned Barry's visit.

"It was strictly business," I said. "He just came to report on what he found out." I gave Mason the short version—basically who lived in the house and that they claimed to be practicing some dramatic dance number. "But I didn't hear any music," I said.

Mason got off at Topanga Canyon Boulevard and drove under the freeway overpass. The street was wide and flat as it passed Ventura Boulevard and headed toward the mountains. "And now comes the confusing part," I said.

The road had narrowed and gotten curvy as we began our ascent up the mountains. In a matter of minutes, we'd left the view of the Valley lights behind us. In the daylight, the long canyon seemed mysterious, but at night it had an eeriness to it. Maybe it was because it was supposed to be a Native American burial ground. The rustic houses here were spaced far apart and lost in the foliage, so that barely any lights were visible.

I began telling Mason about changing the lightbulbs and he interrupted, telling me I was crazy to have been doing it in the dark. He got more upset when he heard that I'd left the lights on and taken the chance of getting a shock.

"That's beside the point," I protested. "I was just setting the scene so you would understand how the new bulb shone all the way into that yard and illuminated something on the ground." I hesitated. "Some*one* on the ground."

"So you're going to tell me that Cheyenne Chambers went over the balcony this time," Mason said. We passed through the town of Topanga. The restaurants and shops on either side of the twisting road had a hippie, sixties sort of vibe.

"It wasn't Cheyenne Chambers or her husband," I said. "I've seen them since and they are both alive and well. I don't know who it was." I realized I was getting ahead of myself and told him about the call to Barry. This time Mason laughed.

"I wish I could have heard that one," he said.

"Right. It took some time and a lot of convincing to get him to go there again."

"I suppose he came over to your place again, too." The unhappy sound was back in Mason's voice.

"Forget Barry coming over to my place. It has nothing to do with anything. The point is that when he came over, he said there was no person on the ground. He said it was just a cushion from a chaise longue."

Mason was going to say something, but I stopped him. "There's more to the story." I quickly added how I'd gone into the yard and found the traces of blood underneath the chaise cushion. "I'm sure I saw someone on the ground. They weren't moving. I mean really not moving. So there's no way they could have just gotten up and left, if that's what you're going to say."

"I wasn't going to say that," he protested. "But if you saw a body and Greenberg saw a cushion, what happened to the body?" Mason asked. "And who is it?"

Everything had gotten out of order by then and I had to backtrack and explain that Barry had talked to the nanny and that Cheyenne and her husband were at a taping of the show she was a judge on. Barry had assured me that he'd looked around the place and that the kids were asleep and that no one else was there. He'd checked the yard, and that was when the nanny said the kids had thrown the cushion off the balcony and she'd forgotten to pick it up.

We left the lights of Topanga behind and began the darkest part of the route. The road snaked around sharp curves as it went down. The mountains here were jagged and empty. Civilization seemed a million miles away.

"I see why you waited to tell me all this. It wouldn't lend itself to being told quickly with interruptions. Let me see if I have this straight. You're sure you saw a body, but you don't know where it is or who it is." He glanced over at me. "This may sound cold, but why is it your concern?"

"Because I know what I saw, and somebody is going to get away with murder."

"Then this isn't just about proving that you're right to show Barry?"

"Maybe there's a little of that, too," I admitted, feeling embarrassed that I was so petty.

"Hmm, proving a detective wrong," Mason said with a chuckle. "As a lawyer, I can certainly get behind that."

Mason pulled the SUV up to a stoplight as we reached the Pacific Coast Highway. Ahead, the dark water stretched to the horizon and blended with the dark sky.

"I can't believe you missed the obvious. It seems to me that the nanny has to know something, since she was there when the body disappeared. I would think the first thing to do is talk to her."

"There's a little problem with that." I told him about her family emergency as we headed up the coast and he pulled into the parking lot of King's. It was our go-to place at the beach. I realized I had to go back and explain that Cheyenne and her sister were in a crochet class we were offering, but Cheyenne didn't know I was the neighbor who kept sending the cops over. I was just telling him about the musical event they were going to do at the bookstore as we were seated at a table next to a window overlooking the water. "You have no idea how much this means to Mrs. Shedd and Mr. Royal. If Cheyenne finds out I'm the crazy neighbor and cancels, I'll never hear the end of it." The server left us menus, and it only took us a moment to decide to just have appetizers and to choose our selection.

"My, but that sounds like a tangled web. I am astounded all that happened in the short time I was gone," Mason said. "Are you sure it wasn't the nanny on the ground?"

"No. It couldn't have been her. That's who Barry talked to." The food arrived, and I picked up the platter of stuffed mushrooms. The smell of butter and garlic reminded me how hungry I was. After sliding several onto my plate, I handed the platter to Mason.

"I still say the place I would start with is getting in touch with her." He traded the plate of caprese salad for the mushrooms. There were bruschetta and roasted vegetables, and a selection of olives, too. For a few minutes we just ate. As I polished off the last mushroom, I went right back to where we'd left off.

"But how do I do that?"

Mason chuckled. "I love your persistence. I'm sure we can figure out a way to get in touch with her." He waved the server over, and we ordered a sampler tray of desserts.

"I'm sorry. All we've been talking about is my stuff. What about your trip?"

Mason took a sip of his wine. "I'd much rather talk about your *stuff*, as you call it, than my client. He couldn't get through the wrap party without getting in trouble. He trashed a hotel room and left it to me to figure out a way to get them off the hook." Mason stopped talking as the server cleared the table. As soon as he walked away, Mason reached over and squeezed my hand. "It is so good to be back here with you talking about a now-you-see-it, now-you-don't body. When I think of the dull conversations I used to have on dates." He gave my hand another squeeze before letting it go. "If you're going to talk to the nanny, it would be good to know her name."

"I think I heard someone call her Jennifer Clarkson." I looked out the window at the ocean. I could see the waves breaking nearby, thanks to a spotlight from the restaurant. There was nothing between us and the waves but a pile of rocks. I'd been coming to King's for years and remembered a storm that had sent the water literally pouring through the restaurant. The rocks had been added after that to break the power of the surf.

"It was just like that," I said, pointing to the pool of light on the most distant rocks where a seagull was roosting. "You can certainly tell the difference between the bird and a rock, right?"

"You don't have to convince me, Sunshine. I believe you."

"I guess I don't completely believe myself." I took another look at the light on the rocks. "But of course, I did find the blood." I was speaking more to myself than to him. Cushions didn't bleed—victims did.

The tray of desserts came, and we put it between us and began to nibble on the assortment of cheesecake, flourless chocolate cake and fruit tarts.

Mason started to talk about Cheyenne. Since he dealt mostly with celebrity clients, she was part of his world. "She's definitely the leader of the group," he said.

I nodded, thinking back to the album cover and how she was actually standing a step in front of the other two. "She's a hustler, too," Mason said. "She hosted that talk show for a while, she's been on a number of reality shows and now she's a judge on that show tune competition."

"I suppose she's trying to keep her name in front of the public," I said.

Mason pushed the last piece of cheesecake toward me.

"That's part of it, but maybe a bigger part is the money. Since her husband is her manager, he only makes money if she does. He manages the group, too, but they can't be making much right now. Like I said, she's a hustler."

"But they just bought that big house," I said.

"Right. And now they have to pay for it." He put down his fork and let out a satisfied sigh before continuing. "Ilona does some acting. She seems to be practically a regular in the movies on the Sweet Romance cable channel. It's not big money by show business standards, but compared to the income of your average person, it is a nice piece of change. Not that she has to worry. Her husband is the darling of country music at the moment."

The server dropped off the check, and Mason fished for his wallet. "Funny, I don't really know much about the other sister." He seemed to be searching for her name.

"Her name is Lauren," I said. I described how she'd come to the crochet class and never told us who she was. "All she said about herself was that she was divorced with two kids and she'd learned to crochet when she did a lot of waiting around. She really seemed to want to appear to be just an ordinary person. It was only when Cheyenne joined the class that we found out who she was."

"I think I know why," Mason said. "People tend to think celebrities are all rich. Lauren isn't hosting talk shows or acting as a judge like Cheyenne, and doesn't have an acting career and a superstar husband like Ilona. You said she was divorced, so she doesn't even have a husband supporting her. She's probably struggling and deals with it by keeping a low profile." Mason signed the receipt, and we got up to leave.

"Shall I tell Spike I'll see him in the morning?" he said, taking my hand as we walked to the car.

CHAPTER 9

"YOU HAVE A NEW HOOKER," MRS. SHEDD SAID, intercepting me as I crossed the bookstore on my way back from my break. It was late afternoon and I had really needed the jolt of a red eye. It had been a late night with Mason, and I'd been at the bookstore since it opened.

"Huh?" I said, looking up. Mrs. Shedd gestured back toward the yarn department and repeated what she'd said.

Lauren was sitting at the table with her head bent over her work. "She brought her kids to story time and then asked me if it was okay if she hung out at the table. She said you told her about the happy hour gatherings."

I nodded in acknowledgment, and Mrs. Shedd continued. "Who would have thought that the crochet group would have led to so much excitement? They came to crochet and now they're going to perform here. Do you suppose the third sister might pick up the hook?"

"Ilona?" I said. "I wouldn't get my hopes up. Both

Lauren and Cheyenne were already crocheters when they signed up for the class. Ilona made a point that she didn't do any handicrafts the time she came in. And that she had no interest in learning them, either."

Mrs. Shedd let out a disappointed sigh. "Too bad. It would be so nice to get a picture of all of them together in the yarn department. Joshua is very excited about having them as customers of the bookstore. Just last night, he was going on about their upcoming event and how he'd like to make it just the first of many musical events. I have never seen him as enthused about any event we've ever done here before."

I held back a smile. She was always making it sound like she and Mr. Royal went their separate ways when they left the bookstore, but we were all pretty sure they were living together, or at the very least spending a lot of time together.

After what she said, I certainly didn't want to do anything that might mess up the event, but I still wanted to get to the bottom of what was going on at Cheyenne's house. And there was still some time before the Hookers' get-together time. "Hi," I said when I got to the table. Lauren looked up from her crocheting. I could see she was making a child-size jacket in blue yarn. Her hook moved with the ease of someone who crocheted a lot.

"I hope it's all right that I came a little early. My girls are at story time and this is a little me time." She glanced toward the children's department. I heard the sound of laughter and imagined that Adele was in the middle of her usual show. This was the after-school version, aimed at older children. They seemed to enjoy Adele's theatrics even more than the younger kids who came in the morning.

I was about to ask what she was going to do with her girls when story time ended and the group got together, but before I could say anything, she stood up and waved toward a young woman who had just walked into the store.

"Your nanny?" I asked.

She let out a sarcastic snort. "I wish. No, she's just the babysitter."

"Sorry," I said, thinking of what Mason had said about her. He was probably right that she was not on the same financial level as her sisters. The woman came back to the table, and Lauren pointed out the children's department. I heard Adele voice call out, "The end," and then there was the sound of kids clapping and yelling out their approval. A moment later, a flood of seven- and eight-year-olds came into the main part of the bookstore, looking for the adults who'd brought them. Lauren's babysitter caught her two daughters before they got to the back table.

"Well, at least you don't have to worry that she'll run off," I said, trying to make it sound like a positive.

"You mean like Cheyenne's nanny," she said, getting back to her crocheting.

"Right. That is who I was thinking of." Inside I felt like jumping up and down. Lauren was following along as I'd hoped. Now to see what I could find out.

"It must have been a shock to have her leave so suddenly. Did she work for your sister for a long time?"

"It depends what you mean by a long time. I think she was with them for about a year."

"I suppose being a nanny wasn't her life's goal," I said, hoping she would keep talking and not wonder why I was so interested in nannies.

"Probably not," she said in a disinterested voice. I plowed on, thinking that at any moment she would probably cut off the conversation.

"Then you didn't know her very well?" Lauren

continued to work on a sleeve, and I wondered if she was going to answer.

"I left my girls with her when the group did some gigs. She seemed nice enough. I think she was from the South somewhere. Cheyenne was generous about letting my girls stay there. Ilona is another story, but then nannies seem to move through her place like it's a revolving door."

"How come?" The words were out of my mouth before I could stop them. I knew I might be pushing the nosiness button too far.

She gave me a strange look. "If you're so interested, why don't you just ask my sister?" There was an awkward moment, and she seemed to be expecting some kind of explanation. I was actually relieved when Adele rushed up to the table in the midst of some sort of upset.

She was dressed as some kind of sorcerer, with a cape dotted with stars and a pointed hat. She looked past me to Lauren and held out several pieces of paper. "The woman over there insisted that I give these to you."

I saw that Adele was pointing to the babysitter, who was on her way to the front door with the kids in tow. Lauren took them reluctantly. "What are they?"

"They're membership forms for the story time gang," Adele said, as if it was an absurd question.

"Membership forms?" I said, surprised. It was the first I was hearing of it.

"You know, Pink, we get one for each kid that comes to story time so we can give them their very own membership card." She had that stilted sound to her voice, like I should pretend to know what she was talking about.

"What's the—" Before I could add "point?" Adele had grabbed my arm and almost dragged me away from the table.

"I couldn't say it in front of her, Pink," she began. "It's not about the kids, but the adults who bring them. I get them to leave a cell number so we can reach them if they wander off while the kids are at story time. It's usually parents or grandparents." She shook her head. "I don't know how I let Lauren drop the kids off without getting her to fill out the forms." Adele's face lit up. "There's an added bonus. Once I have a cell number, I can send them text reminders of sales and new arrivals. The kids aren't the customers. The parents are." Adele got a haughty stance. "It's marketing 101." She started going off that we should do something similar with the yarn department, but I cut her off.

"And you get one filled out for every kid who comes?" I said, getting an idea.

"Of course, no exceptions," Adele said. She pointed to the table where Lauren was filling out the information. The Hookers began to come in and find seats around the table. Dinah saw me standing with Adele in her crazy outfit and rolled her eyes while she stifled a laugh.

When CeeCee headed toward the end of the table where the group leader generally sat, Adele dropped our conversation and rushed to grab the seat at the opposite end. Would their fussing over leadership of the Hookers ever end?

Dinah had saved the seat next to her for me. "What was the problem with Adele this time?"

I looked at my friend. "Actually, I think she may have given me a solution to one."

Dinah wanted details. "Later," I said in a near-whisper.

The crochet get-together was supposed to be an hour when we all relaxed from our day, but it didn't work out that way this time. I introduced Lauren around, but she balked when I said the group generally spent the hour working on charity projects.

"There's no point for me to start anything, since I don't know how often I'll be able to come." She barely looked at what the others were doing and kept working on the jacket. She really did mean it when she said it was her "me" time.

CeeCee kept giving Lauren sidelong glances, and it was obvious our actress crocheter wasn't happy the singer had joined us. Even the usual cheery tinkle in CeeCee's voice was missing. She sounded almost snippy as she asked Sheila to push the bin toward her. She fished through it with choppy, annoyed movements, looking for some odds and ends to embellish her bear.

I knew she felt upstaged by having two members of ChIlLa invading her crochet world. And then to have Lauren not even go along with the program must have pushed her over the edge.

Meanwhile, Adele had seized the moment and started wailing about her ruined wedding plans. Rhoda threw her an impatient groan and in her usual direct manner cut through all of Adele's dramatics. "You do realize that complaining about the place going out of business isn't solving your problem. Why don't you use that energy for something positive?" Adele's response was to say that Rhoda couldn't possibly understand what she was going through.

Eduardo tried to stay out of it, working in silence on an Irish crochet scarf for Rhoda's bear. But his strategy backfired when Adele started to wail anew, claiming the white, lacy piece reminded her of a wedding veil.

Sheila was trying to avoid the group's bad vibe and had started on a new toy. She was working without even looking up, but I noted that her stitches seemed erratic and uneven. It was lucky that crochet stitches were so easy to rip out.

Elise tried to make conversation with Lauren. Elise had a spacey, wispy manner that made her appear scattered, but really she was always pitching something. "You know my husband is in real estate," she said. "I know you celebrities have special needs when it comes to houses. Logan said your sister is going to put a recording studio in the garage of their new house."

Hearing Elise mention Cheyenne's house put me on red alert. Elise knew she wasn't supposed to let Cheyenne know I was her neighbor, but I didn't know if she would realize Lauren shouldn't know, either.

Is it too corny to say I was saved by the bangle? I was never so glad to hear the jangle of my mother's bracelets as she came through the door of the bookstore and walked up to the table and distracted everyone. "Molly, the girls and I were in the neighborhood, and I wanted to show them the layout of the store. We need to tailor our choreography to the space." Without missing a beat, she turned to Lauren. "You girls nowadays don't have to worry about dance steps. You just go with the feeling. Back in the day we all had to be in step in an exact routine. And our fans still expect it." The other two She La Las were standing next to her. My mother turned to her group mates. "Let's show them," she said.

As usual, things got out of hand with my mother. Without an okay from me, the three of them lined up one behind the other and alternated sides as they jumped out, gyrating their arms and singing a cappella.

Mrs. Shedd appeared out of nowhere and clapped wildly when they finished. "Let's find Mr. Royal," she said to the She La Las. "He can take some photos of you dancing for the front wall." As the four of them rushed off to the front of the store, I understood how CeeCee felt. My mother had just upstaged me.

The group broke up right after that, but Dinah stayed behind with me. I started to clean up the odds and ends of yarn and stray pieces of equipment, and Dinah took out some rose-colored yarn and the beginning of a project. She saw me looking at it. "It's a bow tie for Commander— for our wedding." She seemed almost embarrassed. "Adele kept going on about the one she was making for Eric . . ." Her voice trailed off.

"So you are softening up about your wedding," I said.

"I don't know—maybe. Weren't you going to tell me what was going on with Adele?" she asked, taking the opportunity to change the subject by reminding me of what I'd promised earlier.

"The solution won't mean anything if you don't know what the problem is," I began. I told her how Mason had surprised me the night before. She listened to my description of the ride and laughed when she heard what we were talking about.

"A disappearing body. How romantic," she joked.

"For us, I guess it is romantic conversation," I said, smiling at the absurdity of it. I was surprised to note Dinah's unhappy expression.

"I don't know why I'm commenting on your conversation. I'd probably rather Commander talked about finding blood spatter than his current topic."

"And that is?" I prompted.

"He keeps going on about our honeymoon. I didn't really have a honeymoon with my ex. We went to Las Vegas and he spent all the time at the tables. Commander wants us to go to a posh hotel in Hawaii, the Big Island. It's all about having breakfast on our balcony overlooking the water, walking along the beach, watching the sunset, just the two of us wrapped up in each other's company." She looked like she might cry. "It's too much whipped cream," she said at last.

"Huh?" I said.

"When I was a kid my mother used to let me lick off the beaters and the bowl when she made whipped cream. There was always just a taste of it, but never really enough. Then one time she made too much and when she handed me the bowl there was a fluff of whipped cream in the bottom. At first it seemed wonderful, but very quickly the richness got to me and I couldn't eat anymore. It was too much of a good thing."

"Oh," I said. "I think I understand." Dinah shook her head from side to side as if to banish her thoughts.

"I'm being crazy. Commander is what I've always wanted." She seemed to have recovered. "And you were going to tell me about a problem and a solution."

I glanced toward the children's department. I could see Adele moving around the low tables. "I'll just cut to the solution. If you can back me up."

"Dr. Watson at your service," she said, putting her crocheting away.

As soon as we crossed into the children's department, the carpeting changed to cows jumping over the moon. Adele had taken off the purple cape and pointed hat and left them on a low table. She was walking around, muttering to herself. From the few words I caught, it seemed like she was practicing for her next story time. She seemed startled when she noticed us.

"Do you want something, Pink?" she said, with a little edge in her voice.

"I was thinking about how you handled making the kids have membership cards to come to story time. You could be right about doing something like that for the yarn department."

Nothing made Adele smile more than when it seemed somebody appreciated an idea she'd come up with.

"Great. You realized the genius of my plan. I bet the bookstore has sold a ton of books thanks to all those texts I've sent."

Dinah was listening, waiting for her chance to be my sidekick. She knew my moves well enough that all I'd have to do was give her a little gesture and she would figure out what to do.

I went on a little longer, telling Adele how much I liked her plan. I had to make sure I didn't lay it on too thick or she'd figure something was going on. "It would really help me if I could look at the records you have."

"So you can copy what I did?" Adele said with a haughty jiggle of her head. "Pink, you're finally seeing the light." She went to the cabinet that ran along one of the walls and came back holding a file of papers. "You can probably just look at the top sheet."

My disappointment must have shown in my expression. Dinah got that I wanted to look at the whole file, even if she didn't know why.

Dinah swung into action, going to the table and picking up the cape. "Adele, are these stars crocheted or knitted?"

Saying the words *knitted*, *knitting*, or even *knit* to Adele was like waving a red cape in front of a bull. It stirred her up and made her forget everything. Her eyes flashed as she tossed the file on the table and marched over to the cape.

She wasn't paying any attention as I picked the file up and started to thumb through the sheets. "How can you even think they could be knitted?" she said, holding it out and displaying the silver stars. Dinah kept her occupied by asking if they were hard to make. Adele let out a snort and found her crochet things. When I glanced over she was demonstrating how to make a star.

I was surprised at how many kids she had signed up for story time. I kept thumbing through the pages. She'd said there were no exceptions, so the sheets must be there. Finally, I saw the last name *Mackenzie*. I held my breath hopefully as I looked at the contact information. Yes, I was right. I wanted to give my fist a triumphant jerk, but I contained myself. It was better to keep my enthusiasm on the down-low or Adele might figure something was up.

The sheet in my hand had Jennifer Clarkson written as the contact, and there was a phone number. Knowing Adele, she would have made sure to get the number of the person who had brought the kids, rather than Cheyenne's home phone number. Adele was talking and crocheting and didn't have a clue I was writing anything down.

I gave the all clear to Dinah, and she used her experience as a teacher to get Adele to wind it up. When Adele looked back at the table, the file of papers was lying just where she'd left it.

"Thanks, Adele. I got what I needed," I said brightly as Dinah and I walked out of the department. Adele said something about inputting data, but I wasn't listening anymore.

We didn't stop until we found a corner table in the café. "Are you going to tell me what I just helped you do?" Dinah said, all smiles and good cheer.

I finished the story about the night before and how Mason had suggested I talk to the nanny since she was there when whatever it was had happened. "I had no idea how to get her phone number until I heard about Adele's story time sign-up thing. The nanny is their contact on the sheet and there's a phone number. I have to believe it's hers."

I had set the paper with the number on the table and set

my smartphone next to it. For a moment, both of us just stared at the items.

"What are you going to say?" Dinah asked. I had already thought about it. I needed a story. A reason why I was asking her questions. And I needed an identity other than my own.

"I've got it," I said, wanting to give myself a high five. "I'll say I'm her replacement."

"Brilliant," Dinah said, pushing the phone closer to me. I took a deep breath to calm myself and punched in the number. All the lead-up turned out to be a waste of energy. I got a recording. When the beep came I just left my number and asked her to call.

"Well, I guess that's that. A lot of effort for nothing," I said, setting the phone on the table. "We might as well have drinks." I was about to get up to place our order when I felt the table vibrate and realized it was my phone. We both stared at it for a moment.

"Aren't you going to answer it?" Dinah said. "It has to be her."

"Hello," I said tentatively.

The voice that answered sounded slightly Southern. "This is Jennifer Clarkson. I got a message to call this number."

I took a deep breath and let the deception begin. I tuned up the speed of my speech so it sounded a little gushy and explained that I was the new replacement with the Chambers-Mackenzies and I was trying to get some info.

"What do you want to know?" she asked.

"The service just said you had to leave suddenly. Was it something with the family? Did something happen that night?" I asked.

"No," Jennifer said almost too firmly. "The police did come to the door. One of the neighbors called. But it was nothing. I had a family emergency. My mother is sick, and there was no one to take care of her."

"Where exactly did you go?" I asked, and then cringed, wondering if she would answer.

"I don't know why you need to know. My mother was vacationing in San Francisco. I caught the nine fifteen Speedy Shuttle to Burbank and I took the last Pacific West flight of the day to San Francisco."

"So there wasn't some kind of upset that made you want to get away?" I pressed.

"No, absolutely not. I just told you, my mother is sick. Do you want to know the name of her exact illness?" she said. "Because it's streptococcus pneumoniae."

"Okay, I got it," I said. "Just one more thing. Do I have to worry about Garrett Mackenzie?"

She sounded like she was getting impatient. "What do you mean *worry*?"

"I mean, is he going to get all touchy-feely? Like expect me to have a relationship with him?"

"You don't have to worry about him. He wouldn't do anything like that to you." She put an awful lot of emphasis on *you*. It made me wonder if there was something going on between them and she believed she was special. But there was no way to pursue it, and I could hear the impatience in her voice. "I have to go. It's time for my mother's antibiotic. Just tell them I'll be back as soon as I can." Before I could say good-bye, she'd hung up.

"Well?" Dinah said.

"She gave too many details. And we know what that means."

"She's lying about something," we said in unison.

CHAPTER 10

"I HOPE YOU DON'T MIND THAT I'M HERE," BARRY said when I walked into my kitchen. He was leaning against the counter dressed in his off-duty clothes of faded jeans, a green pocket T-shirt and a plaid flannel shirt left open. Jeffrey looked up from the floor. He was holding a dog brush, and Cosmo was draped across his lap. Felix was trying to get in the middle of it.

"I'm trying to do more father-son things," he continued. "So instead of dropping Jeffrey off to do his dog duty, I thought I would stay." I noticed Jeffrey making a face when Barry mentioned the *father-son* thing. But I had a feeling that underneath, Jeffrey liked that Barry was making the effort.

It hadn't been easy for Barry to suddenly take on full fatherly duties when Jeffrey came to live with him after things didn't work out living with his mother. It only got worse when Jeffrey made it clear he wanted to be an actor and go by the name of Columbia. But that was another story.

"Sure, no big deal," I said, stepping around him and preparing to go across the house.

I had really hoped to come home to an empty house, put on some sweatpants and throw together some dinner. It had been a long day at the bookstore, and it wasn't going to let up tomorrow. I liked being assistant manager, but it was overwhelming at the same time.

"Staying out of trouble?" he said before I got across the room. It wasn't his cop voice, and he sounded friendly. "I'm sorry if I snapped at you the other night. I'm sure your intentions were good when you sent me to your neighbor's."

"But I was wrong," I said, finishing his thought. Jeffrey got up and took Cosmo and Felix outside, shutting the door as he did. I had a feeling it was more about giving Barry and me privacy than keeping the cats inside. Even though Barry and I were never married and Jeffrey wasn't my son, he still had that desire kids of divorced parents had—that we would get back together. I really cared about Jeffrey, but he had to accept that it wasn't going to happen.

"I wasn't going to say that," Barry said, still in the friendly voice. "It was dark, and I can see how you might have thought the cushion was a person. And since cushions don't move, it certainly would have seemed to be dead."

I had to bite my tongue to keep from saying that it *had* been a person and bringing up the traces of blood that I'd found—but that were now probably gone, too.

"But don't you think it was strange that Jennifer Clarkson left right after you went there?"

Barry put on his cop face, which meant that I had touched a nerve. "Jennifer Clarkson? Is that the nanny?"

I nodded. "I didn't file a report, since there was nothing to report, and I guess I forgot her name."

"If you're not sure who you talked to, what did she look like?"

"Molly," Barry said in a warning voice. "I'm a homicide detective. I know who I talked to. She had long blond hair, and it was hard to gauge her age. The jeans and hoodie made her look like a teenager. And I'm sure she said she was the nanny. What do you mean she left?"

"Just that she had a family emergency. She must have taken off right after you were over there."

He was concerned that she'd abandoned the children, but I explained that she'd gotten the service to send an immediate replacement.

"How is it that you know all this?" he asked with concern in his voice. He seemed to relax when I told him I'd overheard Cheyenne talking. I certainly wasn't going to mention talking to Jennifer Clarkson. He thought it over briefly. "I don't see any reason for me to follow up on her leaving, since we all agreed that you were having a *Rear Window* moment," he said, referring to the Alfred Hitchcock movie.

All agreed? It seemed to me that the only one who had agreed was him, but I kept that to myself. He glanced at the yard through the large pair of windows at the back of the kitchen. The floodlight I had replaced illuminated the middle of the yard, where Jeffrey was playing fetch with the dogs, but then there was just darkness near the garage where the two burned-out bulbs were.

Of course, Barry noticed the dark spot and offered to change the bulbs, to keep me off the ladder and probably out of snooping into the neighboring yard, but I said I needed to get replacements first. I think he was glad to change the subject, but I wasn't ready to let it go.

"So you really don't think it was strange that the nanny left so suddenly? Maybe you want to check up on her story. You could check a few things like her credit card charges, a shuttle pickup, and maybe the Pacific West flight manifest."

Barry's mouth fell open. "You're joking, right?" He didn't wait for my response. "How is it that you know she was picked up by a shuttle and took a Pacific West flight?" He shook his head. "I knew it was too good to be true that you had let go of investigating." He saw the detective kit sitting on the kitchen table. He started to shift through the contents. He picked up the magnifying glass and laughed. "This is just a set for kids to play detective with and learn about forensics." He picked up the stack of cards with fingerprints that I'd gathered and the booklet that was with them.

"Don't believe that booklet is going to make it so you can match fingerprints, or even get close, unless they have an arch pattern, which is the least common. You do know there is an art to matching fingerprints, right? We narrow them down by computer, but the final match is made by a person."

"So you do that?" I said, and he looked caught.

"No. I was using the big *we*, not the *we* including me." He seemed to want to change the subject. "All I can say, Miss Junior Detective," he said, looking at the box the set came in, "is that if there was a body, then where is it now?"

"You have a point there," I said. "I'll have to figure that out."

"No you won't. Don't even say that," he said with genuine concern. "I don't want to have to bail you out when you get arrested for stalking your neighbor. Celebrities get pretty testy when they find strangers hanging around their property."

I began to take out some things for dinner. I noticed Barry watching me and decided it was time to change the subject.

"I'm impressed by how you can subdue your hunger," I said.

"It's a by-product of the job," he said wearily. "I've taught myself how to simply ignore feeling tired, and as long as I'm not in the vicinity of food, I don't even think about eating."

"So you just shut off all your feelings?" I asked. I thought about how I still felt something whenever I heard his voice on the phone.

"It's about self-preservation," he said. "If I didn't keep them under wraps, I'd fall apart every time I had to tell someone their son or husband was dead. They fall apart, but I have to be stoic." Barry seemed okay with the topic, which surprised me. He'd always brushed off any conversation like this before. "Other guys drink or do things they regret. Me, I just keep it cool."

"So, I'm guessing you don't feel even a tinge of something when you see me." I hadn't planned to make it personal, but I couldn't help myself.

"No," he said, looking at me directly. "It's called accepting what I can't have."

I probably should have let it drop, but it was so far from how I operated, I wanted to understand. "What about with Jeffrey?"

His emotionless face collapsed in distress. "You hit my Achilles' heel. It doesn't work well with kids. Or a dog," he said, glancing out the window as Cosmo ran across the yard.

"Have you ever wondered what would happen if you just let loose on all your pushed-down feelings?"

There was a flicker in his eyes as he considered what I'd said, and then he let out a low laugh.

"I'm afraid it's too dangerous, like opening a door that can't be closed again. The image of an erupting volcano comes to mind, or maybe dropping a lighted match on a pool of gasoline." His eyes were still on me. And for that moment it seemed that he wasn't so successful at keeping everything wound up. The flash of emotion in his dark eyes made it seem like the lava might have started to flow. This was suddenly getting too hot for me.

"Maybe when you retire," I said, trying to lighten the moment.

Before he could reply, Jeffrey finally came back inside. I think he'd tried to give Barry and me as much time alone as possible, but he just got too cold. He gave both Cosmo and Felix a last brushing, and then he seemed to be winding things up. Barry never moved from his spot against the counter.

Jeffrey nudged his father. "We'd better go," he said. "Remember I have a rehearsal."

Jeffrey came and gave me a hug. Barry seemed not quite to know what to do with himself, but I think he wanted to do the same.

Oh, the complications of life.

CHAPTER 11

"MAYBE YOU SHOULD HAVE TOLD BARRY ABOUT finding the traces of blood?" Dinah said. We were in the bookstore café loading up on caffeine before the Tunisian class. Between the evening time slot and the fact it was almost too relaxing, we needed a jolt to make sure we were both alert.

She knew that Barry had come over with Jeffrey for dog care. She thought it had more to do with his wanting to see me than any father-son thing. Dinah was convinced that his life was a gloomy mess without me. "No matter what he says, he has a soft spot for you. I bet if you cajoled him he'd check it out."

I shook my head in reply. "I used up whatever soft spot he had when I got him to go there the second time. I have no proof of the blood to show him. And whatever was there has been washed away."

"But you thought there might be some on the cushion," my friend offered.

"*Might* is the key word there, and even if I somehow convinced him to check it out, how would he do it? He couldn't get a warrant, or even claim probable cause, since no one believes a crime even happened."

"You're right. Forget I even brought it up," Dinah said. "But what about getting him to check up on Jennifer Clarkson?"

I groaned. "You should have seen the look on his face when I suggested it." I flipped open the cover on my drink to see how much was left. "I'm going to have to do any investigating on my own until I can show him something that will convince him it wasn't all my imagination." I glanced at my phone on the table and smiled. "I just thought of something. I know how to get some information."

"How?" Dinah asked.

"Watch me." My next move wasn't quite as instant as I would have liked. It took me a while to find the phone number. "Okay, watch me now," I said as I tapped in the number.

There was more delay while I went through numerous menus, pressing keys as I went. Finally, a human person answered. Dinah moved closer, not wanting to miss anything.

"Hello, this is Jennifer Clarkson. I took one of your airport shuttles Tuesday evening and I think I left a pen in the van. It has great sentimental value to me. It was the last gift from my Aunt Trudy." Dinah was finding it hard not to laugh. "I wonder if you could check the van and see if it's there."

The woman on the other end had a disinterested voice and said she could turn me over to the lost and found.

"Thank you so much," I gushed. "But I already talked to them and it isn't there. It's probably still on the floor in the van."

The woman finally relented and then asked for the pickup time and address. I was really into it now and almost believed I had an Aunt Trudy and an irreplaceable pen. "It was around nine o'clock. Can't I just give you the address and you can check your records?"

"We're not supposed to do stuff like that. But I guess I could this once," she said. There was silence, and I imagined her scrolling through a list on a computer screen. "Okay, there you are. We picked you up at 9:14 and dropped you off at Burbank airport. I see the number of the van. When it comes in tonight, I'll tell them to check it out."

She started asking for information on how to reach me, and I panicked, unsure what to tell her. Dinah figured out what was going on, and she seemed at a loss, too. Then it hit me, and I squealed, "The pen just fell out of my bag. Silly me, it was here all along."

I clicked off the phone and set it down. "Well, I guess that part of her story was true." I reminded Dinah that we had thought she was lying because she had given so many details and her sudden departure seemed suspicious. "I think I know how we can check out the rest of it." I picked up the phone and called Mason's office number. I loved how they put me right through.

"I don't know why I didn't think of this to start with," I said to Dinah while I waited for him to come on the line.

"Sunshine, what can I do for you?" he said in a cheery voice. We hadn't seen each other since the night he got back. He had come back to a pile of work waiting for him, and I'd been working late hours at the bookstore. We'd talked numerous times on the phone, but it had only been personal stuff, and I hadn't mentioned Jennifer Clarkson.

I could be completely honest with him, so I told him all about my phone call with Jennifer and that we thought she wasn't telling the truth.

"Just tell me what you want me to do."

"I checked out that a van took her to the airport, but I'm wondering if she really went to San Francisco. I know you have all kinds of secret ways to find things out."

"I love that you appreciate my craftiness," he said with a chuckle. "So you want to know if she was actually on a plane." He asked for the airline and time of day and promised to get back to me.

We barely had a chance to get a few sips of our drinks before the table began to vibrate and I realized it was my phone. Mason confirmed that Jennifer Clarkson had been on the last Pacific West flight of the night to San Francisco. "And with all the security at the airport, it was definitely her."

Dinah and I looked at each other. "Maybe she's just one of those detailed people and she was telling the truth," Dinah said.

"And it was all just a coincidence that her mother got sick the same night that someone died at Cheyenne's?" It was the first time I had actually said that someone had died. Before, I'd referred to it as a body, which somehow kept it at a distance, but saying that someone had died made it all too real.

We were both hyper alert from our drinks when the Tunisian class began. We could have probably forgone the caffeine, as the class was hardly relaxing. Susan fussed from the start that Adele should be teaching us more advanced stitches instead of just supervising our work on our multicolored scarves. Adele went into harrumph mode and said that it was a beginners' class. Oscar jumped out of his dog stroller and took off across the bookstore, which gave Susan new reasons to fuss.

Lauren continued to work with different yarn than the rest of us, and again Adele warned her that the yarn was going to be tricky to work with.

Elise, Rhoda and the two-for-one pair of Melody and Terri crocheted in peace. CeeCee seemed a little happier. Mr. Royal had taken several photos of her, and he'd just hung them and had put "Academy Award–Nominated Actress CeeCee Collins" in bold type below them. But her mood changed when Cheyenne made an entrance when the class was halfway over. She definitely beat Adele when it came to a big personality. Cheyenne seemed to send a ripple through the air as she walked through it.

"I wanted to come so you didn't think I was skipping, but I can't stay. I'm doing a cameo on the *Life with Lorie Show*," she said, addressing us all. "I'm sure you know who she is. This is like her third reality show. I wish I knew how she did it. All I seem to get are guest spots." She looked to Lauren. "We ought to get Garrett to pitch a show idea about the three of us." Cheyenne flipped her hair off her shoulder and went back to talking to the whole group. "I'm supposed to just drop in to wherever they're taping. Supposedly the public just loves it when celebrities meet other celebrities someplace normal, like a yogurt shop." Then she pulled open her jacket and showed off the T-shirt she had on underneath. Right in the center was the artwork from ChIlLa's current album. "They pretty much throw these shows together with just a little editing, so it should begin airing on Monday, and our appearance here isn't until Thursday."

Cheyenne looked around for Mrs. Shedd. "Be sure to tell Mrs. Shedd that I will get some kind of plug in." Cheyenne turned to me. "And tell your mother I'll mention that the She La Las are going to be here, too. We girl groups have to stick together." She looked at her watch and then said she had to hurry. "They're just going to be there for a few minutes. This isn't one of those setups where they do things over and over or even have special lighting. They just shoot and move on."

She went over and gave Adele a theatrical hug. "Maybe I can make up the class somehow." She turned to her sister. "C'mon with me." Lauren shrugged as she quickly put away her things and got up to leave.

Terri and Melody looked up. "Too bad she couldn't get Lorie to come here and we could all be on the show."

"Then this class would be a complete circus," Susan snapped.

AN HOUR LATER I GRABBED MY COAT AND THINGS and left the bookstore. What an evening. After the class had ended, Adele had fallen apart with worry that Susan was going to complain about the class to Mrs. Shedd. "And what if Cheyenne says she wants a refund because she missed the first class and left in the middle of this one? Maybe she won't even come back.

"My whole world is crumbling," she wailed. "Pink, what am I going to do?" In her usual overly dramatic manner, she had put the back of her hand to her forehead. She might have looked like some old-time actress in a melodrama, but I still felt for her. As I have said before, Adele was difficult, but like family at the same time. I promised I'd help her work things out.

"You are my best friend," she said, grabbing me in a frantic hug.

It was a relief to get outside and away from the drama. Mason and I had agreed to meet at Gelson's. The plan was we'd buy food and go to my place and cook it together. He was standing outside his SUV when I pulled the greenmobile into the grocery store parking lot.

He had obviously stopped home first and changed into jeans and a pullover top under a leather jacket. The casual clothes made him look much more approachable than the beautifully tailored suits he wore for work. But no matter how he combed his hair, a lock of it always broke free and dangled over his forehead, somehow making him look earnest and hardworking.

He greeted me with a warm hug and we went inside the store. It only took a few minutes of us pushing a cart around to change our plan. As appealing as the idea of cooking together was, we both realized it was late and we were impatient to eat. We headed to the prepared food counter and bought poached salmon and a selection of salads, along with a baton of French bread.

"And now for a peaceful meal," Mason said as we carried the bags across my backyard. I should have figured something was up by the number of cars parked on the street, but I assumed one of the neighbors had company.

"Or maybe not," I said as I opened the kitchen door and heard a bunch of racket. We put the bags down on the counter and went to investigate.

My mother was supervising as Samuel and one of his friends moved one of the couches across the room. The coffee table had already been pushed against the fireplace. A keyboard had been set up on the side of the room and I saw a microphone stand. Cosmo and Felix were having a field day with all the activity and were jumping on and off the couch as it was moved. As usual my other terrier mix Blondie was absent, and I was sure she was hiding out in my bedroom. She rarely mixed with the other two dogs or anyone else. That was why I called her the Greta Garbo of dogs. Mr. Kitty and Cat were nowhere to be seen and had probably hidden themselves away. I could see their point.

My mother noticed us and hurried over with a frantic expression. "Molly, I'm so sorry for all this, but it's an emergency. We're going to rent a space to rehearse, but in the meantime we were going to use the rec room where we're staying. But it's booked out all week and the girls and I have to do some run-throughs before the bookstore event. You wouldn't want me to embarrass you in front of your people, would you?" She stopped for a breath. "You understand, don't you? Samuel said you wouldn't mind."

The doorbell rang, and my father let the two other She La Las in. There was a bunch of gushing and hugging. Mason and I looked at each other and put up our hands in helplessness.

"How is it that we have two big houses between us and we can't find a quiet corner to have dinner?" he said when we'd retreated to the kitchen. Samuel had already started playing some chords on the keyboard, and I could hear the She La Las doing vocal exercises as my father tapped on the microphone and said, "Testing, testing." He kept repeating it, apparently not realizing the sound was booming all over the house.

"It's works," I yelled toward the living room—not that he heard me over all the ruckus. Mason chuckled at the absurdity of the situation. But then his eyes lit up.

"I have a plan."

A few minutes later, we closed the kitchen door behind us

and left all the chaos behind. We'd carried the bags of food with us, and we settled them on the umbrella table in the yard. Mason put some wood in the fire pit I'd had for years and never used. He lit it and it instantly gave off warmth.

"There's nothing like a nighttime picnic," he joked. "And we can play with this for entertainment," he said, holding the box with the detective set. I hadn't noticed that he'd grabbed it on our way out the door.

While I set out the food, he opened the box and looked inside. "What's all this?" he said, looking at the cards, bags and containers that I'd been dropping into it.

"My evidence," I joked. I picked up one of the booklets that came with it and showed him the line that said the set encouraged the junior detective to gather evidence to get experience examining it. "I got some of the fingerprints at my party. Except for this one." I extracted the plastic bag with the chocolate smudge I'd put inside a paper one, hoping to keep it intact. "And the fibers are from some horrible yarn Adele was using. I picked the pink strands off my sweater and the chairs at the class.

"And that," I said, pointing to a plastic bag within another one. The inner bag had the dog hairs I'd collected. I smiled, thinking of what else it had. "Barry found it in the yard behind us when he was checking things out the second time. When he handed it to me, I realized it was a chance to see what it was like to get a fingerprint off a plastic bag and get a sample of his. I don't think he realized what I was doing when I had him set it on the table instead of handing it to me. Then I used tweezers to drop it inside the other bag. I haven't had time to try to dust it yet."

Mason thought it was too funny that I had snagged Barry's fingerprints without him realizing it.

We put the set aside and finally got down to eating. With

our jackets and the fire pit going, it was actually quite comfortable outside. "I think there are some cookies in the kitchen," I said. "And I could make some coffee."

Mason liked the idea, and I went into the house. My mother had made pitchers of her green drink and there was a tray with hummus and vegetables. I could hear singing coming from the living room as I quickly made a pot of coffee and put together a tray of cookies.

"Ah, the peace out here," I said when I rejoined him. He was looking over the backyard to Cheyenne's house. The trees blocked some of the view, but the patio and balcony were still clearly visible.

"I'm hoping when they put up a solid fence, it will be better," I said.

Mason shook his head. "With the way they created that hill, a fence won't do much good. We'll have to figure where to plant some strategic privacy bushes."

I poured the coffee and we had our dessert while looking back toward Cheyenne's house. I pointed out the balcony. "That's where all the action was. The so-called dancing couple and the spot where the chaise cushion came from."

I looked through the chain-link and the scraggling of ivy on my side. It was invisible in the darkness, but that part of Cheyenne's yard was almost on the same level as mine. I had a good view of the workmen when they worked on the yard. "At least the workmen and their music aren't there now. It's not bad enough they play the radio—they sing along, too."

Mason chuckled. "Maybe they're hoping that Garrett Mackenzie gets them a record deal." I was already back to thinking about the chaise cushion.

"If only I could get a look at it again. If there was blood underneath, I bet some got on the cushion."

"Whoa, Molly. You can't sneak up on that balcony. I don't want to have to defend you for being a stalker."

"That's practically what Barry said to me," I said.

"When?" Mason said, sitting forward and turning to me. I mentioned that he'd come with Jeffrey for their dog care duties.

"That's something new. I thought Jeffrey usually came alone." Mason seemed agitated, which was unusual for him.

"Barry said he's trying to turn over a new leaf with his son."

"As long as it's only his son he's trying to work things out with," Mason said. "Maybe they should just keep Cosmo at their place."

Now I sat forward. "Aside from everything else, like the fact that they're not really home to take care of him, he's really my dog. Cosmo just goes along with the program when they come over, but believe me—he never tries to leave with them. That dog knows where his home is."

"Sorry," Mason said, putting up his hands to fend off my attack. "What was I thinking? I know how I feel about Spike, so I should understand your feeling for Cosmo."

"I might occasionally complain about the menagerie at my house, but I love each and every one of them, no matter how they ended up living with me." Mason made an understanding sound.

I knew it was not the dog he was really concerned with.

CHAPTER 12

I WAS DRAGGING THE NEXT MORNING WHEN I came into the bookstore. The night before, the fire in the fire pit had burned itself out and we'd taken everything back inside. The music had still been coming from the living room as we decided to call it a night. When I went across the living room to my bedroom, the three She La Las were still gyrating across the floor. Maybe there was something to my mother's green drink after all.

Now I'd barely dropped off my jacket and bag and was checking some things at the information counter, which was as close as I got to an office, when I heard a commotion coming from the direction of the children's department. When I looked toward the noise, I saw Adele fussing with another woman.

My eyes stopped on Adele—the other woman was really an afterthought. I always thought that Adele couldn't get any more outlandish with her story time outfits, but once again she had proved me wrong. She had on some long white thing that I had a feeling was a bedsheet she'd turned into her impression of an ancient Egyptian dress. She had cinched it with a gold belt and made a necklace out of the jangling pieces belly dancers wore around their hips. She topped it off with a stylized black wig and makeup I could see across the room. Her eyes were outlined in heavy black and she had eye shadow on practically to her eyebrows. She'd been generous with the blush and lipstick, too.

I didn't recognize the woman she was fussing with. She seemed a little old to be a mother bringing young kids to story time, but too young to be a grandparent. It was obvious from their body language that she and Adele had reached some kind of impasse. I didn't see Mrs. Shedd or Mr. Royal and decided that it was my duty as assistant manager to step in and see if I could smooth things over.

As I approached, I saw that Adele was holding a sheet of paper that I assumed was one of her membership forms. She looked up as I reached them. Apparently, she thought it was her outfit that had brought me over, since she flashed her heavily made-up eyes and said she was going to read *Aunt Ellie Meets Cleopatra*. Now it made sense.

Adele read a lot of books from the Aunt Ellie series, probably because of the opportunities for different costumes. Aunt Ellie had a time machine and zoomed around history meeting up with famous people. I chuckled, inwardly remembering when Adele had read *Aunt Ellie Meets Abraham Lincoln*.

"Excuse me, are you in charge?" the woman said. "I was explaining to her that I'm just the temporary nanny for the Mackenzie children, so there is no reason for me to fill out anything." She waved her hand toward Adele.

"She keeps insisting she needs my cell phone number. I will be standing right outside here, waiting for the children."

I looked at her with new interest. She was a lot closer to Mrs. Doubtfire than Jennifer Clarkson was, with serviceable dark slacks, white polo shirt, and long blue sweater. She had a broad face, no makeup, and light brown hair pulled into a low ponytail.

"Why don't you let me handle this?" I said to Adele. Just then an athletic-looking young man came out of the children's area and handed Adele a sheet.

"It's all there," he said. "See you in an hour."

"Harumph, a manny," the nanny said.

"Excuse me? Who is Manny?" I asked, confused. She put her hand on her hip and turned to face me.

"I wasn't speaking of the name, but rather the position. That's what they're calling male nannies. Personally, I think it's a sexist remark. The nanny title should go with everyone who does the job, although I would prefer a more formal designation, like full-time child supervisor." She looked toward the young man, who was headed toward the café.

"He just started taking care of the Mackenzie children's cousins." She made another dissatisfied sound. "I understand he's the second replacement in six months, and the first male one. Maybe he'll work out better. I heard that their father is a country singer and quite the flirt. I wouldn't have gone there if they'd offered it to me." She drew a circle in the air with her finger, pointing at herself. "This is strictly off-limits to anyone I work for."

I had to hold in a laugh. With her formidable appearance, I didn't think she had to worry. Adele looked into the children's area. She'd arranged the kids on the floor in front of the story throne, as she called her highly decorated chair. But they were getting impatient and had begun to roll around and tease each other.

"I'd better get in there," Adele said. "Pink, I trust you to get what we're after." She pushed the paper on me and then, amid her swirling sheet dress, marched in, clapping her hands to get their attention.

"Thank you for stepping in," the nanny said to me. "I think all that eye makeup must have gone to her brain." She held out her hand for me to shake it. "Ursula Johnson, at your service."

"Molly Pink, at yours," I said, accepting her handshake. It was hard for me to contain myself. I felt like a kid in a candy store of information. I was sure Ursula could be a great source of information if I could get her to talk.

"It must be difficult stepping in at the last minute," I said. I made sure she knew that I had heard Jennifer had left suddenly.

"I'm used to it. I'm like a transplant surgeon—on call twenty-four-seven, three hundred and sixty-five days a year. Things happen. Nannies get sick, or quit and walk out. Someone has to be able to step in with no warning. I certainly had to hustle to get over there. The shuttle had just pulled up when I was getting out of my car. I barely got a chance to ask her the most basic of questions."

She shifted back and forth and muttered something about being on her feet all the time, and I offered her a chair at the yarn table. She seemed a little hesitant, but I explained that she'd be able to see the children's department from there and she accepted the seat. I saw her glance at the paper in my hand. The way her eyes fluttered I figured out that she was hoping I'd forgotten about it and was going to do whatever she could to distract me. All fine with me.

"You're right. I have a clear view." Ursula kept her eyes

glued on the spot where the carpeting changed to the cows jumping over the moon. "Some of us take the care of children very seriously," she said. "More seriously than their own parents." She shook her head, as if she'd thought of something disagreeable.

"That house is an absolute danger zone. I don't understand why they moved in there before it was all finished. They can't even put the cars in the garage. Apparently it's full of the workmen's supplies. Their mother has no sense. She lets them go in there and help themselves to ice cream treats. I was going to overrule her. Letting small children eat unlimited ice cream treats is a recipe for future problems. I was so glad when the husband stepped in and told them there was too much stuff in the way. If this job wasn't temporary, I would get that household into shape."

There was a pause in the conversation and she looked down toward the paper. I realized I could probably ask her anything if she thought it was keeping my mind off getting her to fill out the sheet. "What is Cheyenne Chambers really like?"

Ursula was glad to talk, though she prefaced it by saying she didn't believe in gossiping about the people she worked for. "There's definitely something going on there," she said. "The husband keeps looking at her like he's worried about something. I'm staying in a room off the kitchen, but I can hear someone pacing upstairs at night."

"What about arguing? Do Cheyenne and her husband get along?"

"I'll just say this. She's the one with a temper. I can't hear words, but I have heard her voice—it sounded like she was in a fury."

"What about dancing?"

Ursula's mouth fell open in surprise. "All I can say is

that they don't as far as I've seen." We talked a little more, but it was mostly about how she operated as a nanny and of no use to me. She kept her eye on the entrance to the children's department and let out a sigh of relief as the kids began to come out. "Time to go," she said, getting up quickly. "It was nice talking to you."

She thought she had gotten away with something. But actually she had given away a lot of information.

Adele wasn't happy when she realized the sheet of paper was still blank. "She's only there temporarily, until Jennifer Clarkson comes back, and you have a sheet on her," I said. Adele made a face and then collapsed at the yarn table. "Everything is falling apart. You let the first person slip through without filling out one of my forms. Any minute now Susan or Cheyenne is going to call Mrs. Shedd and complain about the Tunisian class.

"And now this," She looked toward the front door just as Eric Humphries, also known as Cutchykins, came in. He was wearing his motor officer uniform, which made the tall, barrel-chested man seem even more imposing. "You have to help me. I haven't told him about the wedding disaster yet."

"I don't know if I can help you with that, but I think I can help with Cheyenne," I said. What I left out was that it might be a solution for me, too.

CHAPTER 13

"MY BEST FRIEND, MOLLY, HAS COME UP WITH A way for me to keep Cheyenne happy with the class," Adele said. She was standing next to me with her arm around my shoulder. The happy hour group had gathered in the yarn department and was already working on their toys. I was surprised when Adele gave me the credit. When I shared the idea, I was sure she'd claim it as her own. Adele never ceased to surprise me.

"I thought the only problem was with your wedding," Rhoda said, and the whole group prepared for Adele's onslaught of wailing, but she maintained the same expression.

"Molly helped me break the news to Cutchykins." She looked at me. "Tell them what happened."

Being considered Adele's best friend seemed to come with a lot of duties. "Eric was very understanding. He said that all he cared about was being with Adele and how it happened didn't matter. He also promised not to tell his mother." A wave of *aww*s went through the group, and Adele basked in the attention.

"What about the other thing? I didn't know there was a problem with Cheyenne," Rhoda said in her nasally voice. "Did I miss something?"

Adele looked around the area surreptitiously, and when she was satisfied turned back to the group and turned the floor over to me. "You tell them, Pink." Apparently my best friend status only came with my first name sometimes.

"Those of you in the Tunisian class probably remember that Cheyenne didn't come to the first class and left in the middle of the third one. Adele was afraid that she would think she was so far behind that she would give up the class." I was going to leave it at that, but Adele urged me on.

"Tell them about Pamela," Adele said. She had picked up the flying pig that she was crocheting and was beginning to stuff the body. She thought it would give someone feeling down and out hope because of the saying *when pigs fly*.

Adele was the only one to call Mrs. Shedd by her first name. She had actually encouraged all of us to do it, but the rest of them agreed with me that it somehow felt wrong to call her anything other than Mrs. Shedd.

"Mrs. Shedd seems to be delighted about having Cheyenne be part of the group," I said. "She's excited about their event next week, and she would be upset if anything made Cheyenne back away from it."

"What about her sister? Isn't Lauren in the group, too?" Elise asked. I wasn't sure how the toys she chose to make were going to be received. In accordance with her passion for Anthony, the fictional vampire who crocheted, she kept making little vampire dolls. She used sparkly white yarn for the head, added a frizzle of black hair and made the body out of sparkly black yarn. The faces were all smiling, and thankfully she didn't have any red yarn stitches coming from the mouths. She did, however, add a bright red scarf to each one she made. The best possibility was that whoever we donated them to wouldn't realize what they were.

"She's not a problem," Rhoda said. "Unless her sister makes one. Cheyenne seems to be the decision maker and the one to please." Rhoda turned to me. "So what's the big plan?"

"I'm not sure it's exactly a big plan, but you know how celebrities like to be coddled."

"Not all of them," CeeCee said. "I have never asked for special treatment around here. The only time I made a fuss was when Mrs. Shedd seemed so anxious to hang pictures of Cheyenne, and even her entourage. It kind of made me feel taken for granted."

"Then it's some celebrities who need coddling," I said. "So, I thought that if Adele and I offered to go to her house and give her a private lesson, she might be more likely to stick with the group."

Dinah was sitting across the table. She knew that I probably had an ulterior motive, and she gave me a knowing smile. I gave just the slightest nod to acknowledge she was right.

"What about that Susan? If she hears, she'll probably expect an at-home lesson, too," Rhoda said.

"No. She doesn't have to know about it," Adele chimed in. "As for all her fussing, I'll just have to cozy up to her during class." There was a momentary pause, and then everyone but Adele laughed. She looked confused. Nobody had the guts to tell her that we were laughing at the idea of Adele cozying up to anyone, let alone someone like Susan.

"Dear, I should accompany you, too. If anybody knows how to deal with celebrities, it's me," CeeCee said, giving her perfectly styled brown hair a pat. She'd figured out a long time ago that one way to appear not to age was to keep the same hairstyle. She'd had the bangs and a length just below her ears since she'd starred in *The CeeCee Collins Show* back in the seventies.

"I'm coming, too," Rhoda said. "No reason other than I'm nosy."

"You can't leave me out," Elise said. "I want to see the inside of the house. My Logan is in real estate, and he almost had the listing for it."

Dinah looked at me, and I tried to convey the message that she didn't have to go. She seemed relieved. "I have a lot going on. I have to meet Commander about—" She stopped herself when she glanced at Adele. I was sure she was going to say it was about their wedding but then realized that word would send Adele into a wailing fit. "About something," she added at last. "And I'm in the middle of a crisis in my freshman English class." She shook her head in disbelief. "They keep topping themselves. I really thought it couldn't get worse than some of them trying to text their papers. They're handing them in printed now, but they are half words and half little icons they're used to using in their social media communications. Some of them I get, like a happy face, but lots of the others I don't. It's like visual slang. I wonder if there's one for unacceptable."

Sheila came into the bookstore just then, and when she heard what was going on, she was happy to let us go without her. "It would make me too nervous," she said.

"Well, then, that's settled," Rhoda said. "When does Cheyenne want the lesson?"

Adele pointed to me. "We haven't exactly spoken to her yet," I said. "There's one more thing—everyone please remember to keep your lips zipped about me being her neighbor."

The *we* became *me* when Adele urged me to contact Cheyenne right away, while the group was all there, so we could arrange the time.

Mrs. Shedd had made sure I got all of Cheyenne's contact information when she first talked about doing the event. I tried a variety of numbers before I reached a real person. Garrett answered, and when I explained who I was and what it was about, he handed over the phone to her.

"A private lesson," she gushed. "That would be wonderful." I mentioned that a number of people were coming to assist, and she just said, "The more the merrier."

"Tell her I'm coming, too," CeeCee said. I passed along the information, which made Cheyenne sound more enthused, and we agreed on a time the next afternoon. She said something cryptic about the light being better during the day, and then we said our good-byes.

"I still can't believe you want to be involved," Rhoda said to CeeCee. "You seemed very negative about her and the way she behaves."

CeeCee took a deep breath. "First of all, I'm doing it to help Adele. And I've reconsidered my opinion of Cheyenne. I think she might be what's happening now. Maybe that's the way you have to do it. Keep yourself out there, no matter what it is. If you don't move with the times, you get behind," she said in her musical voice. "Though I do miss the old days when the publicity people controlled what got out about us actors. They'd go to great lengths to bury something like a photo of someone with spinach in their teeth. Everything was positive."

"You're right about the old days," I said, thinking of my late husband and his PR business. One of his favorite things to do had been creating Ten Best lists and sprinkling a couple of his clients in there. He would never put his clients at the top, and would fill in the rest with even more well-known people. The pieces were easy to place, and even though they were completely fictitious, none of the other people on it complained. Why would they? They were suddenly on lists of the top ten celebrities who had the brightest smile or cutest dog, or who were nicest to waiters or whatever else he could come up with. Who would argue that they didn't belong on the list?

"That wouldn't work now," CeeCee said after I had explained this tactic. "Maybe I could try to line up my own show. *CeeCee Collins Uncensored*, or *Keeping Up with CeeCee*," she said. "I could let the public see me in the morning with no makeup before my coffee." She paused to think it over. "Well, maybe just a little makeup, or expert lighting. And I'd have to have a little coffee or my eyes would droop. I'm sure there's a way to make it look real, but still cover up some flaws. I'll talk it over with Cheyenne when we go there."

The others agreed to meet Adele and me at the bookstore after work and then carpool. "Well, problem solved," I said to Adele as everyone began to pack up. "We all know how much it means to Mrs. Shedd that Cheyenne is in the class." I saw Mr. Royal coming in with some stock. "I think he's the real reason it means so much. He's the one so enamored with the music business. The music and video department is his baby, and Cheyenne's presence is putting a spotlight on it."

"She's not the only person from ChIlLa," Rhoda said. "What about Lauren?"

I suddenly felt embarrassed that I'd forgotten about her. "And her, too," I said, trying to cover for my mistake.

"Whatever," Elise said, packing her mini vampire into her bag. "Until tomorrow, ladies."

"I guess you aren't so worried about Susan," I said to Adele.

"I can handle her. I'll just load on a little TLC next class. It was Cheyenne I was really worried about the most. And now I've solved the problem." So the *we* had now become *her*. It figured.

"Okay, what's going on?" Dinah asked. With Adele back in the children's department and everyone else gone, my friend and I had gone to the café and taken a table in a quiet corner.

"There's so much to tell, I don't know where to begin," I said.

"I have a lot to tell you, too," Dinah said, getting up to get our drinks. We were coffeed out and had gotten what I called party drinks. They were frothy and sweet, and covered with a generous dollop of whipped cream. When she returned I took a long sip of my strawberry frappé before I told her about my mother using my living room for a rehearsal hall again and how Mason and I had ended up huddled around the fire pit in my yard. She started to offer her sympathy, but I stopped her.

"I don't really care about my mother's rehearsing. By now I'm used to there being some kind of circus going on at my house all the time. It was when Mason and I were out there that I realized that I wanted to see that chaise cushion again." I needed another mouthful of the strawberry sweetness before I could continue. "But even Mason warned me about sneaking around in Cheyenne's yard." Dinah seemed confused, and I mentioned Barry's dog care visit and him giving me a similar warning. "I don't know why either of them was worried. It's one thing to slip into the yard with the gate and check out the ground, but totally different to actually go into the house to get to the balcony." I stopped and chuckled. "They can't have thought I'd try to climb it?"

Dinah joined in the laugh as we joked about how I would manage such a thing. "But if when we're giving Cheyenne the lesson, I happen to find myself on that balcony with my bottle of Blood Detector . . ." I let Dinah fill in the rest.

"Now I'm really sorry I won't be there. It sounds like you could use a lookout." She seemed deflated for a moment. "There's the thing with my students, and then I'm meeting Commander about the wedding invitations. He's taking care of everything, but he refuses to do it without my approval of his choice."

She changed the subject back to Cheyenne's house. "The group still doesn't know you saw a body in her yard, do they?" I shook my head in answer.

"It's hard enough to keep them from spilling that I'm her neighbor," I said. Then I mentioned meeting the new nanny. "She implied that Cheyenne has some kind of secret, and she looked at me like I was nuts when I asked if she'd noticed Cheyenne dancing."

"And the plot thickens. Cheyenne seems to put everything out there for the public to see. It makes you wonder if that's to camouflage what she wants to hide. Maybe I should just cancel everything and join the group," Dinah said.

Of course, I would have preferred to have her come

along. She was right—a lookout would certainly come in handy. But she had her own things to take care of.

"Promise you'll let me know what happens," she said as she sucked the last of her creamy drink through her straw with a slurping noise.

CHAPTER 14

SATURDAY MORNING, THE GROUP GOING TO
Cheyenne's met outside the bookstore. I was glad to ride
with someone else. I didn't want to drive the greenmobile
on the off chance Cheyenne or her husband might have
caught a glimpse of it in the driveway. I didn't know what
kind of view they had of my place, and the color and age
of the car made it stand out.

It didn't matter anyway. Adele insisted she was in
charge, and she arranged who would ride with who. She
chose me to ride shotgun in her Matrix.

My heartbeat picked up when Adele steered her car
onto Cheyenne's street. Her house sat at the end of the
cul-de-sac, and Adele pulled the car to the curb. When we
got out, I looked in the direction of my place. From this
angle I could just see the lone palm tree in my front yard
that towered above the whole area.

"They call this style California Cape Cod," Elise said.

"Logan told me that developers say they're building a custom house, but they use standardized plans." She glanced around at it. "This looks like the semi deluxe model."

The front of the house was more interesting than the side view I saw from my yard. It seemed an effort had been made not to have it look like a big white box. A balcony was hooked on in front of what was probably a bedroom, and a portion of the ground floor jutted out so the front of the house had a lot of angles. A driveway led to the garage that was attached to the side of the house.

As we approached the front door, Adele started going on about how she wanted to handle the lesson. I barely listened, since I was busy trying to figure out how I could get out on the back balcony unnoticed. I had mixed a small amount of the Blood Detector powder in the spray bottle and had it in a plastic bag in my pocket.

Garrett opened the door. He looked a little scruffy in his T-shirt and jeans with a couple of days' worth of beard. But that and the shaggy hair were all part of the music business look. He smiled as he greeted us, but there was a slight furrow to his brow, which I gathered meant he had things on his mind.

We all looked around the entrance hall as he brought us inside, so my curiosity didn't stand out. I quickly noted the entrance to the living room to the left of us. Matt Meadowbrook was in there with a bunch of small children. He looked out at us and tipped his ever-present cowboy hat and gave us a dimpled smile. I was as bad as the rest of them, getting all gushy and giggly at the way he seemed to give each of us a personal greeting.

It took me a moment before I realized this was the room I'd seen from my yard. I'd only gotten a sliver of a view, just enough to see Jennifer with the kids. Matt had been there then, too.

"Nanny's time off," he said, gesturing toward the kids, who were rolling around on the off-white couches. He turned to them. "Hey, guys, let's go get some ice cream."

"I know where it is," a little girl in a dress with a feather boa and cowboy boots said, running toward the door. Garrett stopped her. "Off-limits. Uncle Matt means from the store." The kids got more excited at the prospect of an adventure, and Garrett gave his brother-in-law an encouraging pat. "Are you sure you want to take all of them?"

Apparently Matt's charm worked with kids, too. He gave Garrett a nod and then told the kids they were going to play a game called helping him find the ice-cream store. Instantly, all four of them calmed down and lined up next to him. The little girl with the feather boa looked up at him and assured him she knew the way.

I noticed the stairway leading to the second floor as Garrett took us toward the back of the house. The hallway ended in a large den. The whole back was made up of mullioned, windowed French doors, and I could see the patio beyond. Or what would be the patio, when it was finished. Cheyenne was draped across a soft gray suede couch that faced into the room. Another, similar couch was adjacent. My immediate perception was that the house was more about living in than being for show. It didn't have that interior decorator signature of having the color of the throw pillows on the couch be picked up in a bowl on the coffee table.

There were neither throw pillows nor a bowl on the coffee table anyway. Some magazines were scattered among some coloring books and sheet music. It seemed odd that the house had a new smell but the furniture clearly wasn't new.

I was surprised when Lauren came into the room and sat down next to her sister. "Hi, girls," she said, seeming more animated than she'd ever been at the bookstore, almost like a switch had been turned on. Even her appearance was different. I guessed it was the makeup and the leather pants. She glanced toward the front of the house at the door. "Lucky for Matt, my kids are with their dad."

Cheyenne had on a graphic T-shirt and a pair of jeans with shredding at one of the knees. There was a time when that would have appeared pathetic, but now it was the style, and you actually paid extra to get them that way. She glanced toward her husband. "Will you go get Ilona?"

Cheyenne turned back to the group and thanked us for coming, going on about how nice it was that we cared so much.

"I should be next to you," Adele said, taking the spot to her right. "They can sit over there," she said, pointing to the other couch. Elise and Rhoda took the suggestion, but CeeCee seemed reluctant. I could read her expression and could tell that she didn't like being relegated to what amounted to the "children's table."

Ilona came in with Garrett and perched herself on the sofa's other end. There was something catlike and languid about the way she stretched herself out. She was the only blond of the sisters, which made me suspect the color wasn't natural. She had a long face, and her hair was cut into a pixieish style. Her outfit was all-black stretchy stuff, with knee-high boots that had silver buckles.

"Nobody is going to believe I'm doing this," Ilona said, holding out a crochet hook and yarn. Lauren reached over and turned the hook right side up and put it in her sister's hand correctly.

I edged my way to the corner of the room, where I had a view out the glass doors. It was my first close-up daytime view of the patio, and I saw the material that had been under the cushion was irregular slabs of grayish stone, just like I had on my patio. The balcony was directly above it and was my goal. I surreptitiously looked to see if perhaps there was an outdoor stairway, but there wasn't. From here I could see my yard, but since the ground was higher and on an angle, I just got a view of my roof and enough of the kitchen window to see that my gray terrier mix Felix was on the kitchen table sleeping in a spot of sunlight.

Cheyenne saw CeeCee about to take a seat on the other couch. "No, no, you should be here." She turned to Lauren and told her to take the other armrest and patted the spot Lauren had vacated. CeeCee instantly perked up.

"Okay, Garrett, we're ready," she said. He came back in with a video camera. Just as I was figuring it out, Cheyenne started to explain. "We're always looking for something to post on social media. What better than the three of us crocheting with our friends and veteran actress CeeCee Collins?"

With all the activity, no one noticed as I moved along the back of the room and out the door on the other side. It led to a hall that paralleled the one we'd come in. I barely saw the large kitchen and formal dining room as I went back toward the front of the house and the stairway.

As much as I tried to stay calm, my heart was thudding and my mouth had gone dry. I had a cover story ready—the usual, that I was looking for the bathroom, but with a two-story house it was harder to pull off. There obviously was at least a powder room on the ground floor. I hoped it wasn't going to be an issue.

When I reached the top of the stairway, I was relieved to see the second floor had thick carpet to absorb the sound of my footsteps. I stopped for a moment, getting my bearings. A U-shaped hall went around the second floor. An upstairs den was directly in front of me and had French doors like the downstairs ones. It seemed sparsely furnished, with beanbag chairs and a lot of toys.

I took a deep breath as I realized my goal was within reach. I could see the lounge chairs on the balcony before I even reached the doors. I opened the glass door softly and stepped outside. The cushions were all yellow, which was a relief. I was afraid they might have gotten trashed. The tops of the cushions all appeared pristine, so I began turning them one by one. The first two were the same on the other side. The last one had some dirt caked to it. It had to be the one. I ran my hand over it looking for telltale signs of dried blood, but there was nothing. It didn't matter—the Blood Detector would react to any residue. I took out the bottle, prepared to spray. After a moment's pause to make sure I was unobserved, I began to spritz. Then I waited. Nothing showed on the cushion. Was I wrong? I quickly read the label on the bottle, and then I understood. The blue glow needed darkness to show.

I put the bottle back in the plastic bag and got ready to retrace my steps.

"You shouldn't be out there," a voice commanded, and I froze. My mind had gone blank and I stole a look inside to see who it was. Ursula was standing in the doorway. She was wearing her coat and carrying a bag of something. I took a breath, realizing that I had overreacted. I had noted when I met her that she naturally had a tone of authority in her voice.

I used the bathroom excuse and mumbled something about wanting to check the weather. It was nonsense, but the best I could do. As soon as she recognized me, she waved me over.

"I need to talk to you," she said in a stern voice. As soon as I reached the doorway, she took my hand and led me down the stairs. I was sure she was going to drag me into the den and report where she'd found me, but when we got to the bottom of the stairs, she led me to the hall I'd come through before. I hadn't noticed the doors along it when I'd been on way to the stairs. She opened one and brought me into the room.

"I'm sorry if I startled you before, but I was told the balcony was off-limits. We can talk in here," she said, shutting the door. I took in the room quickly. There was a single bed and a desk with some things on it. A wall unit with some shelves sat against one wall, and a dresser was against another. A small suitcase was on the floor. It was open, and I could see that it was full of clothes. There was one chair in front of a small desk, but she didn't invite me to sit.

"I saw that woman from story time is in the den." Ursula shook her head with dismay. "I just can't deal with her. You have to step in."

The shock of being discovered was wearing off, and now I was just listening, waiting to hear what she was going to say.

"I thought I wouldn't have to deal with her again. That Jennifer would have returned before the next story time. But it doesn't look that way. I cannot be harassed about filling out a form with my cell phone number. I will always be there waiting when the children come out."

"What makes you think she's not coming back soon?" I asked.

Ursula ignored me and took off her coat and hung it on the back of the chair before putting the bag she'd been carrying down. She clucked her tongue as she looked around the room.

"There's no reason to be living out of a suitcase if I'm going to be here that long." She opened the closet door. I stood on my tiptoes to see over her shoulder as she pushed some hangers farther to the side and seemed to be looking for empty hangers.

She turned back to face the room and I repeated my question, and this time she answered.

"It's something I just heard from the service," she muttered, glancing around. "You seem like someone with sense. Since I'm going to be here for a while, do you think I should pack the other nanny's stuff up? I'm not one to mess with other people's things, but I think the room should be mine while I'm here."

I sensed she didn't really want my opinion as much as she wanted me to agree with her. Actually, I could see her point. "Sure, you ought to be able to hang up your clothes and get her things out of the way."

"That's just what I'm going to do." She looked back in the closet and pulled out a suitcase. As she did a guitar case started to come forward. She caught it before it fell and pushed it back against the closet wall. "This must be hers, so I'll just put everything in it." She put the suitcase on the bed and opened it. "What's this?" she said, looking down into it. I was curious as to what caused her comment and casually moved closer to get a view inside of it just as she pulled out a bag from a local drugstore.

"Well, if that doesn't beat all." There was disgust in her voice as she held a bottle of pink liquid. I leaned forward to read the label. All I saw were the words "Children's" and "Allergy" before she slipped it back in the bag. It seemed to be hitting other bottles, which made me think there were more in there.

"You seem upset about what you just found," I said, hoping my comment would get her to explain.

Instead, she flashed me a look. "So do you think you

can keep that woman off my back? The children love story time, but I won't bring them back if it's required that I give out my cell phone number."

She began gathering up items on the dresser and desk and putting them in the suitcase. I did my best to see what she was picking up, assuming they must be Jennifer's things. There were some papers and CDs in clear cases that Ursula took from the desk.

She picked up a black purse from the dresser. "She certainly did leave in a hurry," Ursula muttered. "Not even to take her purse." She dropped it into the suitcase. "You haven't given me an answer. Can I depend on you to handle the situation? I wouldn't want to have to tell their parents that the children can't go to something they enjoy because I'm being harassed."

Great, another way I had to worry about Cheyenne or, more likely, her husband being annoyed with the bookstore. "I'm sure I can convince Adele to make an exception," I said, hoping it was true.

She picked up the bag she'd brought in and walked into the bathroom. I didn't follow her in, but once I saw that she was still on her clearing-up mission, I watched from behind her. She made a sound of distaste as she picked up a towel and wrapped it around a toothbrush and open tube of toothpaste and a selection of cosmetics and hair products and pushed them to the end of the counter. She emptied the bag she'd been carrying, and I saw it contained a full-size bottle of mouthwash and a glass cup. She picked off the label from the cup and set it next to the sink before taking her teeth-cleaning supplies out of a zippered bag and putting them in it.

"And they will get their membership cards back. She confiscated them when she saw that someone new had brought the children."

"I'll tell you what," I began. "I'll make sure they get their cards back if you tell me what you found out from your service about Jennifer. And I'll make sure that Adele doesn't bother you again." I almost felt like crossing my fingers. Could I actually deliver on my promise?

Ursula turned to face me. "I can't imagine why you would care, but I'll make that deal. The service said the Mackenzies were very unhappy with the way Jennifer left so suddenly, and apparently they caught her in a lie. She claimed her mother was sick and must have forgotten that she told Mrs. Mackenzie that her mother died when she was a child. I'm not sure what they're going to do when she comes back. If they let her go, I'll have to stay here until the service finds a replacement that suits them."

I wanted to ask Ursula for more details, but she was staring intently at me. "And now I expect you to keep up your end of the bargain," she said with a definitive nod.

"Of course," I said, hoping I sounded more sure than I felt.

She gestured toward the door. "I'm sure you want to get back to whatever it is that Mrs. Mackenzie has cooked up this time. I need some time to put my feet up before my time off is over."

I managed to slip back into the den unnoticed. The three sisters were singing as they crocheted. Adele was looking directly into the camera, seeming to being enjoying every moment. CeeCee had arranged herself so her best side showed. Rhoda and Elise both seemed a little stunned and didn't notice when I sat on the end of the couch.

"That's a wrap," Cheyenne said when they'd reached the end of the song. Garrett stopped videoing and gave his body a little stretch. "We'll do a little editing and have it up by this evening."

I was still thinking about what Ursula had told me as

they got up. They were all abuzz with the excitement of being all over social media. Finally, CeeCee noticed me.

"There you are, dear." She looked out the glass doors at the chain-link fence. "That's your—" It didn't take too much imagination to figure out that she was going to finish it with *yard* or *house*.

"Time to go," I said, cutting her off and hustling her toward the door.

I WANTED TO TALK TO DINAH. I CERTAINLY couldn't tell the group about what I'd heard about Jennifer. I had purposely kept them in the dark about anything negative going on with Cheyenne's place. I hoped she wouldn't mind my interrupting her time with Commander, but as soon as Adele dropped me back at my car in the bookstore parking lot, I headed directly to the Mail It Quick Center, which Commander owned and operated. Apparently she didn't, because as soon as I walked in, she came up and grabbed me as if I were a life preserver.

"Seeing the invitations makes it all a little too real," Dinah said under her breath.

Commander was leaning over the center counter, which was spread with a bunch of samples of wedding invitations. He seemed to have no idea that Dinah had used me to get away from what they were doing. Nor, I suspect, of how uncomfortable she was at having to deal with the invitations, even if it was just picking out the one she liked best.

A man came over from the post office boxes, which were in an alcove near the front door. He saw the invitations. "For you?" he said to Commander.

"Yup. All we have to do is pick the one we like and I'll print them up."

"Congratulations. It's nice that things are turning out well for you."

"And there's my bride," Commander said with so much pride in his voice, looking at Dinah.

The man turned to Dinah and me. I'm not sure if he knew which of us it was, so he spoke to both of us. "You're getting a great guy. I don't know if you have any idea the kind of stuff Commander does for his customers." He looked to Commander and smiled. "A lot of us who have post boxes work out of our homes. There's no gathering around the watercooler to socialize or hanging in a break room for us, and it can get pretty lonely. Commander figured it out and he started arranging get-togethers for us post box people. That's how I met my wife." He gave Commander another pat and then told Dinah she was a lucky woman.

Commander almost seemed to be blushing, but I could tell he was pleased. I already knew the story and that there was really more to it. Commander had been in the throes of grief over the death of his wife, and he'd turned his own loneliness into a way to help others by starting the get-togethers. And he'd continued doing things for senior centers. He was all about making other people happy, and in the process he had found his own.

He'd probably been working since early morning, but the crease in his khakis was still razor sharp, and there wasn't the hint of a wrinkle in his blue oxford cloth dress shirt or a hair out of place in his thick shock of white hair.

"Go on with Molly," he said. "I can tell you two need some girl time."

We went outside and crossed the small strip mall to a tea shop that had just opened up. Dinah hung her head. "I wish I wasn't such a stick in the mud. It was so much easier getting married the first time. I didn't know anything. Now I'm worried about everything."

I gave her a hug and assured her it would all work out.

"I don't see you rushing to the altar again."

"Who knows what the future will bring?" I said. "This is about you anyway. Just be glad you're not in Adele's shoes." We went inside and looked at the menu. We both chose chai tea lattes and stood by the bar while we waited for them.

"I just wish he wasn't so perfect," she said. The barista pushed our drinks to the front of the counter. We picked them up and went to a table. "I'm afraid he's in for a shock when we live together. It's going to start with the toothpaste. He's the kind who carefully rolls the tube up from the bottom, and I'm much more of a random squeezer," she said.

"There's an easy fix—just have your own tubes," I said with a laugh.

But all the talk of toothpaste stirred something in my mind.

"Who leaves a place without taking their toothbrush or their purse?"

"Huh?" Dinah said, giving me a puzzled look. Then she snapped to attention. "Does this have to do with your checking out the chaise cushion? How did that go?"

"It was a bust," I said, telling her about the blue light only showing up in the dark. "But I busted Felix." I smiled. "Sorry for the corny play on words—I couldn't help myself." I described seeing the dog sleeping on the table.

"What about the rest of it? Did anyone slip up and give away that you're Cheyenne's neighbor?"

I brushed over that question and brought up Ursula.

"Who?" Dinah said. "With all this wedding stuff and my students and their pictures in their essays, I'm missing out on everything. By the way, the meeting with them was short and to the point. They told me I was out of touch and needed to move with the times. I told them I'm the teacher, and if they want to pass my class they better turn in hard copies of their papers written in complete words only. No texts, no shortened words and no happy faces, emoticons or emoji."

"Good for you," I said, and then reassured her that she hadn't really missed too much. "Ursula is Jennifer's replacement and also the person who caught me in the act of fondling the chaise cushion." I could laugh about it now that it had turned out not to be a problem. "And all your talk of toothpaste reminded me of something I saw at Cheyenne's." I explained about the war between Ursula and Adele before I got to describing what I'd seen. "Jennifer's purse was on the dresser. All of her cosmetics and hair stuff were on the counter in the bathroom. And the cap wasn't on her toothpaste and her toothbrush was next to it. Her suitcase was in the closet."

Dinah played with the lid of her drink. "What do you think it means?"

"If it was just one of those things, I wouldn't think it meant anything, but all of them? It makes me wonder if Jennifer Clarkson didn't really leave at all."

"But you talked to her on her cell phone," Dinah said.

"I talked to *someone* on her cell phone." I looked at Dinah. "And there's something more. Jennifer's mother died when she was a child."

"Ooh, the plot really thickens," Dinah said.

CHAPTER 15

I WENT BACK TO THE BOOKSTORE IN THE AFTERNOON. Somehow my suggestion of Dinah and Commander each having their own tube of toothpaste after they got married seemed to encourage Dinah. She'd gone back to the Mail It Quick center resolved to pick out the invitations and go forward with the wedding plans with more joy. Who knew it would be so easy to solve the whole issue?

Mr. Royal was busy sprucing up the music and video department. He had picked up the signs announcing the upcoming event with ChILLa and the She La Las from the printer and was positioning one right at the entrance to the alcove. He waved me over as he was finishing up. "How big a crowd are you expecting?" he asked.

"I usually set up for fifty people for our author events," I said. He didn't seem content with that.

"This is going to be bigger. ChILLa is posting about it on their Facebook fan page." He gazed around the bookstore.

"We can roll back the bookshelves and open the middle of the store up. Make it one hundred seats." He stopped to consider. "You'll have to rent some chairs. No, why don't I take care of that. It's going to be great."

In the background, I saw Mrs. Shedd overhear him and smile with satisfaction. As I had thought, she was doing it all for him.

I barely had time to straighten up the yarn department. The romance readers were having a meeting, and I'd had to set it up for them. Usually they just got together to discuss a book they'd all read, but this month I had gotten Eduardo to be a special guest. Even though he'd put his career as a cover model behind him, everyone still thought of him that way.

He got to the event area just as the women were starting to arrive. I had to smile when I saw he was wearing one of the outfits from the old days. The white, billowing shirt was open and exposed his chest. Leather pants and boots finished off the look. Time had been kind to his angular face, and his eyes were as clear blue as ever. We traded looks, and I smiled. His expression dimmed for a moment and I gathered that while the leather pants looked good, they might not be so comfortable—I noted him tugging at them.

"What's going on with the pictures at the front?" he asked. "Was that Cheyenne Chambers with a long crochet hook? And there seem to be several shots of CeeCee."

I got it. He was a celebrity, too. I got Mr. Royal to come over and take some photos to add to the bunch. Eduardo was a master at posing, and it turned out that he didn't have a bad side.

I left the bookstore just as it was getting dark. I wasn't sure what the plans for the evening were, but I stopped home to drop off my things and check on the animals. Of course, with the sun down, Felix had left his sleeping spot on the kitchen table. I looked the small gray terrier mix in the eye. "I know where you were and what you were doing."

Did he understand what I'd said? His tail wag did seem almost apologetic—before he sat down next to my leg and asked for some affection.

I felt the plastic bag still in my pocket. "A lot of good you were," I said to the spray bottle as I pulled the plastic bag out. I went into the dining room, where I'd left the detective set on the table. I was trying to be hypervigilant about keeping things in order. I had marked all the "evidence" I had collected. I laughed at what I was calling it. Evidence of what? There was my fingerprint collection, just in case one of the crocheters committed a crime, and the offending fibers that the group had accused of trying to choke them. I went to put the Blood Detector back in its slot in the box, but when I took it out of the bag, I noticed there was a small bit of caked dirt stuck to the bottom that must have gotten there when I set it on the chaise cushion. "Ah, more evidence," I said, shaking it into the bag and writing where it had come from on the label.

I heard music starting in the living room. Time for me to escape. I left the set and tried to slip through the living room unnoticed. My mother caught me just as I was about to walk into the den.

"Molly, why don't you join us?" She was holding a tambourine and gave it a shake. "We could use someone on the tambourine." I was okay with them using the living room as their practice place, but being part of the group? No way. I had no interest in being in front of a crowd. The closest I came was introducing the authors at the bookstore events.

"Pass," I said. I heard the phone ringing in the den. "Saved by the bell," I said in a voice that said I knew I was using a cliché. They were already back to singing by the time I grabbed the phone.

It was Mason checking in. "They're still practicing, huh?" he said, reacting to the noise in the background. "Why don't you come here?" I knew that would mean dealing with his ex and Brooklyn, but it had to be more peaceful than here.

"I have a lot to tell," I said with a tease in my voice.

"Then hurry on over, Sunshine," he said.

As I went back through the living room, my mother held up the tambourine and gave it another shake as she held it out toward me. I shook my head and quickened my pace.

The traffic was light, but I took the back roads to Mason's anyway. Fifteen minutes later, I pulled the green-mobile up in front of his house. He had the door open before I even reached it. It was certainly nice to feel so welcome.

"I thought they were going out," he said as we walked inside. Unlike Cheyenne's, his living room was almost never in use unless he was having a party. The den was the center of the house and where we always gravitated—and was unfortunately where his ex-wife and daughter also seemed to spend their time. Their claims that he would not even know they were living there had never materialized.

Brooklyn was sitting at the built-in desk poring over some books. Jaimee was on the couch watching a video on a computer tablet. They both looked up when we came into the room. Spike was running alongside Mason, and the toy fox terrier jumped on the sofa. He took one look at Jaimee and jumped back off. They didn't get along.

"What are we going to do about dinner?" Jaimee said, looking up.

I knew the answer had nothing to do with her cooking it. Now that she was a permanent fixture on the *Housewives of Mulholland Drive*, she viewed herself as working and being too busy to do anything more than make a cup of coffee—and even that was instant.

Brooklyn was going to law school and working part-time in her father's office. I doubted there was space left in her brain to think about putting together a meal. Somehow it always came down to Mason, who, despite working long hours himself, seemed to be the only one who could arrange dinner. *Arrange* didn't mean *cook*, though. He had a whole collection of menus from local restaurants that delivered.

He gave his ex-wife a hopeless look and opened the drawer that held all the menus. "What will it be tonight? Indian, Thai, sushi, Italian, Mediterranean, Chinese, healthy American, Mexican, Cuban—or Alfredo pizza?" he added with a chuckle. Both his daughter and ex-wife reacted to the last one, complaining about the calories.

"Don't listen to them," he said to me. "You pick."

The Alfredo pizza sounded heavenly, but I wasn't up for dealing with Jaimee and Brooklyn making a fuss, ordering something else and then harassing Mason and me for eating the decadent pizza. "Mediterranean," I said. He held up a handful of menus.

"Israeli, Lebanese, Persian, or Greek?" he said with a laugh.

"Greek," I said, relieved to have made a choice. Mason

took over the ordering and I did the set up when the array of food arrived.

Brooklyn put her work aside long enough to make up a plate of Greek salad, stuffed grape leaves, spinach and feta cheese wrapped in phyllo dough, rice, and chicken. Jaimee took some salad and chicken, saying something about giving up carbs for beauty.

She took her plate to the table in the big room that looked out onto the backyard. Mason and I grabbed spots on the couch and helped ourselves to the buffet I had set up on the coffee table.

"Ignore them," Mason whispered as his lips curved into a grin. "You were going to tell me something."

"The group went to Cheyenne Chambers's house today," I began. I was about to explain what we were doing there and what I'd hoped to find out, but Jaimee swooped in.

"You went to Cheyenne Chambers's house?" Jaimee put down her fork and turned her chair toward us. "She's like the go-to celebrity on TV. Anything with *Celebrity* or *Star* in the title and she's been on it." Jaimee began to name them. "*Celebrity Wife Exchange*, *Celebrity House Hunting*, *Cars of the Stars*, *Eating with the Stars*, *Celebrity Shopping Spree*—and now she's a judge on that show tune program."

"That's more than I realized," I said, amazed at the selection of shows.

"She's become a personality beyond being in that group," Jaimee added.

"What about dancing?" I said. So far nobody had come up with a reason why Cheyenne would have been practicing on the balcony, but Jaimee seemed to know all the reality shows.

"Dancing? I don't think so. For someone so musical she seems to have two left feet. Her 'husband' on *Celebrity Wife Exchange* took her out dancing, and it wasn't pretty."

"You seem to know a lot about her," I said. "Do you think she has any secrets?"

Jaimee leaned into the conversation. "I have my suspicions," she said. "She has such a big personality, and she's always so up. She comes across as so well-adjusted that even if she flops at something, she's okay with it. There's never a chink in her armor. It makes you wonder if it's real."

Jaimee was still talking when Mason and I started on the rice pudding. Her dessert was two strawberries that she sliced into paper-thin pieces. I heard Mason sighing. I understood—I really wanted to talk to him, too. There was something I had thought of after I left Dinah.

At least Jaimee wasn't being hostile. Mason and I cleared up the food, and when we were alone in the kitchen he grumbled, "I wanted to spend an evening with you, hearing about all your mysterious exploits."

"There's still time," I said, making us some Turkish coffee. We stood in the kitchen drinking the muddy brew and discussing our options.

"We could go to my room," he said. "There's a fireplace and places to sit."

I shook my head. "That makes me feel really uncomfortable. Have you seen your daughter's expression when we head down the hall?" When he didn't answer right away, I came up with a way I thought he would understand. "Think about if the positions were reversed and she and her boyfriend were going to her room."

"I get it. I don't like it, but I get it."

"There's always the backyard," I said.

He rolled his head from side to side. "We both have big houses, and we keep ending up outside."

His yard was set up better than mine. He had outdoor heat lamps that warmed the whole area around our chairs, and there was a pool with a fountain cascading into it that gave off a soothing sound.

"Alone at last," he said, taking my hand. "Now what were you going to tell me?"

After all this time I decided to keep it simple and say it in a few words. "I think the body I saw was the nanny, Jennifer Clarkson."

Mason sat upright as I continued.

"I talked to someone on the phone. All I could really say is that it was a woman with sort of a Southern accent."

"But we checked. She was on the flight to San Francisco. She had to have gone through security, and they would have checked her ID," he said. I brought up what Ursula had said about Jennifer's mother being dead, and how Jennifer had told me on the phone that she had to give medicine to her sick mother.

"I hate to bust your bubble," he began, "but people lie about all kinds of stuff. There's probably another reason why she really left." He turned to me. "No body has turned up, has it?" he asked, and I knew why he was asking. It was impossible to say it was a murder without finding a victim.

"No," I said, feeling cross.

Mason picked up on it. "I'm not doubting you. We just have to find out who it is and where they went." He looked ahead. "I have an idea. The pool is heated. We can come up with a plan while we swim."

When we finally did go down the hall to his room, no one was watching.

* * *

SUNDAY WAS A QUIET DAY AT THE BOOKSTORE. There were no events or groups meeting. Our customers seemed to be at a relaxed speed as they browsed the shelves. It was just Mr. Royal, our cashier and me. He waved me over to the event area.

"We've never had an event like this before and we need to be ready to handle a big crowd. I've decided we should give out tickets, and then when people come in, we give them a wristband that will let them in the area we've set aside."

"That sounds like a good idea. I was beginning to worry how we were going to handle the crowd."

He seemed pleased that I agreed and went off to see about getting the supplies we needed and to alter the signage to urge people to get their tickets early.

TUESDAY AFTERNOON WE HAD A FULL HOUSE FOR the Hookers' happy hour gathering. I was refreshed after my day off. Though I had spent the entire day doing everything I'd neglected all week. Even super sleuths like me had to do laundry and go to the grocery store. And for one night there was no singing in my living room.

Elise and Rhoda couldn't stop talking about being all over social media because of Cheyenne and her sisters. "They even picked it up on the news, saying instead of *whistle while you work* it's *sing while you crochet*," Rhoda said. "My daughter was even impressed."

"Cheyenne was very gracious and said she'd be glad to give me some tips to get myself out there more," CeeCee said.

"And who do you have to thank for it? Whose idea was the private lesson?" Adele was standing next to the table. She was dressed to be noticed—as if she ever wasn't. Black leggings and a turtleneck served as a backdrop for the long vest in eye-popping shades of orange, purple, turquoise, green and fuchsia. It was done in Tunisian crochet and, knowing Adele, she was using it as an advertisement of the class. She pointed to herself and took a little bow.

"But I thought Molly came up with the idea," Sheila said. Adele gave her a stricken look.

"Molly may have helped with the implementation of it," Adele said. "But the germ of the idea was all mine. I am the teacher of the class, aren't I?"

CeeCee turned to me. "And to think I almost spilled the beans and said that was your house. It's lucky you stopped me. That would have ruined things." She spoke to the group. "Cheyenne could drop in to a Hookers gathering. Remember everyone, not a word about where Molly lives."

Sheila seemed confused. "Why can't we say anything?" She asked the question of CeeCee, but CeeCee pointed Sheila toward me.

"I made a mistake and sent the police to her house twice and she thinks she has a crazy neighbor." I reluctantly pointed toward myself.

"Why did you send the police there?" Sheila asked.

"Yes, why did you?" Adele said.

Dinah was crocheting across the table. She looked up and gave me a nod, which I knew meant she thought I ought to tell them the whole story.

I described seeing the couple, who I now knew were Cheyenne and her husband, on the balcony. "To me it looked like they were arguing, and the person I now know was Cheyenne was almost pushed over the side of the balcony." I heard them all suck in their breath.

"So you sent the cops there, and what happened?" Sheila seemed really concerned.

"They claimed they were practicing a dance number. They said it was a dramatic tango that only looked like arguing."

"Oh," Sheila said. "So then that's what it was?"

"I wasn't going to say anything, but it doesn't make sense for so many reasons. There was no music playing. I've asked around and nobody knows any dance show she's going to be on. And I just heard recently that she has basically two left feet." They were all listening intently. "There's more. I also heard that Cheyenne has some kind of secret. It might even be that she's deliberately trying to appear like she's so open about everything so that nobody looks any further."

They had all put down their projects now and I had their full attention. Even Eduardo was listening intently. "You said you called them twice," he said. "Was there more of the arguing?"

This was where it got tricky. It was an involved story with too many hanging details. While I was wondering how exactly to begin, CeeCee said that all this intrigue made her want some chocolate, and she offered to bring something back for everybody from the café.

"Don't say anything until I get back," she said. Everybody started up their own conversations while we waited. Dinah came around the table and pulled me aside.

"It will be better if they know what's going on," she said.

I laughed. "I wish I knew what was going on." I mentioned what Mason had said when I told him I thought the body I'd seen was Jennifer Clarkson. Dinah seemed surprised.

"When you said you thought she hadn't left, I didn't realize that was what you meant."

"It doesn't matter. Mason blew the theory away by reminding me that we had checked and she was on the flight to San Francisco, which was after I saw someone on the ground."

CeeCee returned with a whole tray of Bob's double chocolate cookie bars. They were the best, because instead of chocolate chips, he added hunks of dark chocolate. She passed them around, and then they all turned to me again.

"We're waiting," CeeCee said between bites of the deeply chocolate treats.

"Here goes," I began. "I saw a body on the ground in her yard. I'm sure it was a body."

They had actually stopped chewing now, waiting for the rest.

"So I sent the police there again."

"Was it Barry Greenberg?" Rhoda asked.

"Well, yes," I said reluctantly.

"That man is still in your life, whether you like it or not," Elise said.

"That's all beside the point, but he really isn't in my life anymore, except for emergencies. That and we sort of have a dog together."

They all laughed, but urged me to finish the story. "So, did Barry find the person?" Sheila asked, seeming a little apprehensive.

"Here's the thing. When he went there, Cheyenne and her husband weren't home. Just the nanny was there. She showed Barry the yard, and there was a chaise cushion in the spot where I'd seen the body."

"So there wasn't a body after all," Sheila said, sounding relieved.

"I'm sure there was someone on the ground. I just don't know what happened to the body."

CeeCee reached for another cookie bar. "Dear, that is a mess. If it was dark, your eyes could have played a trick on you. Maybe it was like the other thing. They were practicing for something and it was a mannequin or an inflatable doll, and they were too embarrassed to admit what it was."

"What if I tell you I found some blood?" They all sucked in their breath again, but then let it out when they heard it was only something I'd seen and couldn't show anyone.

"Pink, you have to let it go. If you start investigating, you'll ruin it," Adele said. "Why not just assume what CeeCee said is right?"

Little did Adele know it was too late not to start. Not that I had gotten very far. But I wasn't about to give up. Somewhere, there was someone who deserved justice. I'm not sure how I had expected my friends to react when I told them the disappearing body story, but I hadn't expected them to want to sweep it under the rug. I almost would have preferred if they didn't believe me.

"Forget about everything I said," I said, seeing that Mrs. Shedd and Mr. Royal were headed in our direction.

The group was glad to agree, and they were silent as Mrs. Shedd stopped next to me. "We had a phone call. They asked for you, but when I heard who it was and what it was about, Mr. Royal handled it." She gave her partner a nudge. "You tell her."

Mr. Royal seemed to have a glow of excitement. "It was Garrett Mackenzie, and he said the group would like to do a run-through here before the event. Of course I said yes. They're going to come here when the bookstore closes tomorrow night." His eyes were dancing. "This is just so exciting. You don't know how much I love the music world."

As if to demonstrate, he played air guitar to the piped-in music.

I looked over at CeeCee, who made a gesture in front of her mouth of locking a key and throwing it away. Dinah just rolled her eyes.

By then, the hour was up, and everyone began to pack up their work. I went up to Eduardo as he was gathering up the bear he'd almost finished. Close up, I could see that he had some crinkles beginning to show around his eyes, but he was still an incredibly good-looking man. And he didn't have the ego to go with it. "Maybe you can answer a question for me," I said, standing next to him. He stopped what he was doing and gave me his full attention.

"If it's about doing another meeting with the romance writers—I forgot how uncomfortable those leather pants are. I'll only do it if I can show up in jeans."

I laughed and said I'd make a note of it. "But that's not what I wanted to talk you about," I said. "Since you own a drugstore now, you probably know about all the stuff you sell."

"Drugstore," he said with distaste. "Please, Molly, it is so much more than that." He took a moment to describe the old-fashioned ice-cream parlor, the assortment of nostalgic candies and the luxurious cosmetics and grooming supplies.

"But you sell drugs, too, right?" I said.

"Of course."

I didn't want to go into a long explanation of what I'd seen, so I just got right to the point. "Why would someone have a bunch of bottles of children's allergy medicine?"

"Oh," he said. "I think they call it *mother's helper*. Our pharmacist absolutely doesn't recommend this, but there are people who use it for one of its side effects—it makes children sleepy." Eduardo finished putting his crochet tools in his bag. He waited to see if there was anything else, then grabbed his bag and wished me a pleasant evening.

"What was that about?" Dinah asked, coming in at the tail end of the conversation.

"It was something I remembered seeing when Ursula was packing up Jennifer's things." I started to explain who Ursula was, but Dinah assured me she remembered.

"You don't hear about a lot of Ursulas," she said with a smile. She waited for me to continue, and I mentioned the bottles of allergy medicine that seemed to be in Jennifer's suitcase.

"It was almost like she was hiding them," I said.

"Not *almost*—I bet she was. She probably gave it to the kids to knock them out and didn't want Cheyenne and Garrett to know about it." Dinah began to load up her tote bag. "Not to change the subject, except that I am," Dinah said with a laugh. "I don't know how you did it, but after our tea break, I was okay with picking out the invitations. I could see Commander was really happy about it." She dropped her plastic container of hooks into the colorful reusable grocery bag she used for a tote. "Now I just have to buy a dress." She glanced up at me. "You'll come with me, won't you? Maybe you can work the same magic again."

"Of course I'll come," I said.

"We can go back to talking about the Case of the Disappearing Body now," she said. "Anything else on your mind?"

"I was thinking about calling Jennifer again. Maybe with my vast investigative powers I can figure out a way to get the truth," I said with a grin.

Dinah sat back down and waited while I took out my cell phone. The number was still on the phone from the previous call, and all I had to do was click on it. "Who needs a memory anymore?" I joked.

"Or to know how to spell? Take away spell-check and presumptive typing and my students probably couldn't write a single correct sentence," Dinah said.

I put my phone on speaker, and it began to ring. The ringing seemed to go on a long time, and I was just about to hit the red button to end the call when the voice mail greeting came on. I noticed the message was different this time, with Jennifer explaining she was tied up with the care of her mother and saying she would return calls as soon as she could. Then there was the usual beep to indicate it was time to leave a message.

"Hi, Jennifer," I said in a friendly voice. "It's your replacement at the Mackenzies' again. I wanted to check in with you about your things. I packed all your personal items. Would you like me to send them to you?" I asked before adding my number. Then I did hit the red button, ending the call.

"Thank heavens my phone's outgoing calls just say *private caller*," I said as I put the phone away.

"I get what you were doing," Dinah said. "If she wants the stuff sent to her, she'll have to give an address."

"That's what I'm hoping for, but let's see how she answers—or *if* she answers."

I saw Commander standing in the front of the bookstore waiting for Dinah, and I urged her to go.

The yarn department seemed very quiet with everybody gone. I began to clean up, returning the yarn and embellishments to the bin. There were still stray fibers on the table, and I used a piece of paper to gather them up. I chuckled to myself as I put the paper and all the fibers in one of the plastic bags from the detective kit. "More evidence," I said out loud. It would be fun to look at them with the magnifying glass.

I was looking forward to a quiet evening alone. Mason had something with a client. My mother and the other She La Las were taking a night off from rehearsing. They'd all gone out to a club and taken Samuel with them. My mother had tried to get me to join them, but I'd turned her down. It was hard having a mother who was more lively than I was.

I let out a sigh of relief as I pulled the greenmobile into my driveway. I never bothered parking in the garage. The floodlights were on, and I realized Samuel must have turned them on before he left. As I passed the end of the garage, I glanced up at the two burned-out lights. I didn't even consider dragging a ladder out in the dark, as these lights were so much higher than the others I'd taken care of. I'd have to go all the way to the top step on the eight-foot ladder to reach them. I wasn't up for that in the daylight, let alone in the dark.

My greeting committee was waiting inside the back door. Felix and Cosmo danced around my feet as I came in, and the cats walked between my legs. Even Blondie had come out of her solitude, though her greeting amounted to her sitting and looking up at me. Felix and Cosmo heard something before I did and took off, barking, toward my front door. "Are you really a terrier mix?" I said to the strawberry blond dog as she got up leisurely. I followed her out of the kitchen and watched her head across the house, no doubt on her way to her chair in my bedroom.

I startled as my front door swung open and two people walked in.

"Oh," Barry said, stopping suddenly as he saw me. Jeffrey was right behind him and actually jumped. "I'm sorry if we frightened you. We rang the bell," he said. "But when no one answered, we used the key." He held it up as if to show proof. It was the key I'd given him when we were together. He'd given it to Jeffrey when we broke up.

"I just came in the kitchen door." I looked down and realized I was still carrying my purse and tote bag. "It looks like we surprised each other." As soon as Cosmo and Felix realized who had come in, they started dancing around, looking for affection.

Jeffrey went into the kitchen, with Felix and Cosmo in close pursuit. Barry seemed a little ill at ease as we stood in the entrance hall. "I'm sorry it's so late. Jeffrey wants to come by more often, and as I told you before, I'm trying to make it a father-son activity. This was the earliest I could do it." I heard the kitchen door open and Jeffrey invite Felix and Cosmo into the yard to play fetch. I noticed that Barry was holding a grocery bag.

"Do you want to put that somewhere?" I asked, and he gave me a tired nod. He went on ahead into the kitchen and began to unload cans of dog food in my pantry. Meanwhile, I set my things down and finally took off my jacket.

I hesitated as to what to do. They didn't need me for the dog care, and it was supposed to be a father-son thing. But I noticed that Barry wasn't going outside to join the game of fetch.

I went into the kitchen to see what I could find for dinner. It seemed rude to start cooking something without inviting them to join me. "I was going to throw something together for dinner. Nothing fancy. Do you and Jeffrey want to join me?" I looked up at his face. He had his cop expression on, which was hard to read. I thought he was going to decline, but then the benign expression eased into a grateful smile.

"Yes. Whatever it is, it will be better than the burgers we were going to pick up after this."

"Haven't you heard of vegetables and fruit?" I said.

"Yes, I was going to get one of those salads they have now."

"Don't get me started on that." I shuddered thinking of the iceberg lettuce with some red cabbage and the sprinkling of carrot shreds that fast-food places called *salad*. It was probably soaked in so many preservatives that it would still be green and crisp when we were dead and gone.

Between Samuel bringing over some of his musician friends and the She La Las being at my place all week, my refrigerator was picked pretty clean. I took out a carton of eggs and searched through the vegetable drawer. I had some cook-in-the-bag asparagus, a few green onions, and half a box of mushrooms. I found a few slices of Muenster cheese and some ghee. Barry looked at the jar of hard yellow stuff. "What's that?" he asked.

"It's like clarified butter and used a lot in Indian cooking. It's great with eggs."

Jeffrey came in after a few minutes and stopped in the kitchen to see what was going on. "Molly invited us to eat with her," Barry said.

The relief was apparent in Jeffrey's face. "Thank you," he said, giving me a hug. "He thinks it's okay to eat burgers all the time."

Jeffrey went into the den with the two dogs, carrying their brush. "It's nice how he includes Felix," I said. I had such a soft spot for that kid.

"The least I can do is help," Barry said. "Just tell me what to do." I handed him some place mats and silverware, along with napkins, and suggested he set the table. He obediently went into the dining room with the load.

"What should I do with this?" he said a moment later, with a little edge to his voice. I went in to see what he was talking about and found him looking down at the detective set. I'd forgotten that I'd left the box open. I closed it and stowed it on a shelf, then gestured toward the clear table. I went back into the kitchen, wondering if I'd made a mistake by inviting them to stay.

I'd cooked the asparagus in the microwave and cut up the green onions and mushrooms by the time he came back in the kitchen. "Anything else?" he asked, glancing around. I suggested he have a seat at the table, but he hung around in the kitchen, watching as I swirled some ghee in a pan and added the green onions and mushrooms. I sprinkled in a little seasoning and stirred everything until the mushrooms were soft before adding the asparagus. I set the pan aside and took out my favorite pan for making omelets. It was enamel-coated cast iron and made it easy to turn out a perfect one.

There was probably a way to make all three at once, but I didn't know it. I stuck to what I always did—make them separately. As the eggs began to set, I dropped on small pieces of cheese, moving the still-liquid egg off the top and pushing it to the side of the pan with a spatula so it would cook. The smell was delicious. After a few minutes of dead air, Barry finally said, "So what's going on with you?" The silence had made him uncomfortable and he was trying to make conversation.

I automatically looked toward the two big windows at the back of the kitchen. I could see the lights on at Cheyenne's through the filter of a tree. I considered bringing up the chaise cushion. I had never mentioned finding the blood residue beneath it. Maybe I should tell him now. But I didn't speak my thoughts, and the only sound was still just the sizzling of the ghee as it cooked the eggs.

The silence really seemed to be getting to him, which I found amusing, since I knew it was a technique he used at work to get people to talk.

Ever the detective, Barry had picked up where I was looking. I could practically feel the tension building inside him.

"Okay, whatever you're thinking about, just say it," he said at last.

"If you really want to know, I was thinking about the chaise cushion back there. You do remember it?" I asked.

His shoulders slumped slightly. "Yes, I remember it well."

"I'm just curious. Did you look under it that night?"

"No," he answered, beginning to appear uncomfortable.

"You saw the detective set in there before, right?"

He answered with just an uh-huh. I pushed on and mentioned the spray bottle of Blood Detector. This time he let out a worried groan.

"Well," I said, "I did look under the cushion that night and spray the area with Blood Detector, and you know what happened?" I deliberately paused to build up the tension. "It lit up with a blue glow. So, if there was blood below the cushion, it probably got on the underside of it, too." I hoped he would pick up on it from there, but he didn't.

Barry started to shake his head with disbelief. "Molly, you went back in that yard that night, didn't you? I can't believe you actually did that."

I had continued to cook during our back and forth. I slipped the finished omelet onto one of the stack of plates I had next to the stovetop, poured some of the cooked vegetables over it, and rolled the cooked egg over the mixture. I added some orange slices for garnish. "Why don't you put this on the table and call Jeffrey."

He carried the plate into the dining room and got his son. By the time he returned I was working on the next omelet. His head seemed to be stuck on disapproving-shake mode. "I can't get over the fact that you went back there."

"Well, get past it. I did it. It's over," I said impatiently. "I'm just telling you there was blood spatter on the ground."

At least he'd stopped shaking his head. "And you're basing that on something that came in a kids' detective set? Molly, it's probably just glow-in-the-dark paint. It's a kids' kit, for heaven's sake."

"It is not glow-in-the-dark paint. I'm telling you, I saw a body there. And I think it was the nanny."

"You do remember that I spoke to her, right? She was the one who answered the door. She had long blond hair and was wearing jeans and a sweatshirt with a hood."

"What did her voice sound like?" I asked. I was careful not to give a hint about the voice I'd heard on the phone.

He took a moment to think. "She had a little bit of a Southern accent."

"Well, did you ask for her ID?"

"Now you're getting crazy. Of course not. She let us look around and everything was okay. She explained that the kids had thrown the cushion off the balcony and she'd forgotten to pick it up."

"Did you talk to the kids?"

"No. They were sound asleep in their beds. She was the nanny—case closed."

The second omelet was done, and I handed him the plate and told him to go and sit down.

"I'm sorry," Barry said a few minutes later when I

walked in, carrying my plate. "I seem to be saying that a lot lately, but I mean it." Our eyes met, and the flicker of heat that came off his was so intense, it made me almost weak in the knees. He must have realized how much his emotions were showing, because he quickly glanced away before he continued. "I'm just trying to keep you out of trouble, to protect you. You do remember what I said about not wanting to have to bail you out if you got arrested for being a stalker, right? And you said you were going to let it go." Our eyes met again, and he was back to being the in-control detective. "Truce?"

"Okay, truce," I said, setting down my plate as he reached over and pulled out my chair.

Even though they'd already gotten their food, they had waited for me to start eating. Now that we'd agreed not to fight, the mood had lightened. We all began eating the omelets together, and Jeffrey started to talk about the play he was in.

I heard my cell phone begin to ring in my purse. I was sure it was Jennifer calling back. As much as I wanted to hear what she had to say, I didn't want to hear it with Barry around.

"Aren't you going to answer it?" Barry said.

"No. I'm sure it's nothing important."

CHAPTER 16

"COFFEE FIRST," DINAH SAID WHEN I CAME TO her door the next morning. She had called earlier and suggested we shop for her dress today since we both had the time off. I think she wanted to ride the momentum she'd gotten from picking out the invitations.

I started to walk into her house, but she waved me off. "All I have here is the plain-brewed stuff. Let's go somewhere where they have espresso drinks." I looked askance at my friend.

"Are you sure you're not trying to stall our shopping?"

She shook her head so vehemently that the gelled spikes in her short salt-and-pepper hair began to shake. She stopped her head movements abruptly. "Well, maybe just a little."

"We'll ease into it," I said, waiting while she locked her front door. Her house was conveniently located around the corner from the bookstore, as well as all the shops and restaurants on Ventura Boulevard. I suggested the café at the bookstore, but then realized it was a bad idea. If I was in there, it was all too easy for someone to snag me into helping in the yarn department, and the next thing I knew, our shopping time would be over.

Le Grande Fromage was further down the street and seemed to be a better option. So far I hadn't mentioned Barry's visit, but when we were seated with our drinks, I fessed up.

"I don't care what he says about controlling his feelings and accepting that the two of you are done; he still has something going on," Dinah said.

I glossed over her comment and mentioned we'd had a fuss and how when it seemed to have calmed down my cell phone rang.

"Who was it?" she asked.

"I was sure it was Jennifer calling back, and I didn't want to talk to her with Barry around. Even if I went in the other room, he might have heard a snippet of conversation and start asking questions. When I checked later, I saw that I was right. She left a message. Nothing more than that she was returning the call. But by then it was too late to call back." I pulled out my phone and scrolled through the called numbers. When I got to Jennifer's, I hit the icon, and it began to ring. No surprise—I got voice mail.

"Jennifer, it's me again. Your replacement. Just calling to get an address where we can send you your things." Then I clicked the end call icon and turned to Dinah. "That sounded okay, didn't it?"

My friend nodded. "So what did you and Barry fuss about?" she asked.

I made a face. "I'm not sure exactly how it came up, but when I told him about finding the blood spatter on the ground, he just dismissed it. Imagine him telling me that the Blood Detector in the detective set was probably just glow-in-the-dark paint." I looked at Dinah, expecting her to agree with me, but she seemed to be holding in a laugh.

"Did you listen to what you just said?"

"Yes," I said defensively, and then I actually did think over what I'd said. "Defending a kids' kit. I guess that does sound pretty lame."

We'd decided to be adventuresome and not order our usual drinks. We'd both gotten double espressos with a swirl of milk. I took a sip of mine, and the hot, strong drink was a jolt to my taste buds.

"The box had all these instructions on how to mix the Blood Detector and how to use it. I'm sure he's wrong," I said. I took another swallow. "But what if he's right? Then maybe I'm wrong about everything." The caffeine and the upsetting thoughts were working together, and I was getting a little panicky. Dinah read my expression and reached over, grabbing my arm.

"Calm down—there has to be something we can do."

The strong drink sped up my thoughts, and the obvious answer appeared. "Of course—we just have to test it on something with real blood and something with no blood."

"Maybe we should do that before we go shopping," she said. "You seem so upset about it, why not get it off your mind?"

"I don't think so," I said with a knowing smile. "You're just looking for an excuse not to shop for your dress."

"Guilty as charged," she said, draining her small cup.

We were already discussing how we were going to get some blood to use as a test for the spray as we walked through Topanga Mall. Since Dinah was adamant about not wanting anything resembling a traditional wedding dress, we weren't concerned about finding an actual bridal shop. We passed a bunch of stores, and Dinah kept pointing out ridiculous possibilities, like a pair of board shorts and halter top, or a micro mini skirt topped with a long coat.

"I don't see why I have to get something new. I could just wear something from my closet," she said.

"No you can't. Once you get past the wedding you're going to look back on it as a special day that was a whole new beginning in your life. You don't want to look at photos and see some old dress of yours and say, *Why didn't I wear something special?*"

I heard Dinah let out a low chuckle. "That's pretty funny coming from you. You, who said she never wanted to get married again."

"Never is an awfully long time. Maybe I didn't really mean *never*. When Charlie died, I needed time to get over it, and then I wanted some time to be on my own. I can't say what I'll do in the future."

"Are you just saying that to appease me?" she said.

"Maybe, but also maybe I'm being realistic to know that I might change my mind."

"Okay then, I do see your point about looking back at photographs and being upset that I didn't wear something nicer. It's time to get serious. Let's really start shopping." We went into Nordstrom, and Dinah began to thumb through the racks. She seemed to have done a complete about-face and was okay with holding up dresses to herself. Maybe not one hundred percent, though, since when I asked if she and Commander had decided if they were going to live at her place or his, she got nervous again.

A saleswoman saw us going through the dresses and offered to help. "What kind of occasion are you shopping for?" she asked. I heard Dinah try to talk, but her mouth seemed to have dried out and her words came out in an unintelligible croak, so I answered for her.

"She's getting married, and she needs a dress for the wedding."

The saleswoman began to coo with congratulations and say how wonderful it all was. She never added *for a woman your age*, but since she was somewhere in her twenties, that was what she was probably thinking.

She made an appraisal of Dinah and said that, with her petite size, there were a ton of options. She led us to a dressing room and said she would bring in something for Dinah to consider. "This is like the old days," Dinah said, "when you actually got service." Her voiced wavered a little bit, and I could tell my friend was back to being anxious about the whole situation.

She did what all of us do when we're nervous—she began to talk all over the place about something else.

"Does it need to be human blood?" Dinah said just as the door to the dressing room opened and the saleswoman came in with an armload of beautiful dresses. To say she did a double take was an understatement.

"Well, that's done," Dinah said when we were walking back to the car. The cream-colored dress she'd chosen was in a garment bag. It was ballet length and made out of silk cut on the bias so it draped beautifully. She could have gotten a jacket to wear over it, but instead decided to make herself a long scarf out of fingering weight yarn with some tiny pearls crocheted in.

With the dress shopping done, Dinah relaxed and was quick to bring up my reaction when the saleswoman heard that I was the maid of honor. "I can't believe you said exactly what I'd said about wearing something in your closet."

"Yes, and you used my own words against me," I said, smiling as I remembered her giving me the speech about looking back at the wedding photos and regretting that I hadn't gotten something special.

I looked at the garment bag I was carrying, imagining the dress inside. It was mocha-colored silk made into cascading ruffles, and when I had tried it on I felt like I was wearing air.

We got to the greenmobile and laid our dresses across the backseat. Dinah was restraining a laugh as she got in the passenger seat. "The look on the saleswoman's face when she came back with more dresses just as you said maybe the best option was just to use some of our own blood. I don't think she realized you were joking when you said we could cut our fingers and dribble the blood on a plate."

"While you were trying on that violet number with the spangles on the hem, I checked my smartphone. The substance Blood Detector is supposed to be reacts to the iron in blood—any blood. So we can get a steak and squeeze out the blood and use that."

Squeezing a steak didn't seem very appealing to us, so we opted instead to buy some prepared roast beef that had a lot of juice around it. The deli clerk had given me an odd look when I asked for assurance that there was blood in the juice.

"Just imagine if Elise had come along. All the talk of blood would have gotten her going about Anthony and how he crochets to handle his blood lust. The clerk would have really thought we were a bunch of loonies," Dinah said with a chuckle.

"Maybe we are. We're going to my house to spray

something from a kids' kit on a spot with blood and a spot with none to see if only one of them lights up."

I realized the obstacle to our plan as soon as we got to my house. We needed darkness to see the glow. We were slowed, but not stopped. We simply moved the experiment into my closet. We followed the directions on the kit and mixed up another batch to put in the spray bottle. We re-created Cheyenne's patio by putting some river rocks on two saucers. Getting the juice from the roast beef turned out to be easy, as it had gathered in the paper it was wrapped in.

"I think I might become a vegetarian after this," I said as I poured the reddish liquid into a small cup, then poured it over the rocks on the saucer I had marked B. "It never fully registered before what the juice was when someone offered me a juicy steak."

We put everything on a tray and carried it to my closet. It wasn't one of those giant closets that was like a room, but it had plenty of space. The rod ran down one side, and the other side had shelves. Three overhead lights illuminated it. I cleared off one of the shelves that was at a level that would be easy to see. I had been concentrating on the logistics until now, but as it got closer to the moment of truth, I started getting nervous all over again.

All of my proof that there had been a body was based on having found blood on the ground. I set the two saucers on the shelf, with the Blood Detector bottle next to the one with the blood-soaked stones.

"Are you ready?" Dinah said. She was standing by the door and the light switch, ready to create the complete darkness I needed.

I was telling myself it didn't matter if I turned out to be wrong. Everybody already thought I was anyway. But still . . . I took a deep breath and prepared for my fate. "Okay," I called.

The light went off, and it was so dark I really couldn't even see my hand in front of me. I had to do it all by feel. I lifted the spray bottle and spritzed it over the saucer with the blood, then felt my way to the other saucer and did the same. Dinah had felt her way through the narrow space to join me.

"Well, this is it," she said. "Maybe we should hold hands for luck." She grabbed mine, and we waited.

"Oh my gosh," Dinah exclaimed as the eerie blue glow showed up on the saucer to our left. We turned our heads in unison to check the other one. It was lost in the darkness.

"It works. It really works," I said, almost wanting to jump up and down. "I can't wait to tell Barry." The words were out of my mouth before I thought about it. "Maybe I should just leave it alone."

CHAPTER 17

MY MIND WAS CLICKING AS I WALKED FROM THE parking lot to the bookstore. I was right; I really was right. I did find blood spatter, which meant there had been a body on the ground. I knew that still wasn't enough, though. Barry had told me the cops needed to have a body to believe there had been a murder. I didn't need a body—the blood was enough for me to believe there had been one. I had a whole new resolve to unravel the mystery of who had died and to produce their remains.

Dinah had taken her dress and we'd parted company in the bookstore parking lot. It was just a short walk to her place. As she said good-bye, she said she couldn't wait to look through her stash and see if she had some appropriate yarn for the long scarf. Like the rest of us, she had accumulated more yarn than she could use in a lifetime, so there was a good chance she did. She was sure she had some little pearls, if only she could find them.

It always felt a little strange to me when I started work in the afternoon. It was like walking into the middle of a story. Mrs. Shedd grabbed me as soon as I came in the door. "You have to see," she said in an excited voice. She practically dragged me to the music and video department. "Look at all the customers," she said. "Joshua is so happy, and he's giving me all the credit, because I gave the okay for ChILLa to perform here." I'd never seen my boss so happy, and I definitely sensed it was because of Mr. Royal being pleased more than because of the store having more business. "Joshua said so many people want to come, we're going to have to give out tickets. Joshua never makes any fuss about it, but you know, he's a musician, too. He plays the harmonica."

Two twentysomething women were looking at the sign. "I love them," one of them said. "Their songs are so inspirational. Pretty cool they're doing something here." Mrs. Shedd pushed away from me and told the pair they could pick up tickets at the front.

"You might want to buy your CD or album now. They're going fast," she said. "We may run out the night of the event." They each grabbed a CD and took them to the front. "Be sure and bring your receipt to show you bought it here." She turned back to me. "Remember, we're not allowing in any outside merchandise. They have to buy it here if they want it signed." She drew her hands together in a hopeful pose. "Just think, if even half the people that show buy, we'll be doing great. And in the meantime, everyone is discovering we have a music department. I actually had someone ask me when we added it." Mrs. Shedd put on a world-weary air. "How about twenty-five years ago." She was all serious as she stepped closer to me. "Remember, we have the rehearsal here tonight. We don't want anything to mess this up, do we?"

Why would she even say that? Of course I didn't want anything to mess it up. After assuring her it would be fine, I went back to the yarn department.

Elise was at the yarn table, crocheting. She looked up when I approached the table. "I came in here to work on my bear for a while." She held it up, and I had to laugh. She'd gone from vampire dolls to a vampire bear. "He's going to have a crochet hook in his pocket," she said with a smile. She glanced in the direction of the café. "Logan is sitting in the café on his computer." It wasn't unusual for her husband to stake out a table in Le Grande Fromage or in our café and use it as his office. It seemed to be the style these days. It reminded me that she had said he knew something about Cheyenne's house.

When I brought it up, she shook her head. "I can't really say anything. I think being a real estate agent is kind of like being a doctor or lawyer; everything is confidential."

"Then he sold the house to them?"

She seemed surprised at the question. "Telling you that would probably break the code." She did a few stitches on the vampire bear. "I'm really sorry, Molly. You should talk to Logan. He'll know what he can and can't say more than me."

It seemed like a good idea to talk to him, but a woman came into the yarn department and needed help. When I'd finished assisting her, Elise was gone, and I presumed Logan was as well. There was always another time.

There was no happy hour gathering that night, so I spent the rest of the time helping Mr. Royal rearrange things. He'd decided not to use our usual event area, but to open up the area near the entrance of the music and video department. The plan was that we would move all the bookcases back and have the groups use the front of the music and video department as the stage area. He'd also decided to make a photo gallery of our celebrity customers in the department alcove. His final touch was to rename it the Sight and Sound department.

By closing time, we had everything ready except moving the bookcases, which we'd only do on the night of the actual performance. Mr. Royal escorted the last customer out and locked the door but stood in the front waiting for ChIlLa to arrive. As the minutes ticked away, the tension mounted. They'd asked for the rehearsal, but maybe they weren't going to show. Meanwhile, I noticed a bunch of people gathering around outside the front of the bookstore and peeking in the window. Mr. Royal finally opened the door to see what was going on.

"We heard Matt Meadowbrook is going to be here and that his wife's group ChIlLa is supposed to be rehearsing," a young woman with purple hair who seemed to be acting as spokesperson said. Mr. Royal told them about the group's appearance at the bookstore and started handing out tickets. I was curious how they knew about the rehearsal. Just then, a black Escalade pulled to the curb. The doors opened, and Cheyenne, Ilona, and Lauren got out.

The small crowd went into a frenzy, surrounding the three of them, asking for autographs and taking selfies. I saw Garrett trying to hustle them inside, though it seemed that it was more of an act. The frenzy grew more intense when Matt Meadowbrook and another man came through the crowd.

Matt stopped for a few selfies and signed somebody's cast before moving past them. Mr. Royal held the door open for the two men to come inside.

The three women stayed out there for a while before finally letting Garrett guide them inside. Cheyenne glanced over her shoulder and gave a parting wave to the fans. "I bet they all put it on social media or send it to a news station." She turned to her husband. "We know they use it. It was my tweet that got them here."

I was glad we had waited until the bookstore was closed, because the group totally took over the space. "This is my road manager, Zeke," Matt said, introducing the man who'd walked in with him to Mr. Royal and the rest of us. "He's going to be helping the girls out with the technical stuff." I noticed Zeke was carrying a guitar case and brought it over to the area we were calling the stage.

Garrett glanced around at the set and asked Mr. Royal what they were going to do about seats for the audience.

"I thought we should have them stand. It makes it more exciting," Mr. Royal said. Garrett didn't seemed impressed with the setup, and I heard him ask Cheyenne more than once if she was sure she wanted to do it.

"Go on and get a cup of coffee or something," she said finally as she and her sisters went to confer with the road manager.

"Oh no," Mrs. Shedd said. "We didn't think about refreshments. Do something, Molly."

I got the key to the café and went inside to see what I could manage. It felt strange to be behind the counter—and also kind of fun. Or it would have been if I'd had time to play around with all the equipment. I did a quick search for supplies and brewed a pot of coffee. Bob had a pitcher of iced tea made up for the next day, which I commandeered. As for snacks, I made up a small tray of leftover pastries and set everything out on the counter. I was thinking how unhappy Bob was going to be that we'd messed with his domain when Garrett came in asking for some bottles of water.

I offered to get cups of it instead, and he seemed

shocked to be offered tap water, even when I said all of ours was filtered.

"Fine, whatever you can do. I'm sure you realize the group is accustomed to more sophisticated treatment than this."

I'd found the best way to deal in a situation like this was merely to apologize. He appeared surprised, probably expecting a bunch of excuses, and his expression softened. "That's okay. I'm sure you're doing the best you can." He waited while I started getting cups of water and putting covers on them.

I had never really talked to him before. I wondered what he knew about the night the nanny left. I couldn't ask him directly, but I'd noticed that people seemed to appreciate a sympathetic ear. Maybe all I had to do was to get him to start complaining about Jennifer's leaving and he'd spill some information.

"I was sorry to hear about your problem with your nanny," I tried.

He appeared surprised by my comment. "How did you know?"

"You know how it is when a bunch of women get together and crochet—we all talk about our problems. Cheyenne told us how your nanny left in the middle of the night."

"Leave it to my wife to make it sound more dramatic," he said. "It wasn't the middle of the night. We were at the taping of Cheyenne's show and Jennifer had a family emergency. I suppose I should be grateful that she had a replacement take over. It was still a hassle, though. The kids went to sleep with one nanny, and a different one got them up the next morning."

I was afraid that was all he was going to say, so I rushed in, hoping to keep him talking about it. "It's always hard dealing with help," I said, glancing toward the bookstore as if I were in charge of hiring and firing.

He nodded ruefully. "That's the truth. The weird thing is that our nanny never let on anything about having to leave. I had to come home to pick up a change of clothes for Cheyenne, and Jennifer was reading a bedtime story to the kids. I didn't want to get the kids riled up right before bed, so I didn't go in the upstairs den, but I'm sure she saw me."

"Why did Cheyenne need a change of clothes?" I asked, hoping to stir the pot of conversation.

He explained that they were taping two shows back-to-back, and she needed a different outfit for each show. "She'd left it on the bed. I just picked it up and ran." He grabbed a couple of cups, and we walked back to the stage area together.

"Cheyenne said someone sent the police to your place that night, too." I left it hanging, hoping he would pick up the thread.

"There's some crazy neighbor who needs a life. Twice the cops have showed up thanks to him or her," he said with annoyance. I found myself shrinking back, as if somehow he would know it was me. It took all my courage to keep talking.

"Why does that neighbor keep calling the cops?"

"They seem to have an overactive imagination." He completely ignored the first appearance of the cops and went right to the second. "They claimed to have seen someone lying in the backyard. I asked the cop who called me which neighbor it was, but he wouldn't tell. You'd think he had some kind of personal interest in keeping their identity secret."

"So then you weren't home when it happened?" I set the tray of cups down on a table in the café so everyone could help themselves.

He shook his head. "I was already back at the taping when that detective called me. Of course, I checked with our nanny, and that's when she broke the news to me." He turned to face me. "Personally, I think her taking off had to do with the cops showing up, since she left right after they were there. It's all that nosy neighbor's fault," he said with annoyance before he walked back into the bookstore.

I added a handful of straws and followed him back into the bookstore.

Once the refreshments were settled, ChIlLa started the rehearsal. Lauren accompanied them on the guitar, and they did their songs a couple of times. There wasn't much for me to do, so I went back to the yarn department. Elise had taken out the bin of supplies for the toys, and I thought I'd use the time to clear it up. Matt Meadowbrook was sitting at the table and appeared rather fidgety. He seemed glad for my company as I began straightening up the yarn bins.

"I came along for moral support," he said, sounding bored. "But I'd rather be the performer than doing all this waiting around." He checked out the area. "What is this?"

"A yarn department," I said with a smile. "I know it seems odd to have one in a bookstore." I told him about the Hookers, which got a laugh as usual, and then mentioned that two of the members of ChIlLa were our customers. "Maybe Ilona would like to learn how to crochet," I said. "Or you. It's a good thing to do when you're waiting around."

He chuckled at my suggestion and said he'd keep it in mind. "Cheyenne always says it saved her life," he said.

"Really?" I said, surprised. She'd been vague about how she'd learned, and when. "Do you know what she meant?"

He was lounging back in his chair now. "I'm not sure if that's my business to talk about," he said. "You ought to ask her." He picked up a hook that was on the table and started to play with it. "Maybe I'll take you up on that offer. You could give me a lesson right now." He patted the seat next to him.

How awkward. I was trying to think of a graceful way to say no.

"Matt!" Ilona said in an angry voice. "What are you doing?"

"Hey, babe, I just thought I could make use of my time." He had a slow, sexy way of talking. "I could make one of these for the kids." He reached into the bin and plucked a bear out of the bin that I had left as a sample. "It looks just like Mr. Snuggles." He looked up at his wife with an innocent smile.

"Don't even mention Mr. Snuggles," she said in an angry tone. It seemed as if they'd forgotten I was there and had jumped into what sounded like an unfinished argument. I knew I should slip away, but I was too curious, so I stayed.

I listened, trying to make sense of it. I gathered that Mr. Snuggles was a favorite bear of one of their children that had gotten lost. "I had to find it at Cheyenne's the other day," Ilona said. "Did you even look when you went there that night, or remember to ask the nanny?" She made a *grrr* sound. "Or were you too busy showing her how to hold a guitar?"

"C'mon, honey, there was nothing going on with her, or anyone." I was pretty sure Ilona wasn't talking about Ursula, so it had to be Jennifer. What Ilona said next made me almost choke.

"What happened? What did you say to her? You came home without Mr. Snuggles, and I heard she took off that night."

"There you two are," Garrett said in a loud, friendly voice, clearly trying to drown out their arguing. He saw me standing there and gave me a dark look. Still in the upbeat voice, he said it was time for them to go.

When I was alone at the table I picked up the bear. "So Matt Meadowbrook was there the night Jennifer left. Good detective work," I said to it with a smile. "Maybe I'll make you a deerslayer hat."

CHAPTER 18

THANK HEAVENS FOR BEST FRIENDS WHO STAY UP late and don't mind surprise company. It took a while to shut everything down and clean up after the rehearsal, but instead of going to my car, I walked down the block to Dinah's. When I knocked at her door, it wasn't a complete surprise—I had called first.

"C'mon in," she said. "You sounded like you had a lot to tell when you called."

I glanced around her living room. "Do you have a dry-erase board?" I asked. She seemed surprised by the request and was still processing it when I suggested maybe we should go to my place if she didn't.

"How about a cup of tea first? You seem a little wired."

"Wired? Me? I don't know what you mean." Then it was as if I was observing myself from the outside. I'd rushed over there and was talking fast and making demands. Yes, I was wired. I flopped on her chartreuse sofa and forced myself to take a slow, deep breath and let it out the same way.

"Tea would be good," I said. "You're right; I need it."

Dinah was wise enough to figure out that I needed tea with no stimulants in it and pulled out a box of honeybush tea. I was far calmer by the time she handed me the steaming mug of sweet-smelling drink. "Why do you need a dry-erase board?" she asked, sitting next to me on her couch.

"I was thinking we could use it to write down everything I know about that night at Cheyenne's. We could make a time sequence."

Dinah looked a little sheepish. "I do have a dry-erase board, but there's something on one side of it. Maybe we could use the other side." She got up. "I'll just flip it and bring it in."

"Here, let me help you carry it," I said, following her. It wasn't like her to hide things from me, and I was curious.

"Okay, you might as well know my secret," she said, flipping the light on in the spare bedroom. The whiteboard was on a stand, and there seemed to be three lists. When I got close enough to read them, I saw one was marked "Commander's," one "Here" and the last "New Place."

Underneath each heading was a list of pros and cons. "I thought it would help me figure out where we should live."

"Why were you hiding it?" I asked.

"It seems so lame and unromantic. It's not like it has helped, either. There are pros and cons to all of them. Nothing seems like the right answer."

"What about Commander? Where does he want to live?"

My friend actually blushed. "He said it could be Timbuktu as long as it was with me."

We both said *awwww* together.

I flipped the board over to the blank side, and Dinah handed me a marker. I wrote "What We Know" and underneath I started to make a list—and then Dinah slipped in and wrote "Barry still cares for Molly" on the board in red.

"He does not," I argued and wiped it away with eraser. "We're getting off the subject."

I wrote down that I had seen someone lying in the yard. I tried to remember the time. It was dark, so I guessed it had been about seven thirty. Next I wrote "Called Barry."

"I took a while before I made the call."

Dinah tried to help by asking what I did before calling him so we could figure out the approximate time.

"I stood in the kitchen arguing with myself," I said. "I picked up and put down the phone a few times." We decided to allow fifteen minutes for my dithering.

"Did you look outside while you were deciding what to do?" Dinah asked, and I shook my head.

She asked me questions about the phone call, and I remembered how I had had to talk Barry into it and how, even when he agreed, it had taken him a while to get there. "It must have been after eight when he rang the bell there," I said.

"There was certainly time to move whoever was on the ground," Dinah said. "But to where?"

"We'll just put a question mark," I said. We moved on to how long Barry had been there and came up with half an hour, which put the time at about eight thirty.

"The flight she took left at eleven," I said. "The shuttle pickup was at about nine." I thought about the nine o'clock time. "She had to know before Barry got there that she was leaving." I regretted that I hadn't asked the shuttle place what time she had ordered the pickup.

"She could have called in around seven thirty. They could have added her to a pickup list at the last minute."

"I wonder where the kids were in all this," I said.

"I thought we were only writing in what we knew," Dinah said.

"In that case, Cheyenne wasn't there, but"—I wished there was some way I could play fanfare music—"Garrett was there briefly." I explained the taping of her show and his coming home to pick up a change of clothes for her. "He mentioned that Jennifer was reading the kids a story when he stopped home. Barry said that when he talked to Garrett he was at the taping. And there's something more. Matt Meadowbrook was at their house that night."

"What?" Dinah exclaimed. "How did you find that out?"

I told her the whole Mr. Snuggles story. "But I don't know when it was." I simply wrote in that he was there, with a question mark for the time.

"Maybe we should also write down what we don't know," Dinah suggested. That was easy, and the list was long: Don't know who was on the ground. Don't know where they are now. Don't know what happened to them or who did it. If Jennifer was the victim, how was I talking to her? If Jennifer wasn't the victim, then who was it?

We both flopped on her couch when we were done. "I'm not so sure that was the help I thought it would be," I said. "Maybe we should flip the board and work on your problem."

THE SHE LA LAS HAD HAD ANOTHER REHEARSAL at my house. I found the residue when I got home, but left it until morning to deal with. I was glad my mother didn't know about ChILLa's rehearsal at the bookstore, or she would have felt left out. Samuel was off doing his usual late night with his friends. I envied his energy.

The phone rang as I was about to fall into my bed. "Just checking in, Sunshine," Mason said. "Two days without seeing you. It feels like forever. Anything exciting happen?"

When he'd heard about my day, with shopping for Dinah's wedding dress, finding out the Blood Detector really did work, the rehearsal at the bookstore and Matt Meadowbrook flirting with me and finally the dry erase board at Dinah's, he let out a *whew*. Then he backtracked to Matt Meadowbrook and wanted the details so he'd know if he had to challenge him to a duel.

"I get the feeling he's not too particular with who he flirts with," I said. "It seems like he might have had something going with Cheyenne's nanny."

"That's a new wrinkle," Mason said. "Maybe he's trying to avoid the cliché of being involved with his own kids' nanny." Mason punctuated that with a chuckle.

"I think he had something going with them as well. They have a manny now, and I heard something about the nannies moving through there like it was a revolving door. His wife seemed pretty annoyed, even with his silly flirting with me."

"The trials and tribulations of the rich and famous. In other words, my clients." Mason wanted to make plans for the next night, and we agreed to try to have dinner together. I wondered if I should have mentioned Barry and the dog care that had turned into dinner. But there seemed to be no reason, since I knew it would just upset Mason.

"Love you," he said.

"Me, too." I hung up the phone and was asleep a moment after my head hit the pillow.

CHAPTER 19

I AWAKENED AT MY USUAL TIME EVEN THOUGH I didn't have to get to the bookstore until early afternoon. I made myself some coffee and took it to my kitchen table. Samuel came into the kitchen, and I offered him a cup of coffee.

"Mother, really," he said, rolling his eyes and pointing to the brown apron with The Bean and Leaf written across the top. Of course, his job was coffee. I mentioned breakfast possibilities, and he said he'd grab a breakfast sandwich at work. When I said I hoped he wasn't burning the candle at both ends, I got another roll of his eyes.

"You should talk," he said. He touched his head to make sure his dark blond hair was tied back. Felix and Cosmo were at his feet, and the cats jumped up on the table bench to get closer to him. "I forgot to let the dogs out this morning, and I think the cat box might need attention." He shot me an apologetic look before he grabbed the door handle.

"Grandma, uh, I mean Liza, is having another rehearsal tonight." And then he was gone.

My plan to languish over my morning brew had just evaporated. I waited until Samuel had cleared the back gate and then let the dogs out. They went racing to the back fence and started barking at two workmen walking around in Cheyenne's yard. I just saw bits and pieces of them through the ivy growing on my side. Thank heavens there was no music or singing. I wondered what they were doing, but didn't feel like being on display if I went to the back fence and looked in.

I dealt with the cat box and called the dogs back in. After several rounds of treats, I thought about my breakfast. By then my coffee was cold, so I brewed a new pot. The one bonus of my mother's many visits was that she kept bringing over more of her homemade granola. I found a canister of it and poured some in a bowl. I think she mixed hers with nonfat yogurt and fruit. I poured some half-and-half in mine.

"Why not be fancy?" I said, taking a fresh mug of coffee and the cereal into the dining room. I sat down with a nice view of the backyard through the French doors. I was just going to concentrate on eating, but then I noticed the detective set on the table.

I pulled it over and opened the box. I looked at the Blood Detector, realizing that I'd put it back in the plastic bag after Dinah's and my experiment instead of putting it into the box in the slot made for it. There didn't seem to be any reason to move it now, though.

I was surprised at how many evidence bags I'd added to the box. Other than the fingerprints, they were all fibers. I set them where I could look at them as I worked on the cereal. It was so delicious I didn't know how I'd ever be able to go back to the store-bought kind again. Still, as tasty as it was, I put down my spoon, picked up one of the bags and held it to the light. I could barely make out the bits of fuzz.

I had no idea how crime scene investigators handled evidence, but I found a piece of white tissue paper from my wrapping stash and laid it on the table. I opened a bag and let some of the fuzz fall on it before using the tweezers that came with the set to capture a piece. I used the magnifying glass to examine it.

Maybe the Blood Finder was the real thing, but the magnifying glass seemed a little weak. It worked a little better with the fingerprints, and I was actually able to divide them into three groups of patterns. Just like the booklet said, most of the fingerprints had loops. The next most common pattern was whorls, and there was only one print that looked like it was made of arches, which was the rarest pattern. I went back to looking at the fibers, wondering how anyone could match them up. Then I remembered Peter's old microscope. It was stuck in the back of the built-in cabinets in the den.

I set it up in the dining room, found a package of new slides, and put some fibers on them. The microscope made it much easier to see the fibers. I was going to move on and make up slides of some of the others I'd collected to see if I could match them up when the front door opened and closed.

Felix and Cosmo went into their guard dog mode, and I heard them barking as they ran into the entrance hall to see who it was.

"Mother, can you call your dogs off?" Peter said. I did just that, calling their names until they came into the dining room, probably expecting treats. Peter followed them.

He was dressed for work, which in his case meant a well-fitting suit and a dress shirt. He'd recently dropped the tie.

"I came by to pick up my golf clubs," he said. His gaze flicked from me to the view of the yard. "That house is a real intrusion. You should plant some privacy bushes."

I explained my plan to wait until they put up a fence and we saw how much of their house it covered.

"They'd need to put up a ten-foot fence for it to do any good." He paused for just a moment. "This might be the time for you to sell this place and downsize into a condo."

I tried not to let my reaction show in my face. Peter said something similar about once a month. And I always ignored it. I didn't believe he'd really thought it through anyway. Didn't he understand that if I lived in some place with a carport and a small storage place, I couldn't store the kayak, skis, surfboards, bicycles and golf clubs that he left with me?

I saw him look at the table. His gaze stopped when he saw the open detective set and the microscope. "Mother, what are you doing?" There was a warning sound in his voice.

"Just enjoying the wonderful birthday present you gave me." I grabbed the plastic bag with the bottle of Blood Detector and held it up. "This stuff really works."

It took a moment for it to register, but then he looked horrified. "You've been looking for blood? Where?"

My poor son was so uptight that I wasn't going to tell him about using it in the yard behind us, so I told him about Dinah's and my experiment. It didn't sit well with him.

He reached for the set and flipped the lid back on. "This wasn't a good gift idea. I'm going to take it back and get you a book of certificates for a spa."

"No," I said, putting my hand on it. "I don't care about

massages or facials; I just care about crime." Okay, that last part might have been to tease him, but I really did want to keep it.

"Fine, keep it," he said, with an unhappy face.

"Do you know who lives back there?" I said, noting that he was back to looking through the French doors again, probably trying to figure if the new house would hurt my property value. He shook his head.

"Do you know who Cheyenne Chambers is?"

He gave me a look that said I had just asked him an incredibly stupid question. "Everybody knows who she is. Anytime there's a pitch for a reality show, she's always listed as a possible participant." He looked back there with new interest. "She lives there?" He sounded surprised. "Why would she move in when the yard isn't even done?"

I don't think he was expecting me to answer, so I just shrugged it off and brought up the show tune show. Naturally, he knew all about it. "I've never seen it," I said. "Actually, I don't even know when it's on or how to find out."

"I can help you with that," he said, taking me into the den and flicking on the TV. He hit some keys on the remote and did a search. "There," he said. "I set it to record the show so you don't have to worry about when it's on." I sensed he meant it as a nice gesture, not a reminder of his superior knowledge, so I thanked him.

"No problem," he said leading the way back through to the living room. He looked at the rearranged furniture. "Liza again? The show must go on." Poor guy. I think he wished all of us would go off somewhere and stop doing embarrassing things. He made a last effort to take back the detective set, but I made it clear it was staying. Finally, he went to the garage and picked up what he'd come for.

*   *   *

I HAD THAT FEELING OF WALKING INTO THE MID-
dle of a story again when I went in the bookstore a couple
of hours later, but there wasn't much time to think about
it. I saw there were customers in the yarn department.

As I crossed the store, I noticed a crowd near the children's department and remembered that Adele was having
an afternoon session. As I got closer, I saw Adele standing
in the entrance to her domain, holding a clipboard and
checking membership cards. I guessed that it was fairy-tale
day and that she was reading *Rapunzel* by the long puffy
sleeved dress and the yellowy blond wig that almost
reached to the floor. As she gave the okay, the kids went
in, and whoever had brought them stepped away. A group
of mothers headed toward the café, glad to be free for a
little while. Ursula was in the line with Cheyenne's two
daughters in tow.

I suddenly remembered my promise to her to get Adele
to back off on the form and to give back their membership
cards. The line moved forward, and the two girls with
Ursula reached Adele. Adele's face clouded as the nanny
said something to her. Then they both started looking
around the store and saw me at the same time.

"I said it was okay." I directed my comment at Adele.
Instead of her nodding and letting it go, she appeared more
inflamed.

I hated to do this, and I was sure Adele would not take
it well, but I had no choice. "It's fine, Adele," I said when
I reached them. "As assistant manager, I said she didn't
have to fill out one of your forms and that the girls could
have their cards back." Adele's eyes bugged out, and I realized I needed to pour some water on the situation. "I

understand you need a contact number. Just write in my cell," I said.

It was like when someone runs and stops short and there's leftover energy with no place to go. Adele seemed to be sputtering, and she mumbled, "But, but . . ." Finally, with a small shrug, she let it go.

The two girls went on in, and Ursula stepped aside. "I suppose I should thank you," Ursula said, "but I had hoped you would have taken care of it before there was another confrontation with that woman." I expected the nanny to go on complaining about Adele's persistence about the form, but she surprised me. "I can't really fault her though," she said, looking back toward Adele with her clipboard. "She has her standards."

There were no chairs in the vicinity, so I offered her a seat in the yarn department. She accepted it, and I went up to the customers I'd seen to offer my help.

"We need some needles," one of them said. There was a pause before she hesitantly added, "Knitting needles." Again there was a pause, and she added that they wanted the ones with the cable. I took them to the rack of tools and turned it to display all our needles. "Oh," she exclaimed when she saw them.

Her friend started talking in a low voice. "I told you it would be okay. It's that woman in the costume who goes berserk at the mention of knitting." I didn't have to turn to know who they were talking about.

Ursula had chosen a chair with a clear view of the entrance to the children's department. Ursula was certainly diligent about her responsibility, unlike the mothers I'd seen heading for the café. I saw that Adele had finished checking kids in and story time had begun.

"Do you crochet or knit?" I asked. Ursula looked away

from the entrance for the children's department for a moment.

"No, I never learned. Too bad, though. It would be useful at times like this."

"I could show you how to crochet," I offered. We had some odds and ends of yarn and hooks and I went to the cabinet to get them. I sat down next to her and handed her a size J hook and a ball of worsted weight yarn.

She was an easy student and picked up the chain stitch and single crochet in no time. She wasn't one to just want to make swatches, and she asked if there was an item she could make with what she'd learned. I made up a kit for her with a hook, a skein of yarn and a printed pattern we had for an easy hat and put it in a small canvas tote. She began working on it right away.

"I needed something to brighten up my spirits," she said as she took the label off the yarn and pulled out the end.

"Oh," I said, my interest perking up. I decided I should really stay with her until she got going on the hat. Maybe I could get some more information about what was going on at Cheyenne's house. "What's wrong?"

She seemed to be considering her words. "I suppose it is all right to talk to you. There's a code of not divulging any of the family's business that we all sign. I've tried to follow it, but I think this negates it."

Now she really had my interest.

"I have a right to my privacy," she said, seeming more upset. "Someone went through my room yesterday when I took the girls to the park. With that yard in chaos, they can't play outside there."

"Really?" I said, showing her how to go into one of the chain stitches to begin the hat. "Was anything missing?"

"No. And to a less trained eye than mine, no one would

have known anyone had been in there. But everything was shuffled around on the desk, and a drawer was left slightly open. The closet was the most obvious. I think the nanny's suitcase was pulled out and put back."

"Did you say anything?" I asked. Ursula looked down at her work and smiled as she recognized how the stitches were forming the top of the hat.

"No. I really couldn't, since nothing was missing." She kept on crocheting. "Thank you for this. It's amazing how much better I feel."

"Crochet can do wonders," I said with a smile. And could be distracting. Neither of us had noticed that story time had ended and the children had begun to disperse.

"Uh-hum," a sharp voice said, and both Ursula and I looked up to see Adele in her Rapunzel outfit. "What was it you said about being right there when story time ended?"

She was holding the two little girls' hands.

"I'm sorry," Ursula said. "You're right." She put down her crochet and waved the girls over to her. Adele seemed surprised by her apology, no doubt used to people making excuses instead of simply admitting they were wrong.

"It's my fault," I said. "I taught her how to crochet, and she started making a hat."

Adele's eye rested on the hook and yarn on the table and her expression changed completely. "In that case," she said, "it's okay." She picked up Ursula's work and examined it. "It looks good, but I'm really the one who gives the crochet lessons around here."

The two girls had moved up to the table and were looking at the yarn and tools. "I want to know how to do that," one of them said. "And be like Mommy." The other one nodded in agreement.

"I just happen to have a little spare time," Adele said.

She moved the long blond hair out of her way and sat down at the table. "Pink, get them supplies."

As I was gathering some hooks and practice yarn, it occurred to me that the two girls were there the night everything happened and might know something.

I brought everything back to the table. "My name is Molly," I said to the two girls before asking theirs.

"My name is Merci. It's French for *thanks*," the one who had asked for the lesson said. I recognized her as the one who'd been wearing the boa and cowboy boots the day we'd gone to Cheyenne's. She announced that she was four and her sister was three and her name was Venus.

"Well, now that we all know who is who, we can begin," I said.

"You can go now," Adele said to me, clearly wanting to be in charge.

"I think I'll stay. I'm sure I can pick up some teaching tips from you, since you're the master." Then I reminded her that when we put on children's crochet parties I helped with the lessons. Adele was flustered, but couldn't argue.

Adele really was a master, even though the blond wig kept getting in the way. Both Merci and Venus were good students, and Adele had them making loopy single crochet stitches in no time. "And now you know how to crochet," Adele said, getting up as she maneuvered her long mane out of the way.

"I want to make a red jacket," Merci said, holding up her stitches.

"Me, too," Venus said.

"Pink, I'll leave that to you," Adele said with a chuckle as she pushed in her chair.

"I don't think you're ready for that," Ursula said to the girls. She thanked Adele and started to gather the girls up, while I realized my chance to talk to them had never materialized.

Merci stamped her feet. "I wanna make something."

Ursula was packing her things back into the little canvas tote, and I watched her shoulders drop as she looked to the older girl with understanding. "I'm the same way. I wanted to make something, too," she said. She turned to me. "Could you put something together for them?"

I nodded enthusiastically, since it would give me some more time to talk to them.

"I hate to ask, but could you watch them while I go to the ladies' room?"

"No problem," I said. "Take your time. You can pick up drinks at the café if you like."

The girls heard the last part and called out their orders for strawberry drinks. Ursula looked to me for a last reassurance that it was okay, and then she was off.

The girls were enamored with all the colors of the yarn and the different kinds of tools. "How would you like to make a purse?" I asked. Merci made a last play to make a red jacket, but finally agreed to make a purse, as long as it was red.

"Let's start with giving you bags." I handed each of them a canvas tote like I'd given Ursula. "Next comes your hook." I opened a drawer and took out two blue plastic size P hooks. They were nice for little-girl hands and for little-girl impatience. Their purses would work up quickly with the large hooks.

"How do you like your new nanny?" I asked both the girls.

"She's okay," Venus said. "But I liked Jennifer more. She let us watch the princess movie over and over."

Merci made a face. "Miss Ursula is more bossy. She

made me wear these shoes. I wanted to wear my cowboy boots. But she reads to us."

"It must have been surprising to have a new nanny. Did either of you know that the other one was leaving?"

They both shrugged, and I realized it was too complicated a question. It was better to try to ask them specifics from that night. I began by getting them to remember that their parents were at a taping. Then I asked them what they had for dinner as a way to juice their memories.

They were telling me about the fish sticks and macaroni as we moved over to the cubbies of yarn. I took out some worsted weight yarn in different shades of red and let them pick. No surprise—they both chose a cherry red shade.

"Was Jennifer there when you went to sleep?" I asked as I dropped the yarn into each of their bags. They both nodded.

"Do you think she was upset?" They were far more interested in their tote bags, and I got shrugs for answers. I picked out a pair of our kid-size scissors and a big plastic tapestry needle for each of them and put them in their bag. Then I remembered the whole thing with Matt Meadow-brook and Mr. Snuggles. "Did your Uncle Matt come over looking for a bear that night?"

That got their attention. "We love Uncle Matt," Merci said. "He's so much fun. Mr. Snuggles is Bradley's bear. He's always losing it." Then she shook her head. "No. Uncle Matt didn't come over. He would have asked us to help look for Mr. Snuggles."

I was trying to sort through what she'd said as I took out two of the pattern sheets we had for the crochet parties we put on. They had drawings and written instructions. "Your mother or Aunt Lauren can help you." I folded the sheets and put them in each bag. "Well, that's it. Now you have everything you need." Venus opened the bag and poked through everything. Merci stood off to the side with a furrowed brow. I felt her tug at my arm. "That night I had a dream that someone was arguing."

"I'm back," Ursula announced. She handed each girl a small cup of Bob's special strawberry lemonade. The girls showed off their bags and told her about their purses. I made sure they understood they could come back anytime they needed help, including Ursula.

"Thank you," the nanny said. "This will be a wonderful way to keep them occupied. And it's something for me, too." She led them to the front to pay for everything.

Now that I was alone I had a few moments to think it all over. It was a win-win—I got business for the bookstore, and I knew a little more about that night. Either Matt Meadowbrook was lying about going there that night or he'd been there after Garrett, when the girls were asleep. And Merci's dream might not have been a dream at all.

CHAPTER 20

"WE NEED TO GENERATE MORE EXCITEMENT about our musical event," Mr. Royal said as he draped a banner across the sign we had at the entrance of the store. It read "Limited Supply of Tickets. Get Yours Today."

"I can't wait to replace the banner with one that says 'Sold Out.'" Technically, since the tickets were free, I wasn't sure that would be accurate, but if it made him happy, I wasn't about to say anything.

The door whooshed open and I automatically looked up as Barry came in. The suit and tie meant he was working. He had on his cop face and I assumed he was there looking for *bad guys*, as he called them. I put my hands up. "I'm innocent. I didn't do anything," I said, joking.

The cop face broke into a smile. "Are you so sure?" He paused for effect. "But then, I haven't gotten any more calls about weird activities at your neighbors', so maybe you are."

Mr. Royal nodded a greeting and then went back to the music department. Barry read the sign and seemed a little surprised that my mother's group was on there along with ChIlLa. "Does this mean you and Cheyenne Chambers are friends now?"

I made a shushing sound and pulled him over to the side. I quickly explained that Mrs. Shedd was very excited about the upcoming evening and didn't know that I had sent him to Cheyenne's twice, but would have a fit if she did, because she'd worry that it was going to mess things up. And Cheyenne still didn't know that it had been me. "And that's the way I'm trying to keep it."

"Your life is a web of deception," he said with a tease in his voice. "As long as you're done with your poking around their backyard, my lips are sealed."

My immediate response was to insist that there was something going on back there, and there was a long pause while I thought of all the things I could say. There was the fact that the Blood Detector really did detect blood, which meant I had found the real thing. Or I could tell him about all the personal stuff Jennifer had left behind. Thinking it over again, it seemed all she'd taken was her phone and her wallet. I could mention Ursula's claim that her room had been gone through. I could bring up the supposed visit of Matt Meadowbrook to look for Mr. Snuggles. I stopped on that thought. I was not going to mention a famous country singer looking for a teddy bear.

"So if you're not after a perp . . ." I left it hanging and he shook his head.

"At least get the terms right. Nobody really calls them *perps*. I stopped by to pick up something for Jeffrey. He called it in. Do you know where I could find it?"

"Let's try the information desk," I said, leading the way.

It was a small enclosed area in the heart of the store. Stepping behind the desk, I tried to act like Barry was just
another customer, but I still felt an awkward vibe.

"There you are, Pink," Adele said, coming into the
small area. She had taken off the Rapunzel wig and
changed into her normal attire. I was expecting some kind
of reproach from her about offering my number instead of
Ursula's, but she seemed to have forgotten all about it. "As
my matron of honor, you have to come with me."

I was trying to figure out what she was talking about
when a woman bustled in behind her. "Adele, you shouldn't
have rushed on ahead," she said, sounding both annoyed
and breathless. It was Leonora Humphries, aka Mother
Humphries.

Adele grabbed my arm. "Sorry. I was just gathering up
my best friend Molly so she could come with us." She
caught my eye with a pleading expression. "I want Molly
to see this place you picked for us."

I was mildly stunned that she'd called me by my first
name, but I managed to call her shenanigans to a halt while
I looked for Jeffrey's order. Adele had been too wrapped
up in her moment to even notice Barry's presence. As I
handed Barry the book, I saw that his eyes had gone skyward and he had an amused smile. "I forgot how crazy
your life is." He turned to go, and it sound like he muttered,
"And I miss it."

Adele had already gotten the okay from Mrs. Shedd for
us to leave, so I was on the way out the door with the two
women before I knew it. Adele wanted me to sit in the front
seat with her, but Leonora claimed she had to be there to
direct the way. Personally, I was glad to be in the backseat,
as far away from the action as possible.

Poor Adele. She had been so thrilled about getting

engaged to Eric and had thought her happy ever after had already begun. But first there was the news that Eric's mother had moved in with him—permanently, as in forever, even after they were married—and then the wedding venue went under, taking both her dreams of a romantic wedding and the money she'd paid in along with it.

"Mother Humphries, just tell me the address," Adele said. I couldn't believe that Adele missed how that woman cringed every time she was called that name.

"Turn right at the next stoplight," Eric's mother said, ignoring Adele's request. And so it went, with Mrs. Humphries instructing Adele to *turn here, go there*. The headrest blocked my view and I couldn't tell where we were, other than noting that we'd turned off Ventura Boulevard and were on a residential street. Trying to get my bearings, I leaned around the headrest and recognized our location. The cross street ahead had businesses on it and they spilled around the corner.

"Turn right at the driveway," Leonora commanded, and Adele pulled the car into the parking lot of a cream-colored single-story building that had "Parisian Banquet Hall" written on it in white letters that looked like frosting. The arched windows that faced the street had been filled in, just leaving their outlines. In an effort to give the plain building a more romantic appearance, light fixtures were spaced around the front. The poles, with their lanternlike tops, looked like a scaled-down version of something you'd see in Paris.

Adele pulled her Matrix into a parking spot that faced the entrance to the hall. Here, the arched windows had been left intact.

"It's a famous place. Eric will love it," Leonora said, leading us to the door. She knocked, and a man in a dark suit opened it. He introduced himself as Tony and invited us in. It took a moment for my eyes to adjust to the dim interior. The curtains over the windows cut down the natural light and the few overhead fixtures barely illuminated the large open space. There were columns spaced around the room, and I was sure they were more about holding the ceiling up than about looks.

The walls had a combination of murals of trees in pots and fake ones in pots. The fake ones were strung with tiny white lights.

"Don't you recognize it?" Leonora asked. Adele looked stricken and shook her head.

"I understand you're interested in a wedding package and your budget is limited," Tony said. He called over to another man skulking in the corner and told him to bring something out. A moment later, the man rolled in an archway covered with fake foliage. "This is what we use for the ceremony."

He walked us to the front. "We set up a wine toast and some appetizers, followed by a pasta buffet." He demonstrated where a long table would be placed. "You just say *go* and we take care of everything." The other man handed Tony a floral centerpiece, which he waved in front of Adele. "All included. They look so real you can almost smell them," he said with an oily smile.

He stepped back into the open space. "We can set up the tables any way you want. When we know it's for a shooting, we set it up so the important people can see the door."

Shooting?

"Can't have a wedding without a cake, can we?" he said. "We roll in a plaster one with a layer of real cake on top for photos. Your guests are served from the finest sheet cake, baked fresh that day at the grocery store around the corner."

Leonora gave Adele a sharp look. "I say grab this place. It's such a deal."

Adele was almost in tears. It was not the beautiful place she'd imagined, where the trees were real and the dinner was served in a room with windows looking out on a pond with swans.

"What about music?" Adele asked, clearly looking for anything to stall.

"Provided by my nephew," Tony said. He took us over to a table set up in the corner. "That's Victor. When he's not working here, he's doing a gig in Vegas." He pointed out a photograph of his nephew dressed in an Elvis jumpsuit. "If you want, he can compose a song just for you—for an extra fee, of course. He's gonna be a big star any minute."

I saw some CDs in boxes on the table. "Are these his?" I asked.

"You mean like for sale?" Tony said. "Hey, that's a good idea, we should do that. Those are for him to send in to that rights place. He knows all about that stuff. How you gotta send a CD of him performing it, and the lyrics and music written down. You know, to protect his rights. You should hear the songs he writes. So much emotion it will make you cry." He looked at the three of us. "So, can we get down to business?"

He pulled out his phone and pulled up a calendar. "We don't have any weekends left in the next few months. People love the authentic ambience and the fact that we're famous now. I understand you have a budget crunch. I could give you a real deal on a Thursday, though we might have to slide it one week either way. We give first priority to a shooting."

"What do you mean a shooting?" I asked, and Tony looked at me as if I'd asked a stupid question.

He mimicked shooting an automatic rifle. "It's kind of like a double meaning." He laughed like he was making a bad joke. "That's why you came here, right?" He looked over the three of us. "If you want we can even set up an ambush, like that detective does." He gestured around the place with a proud smile.

"No, thanks, Mr. Tony," I said, putting my arm around Adele's shoulder and leading her outside. "Don't worry, Adele. We'll find some other place."

"I don't understand what's wrong with you two," Leonora said, following behind us. "I tried to help you. I found a special place at a price you could afford."

Adele was sniveling all the way back to the car, and I had to carry the conversation.

"You do know your son is a police officer and that man was talking about arranging killing people," I said sternly. Leonora began to cackle.

"The ambushes are all fake, like the trees in that place. When he said *shooting* he meant shooting the *Jack Hunter* show. That's what I meant when I said the place was famous." She turned her attention to Adele. "That's Eric's favorite show. I would have thought his fiancée would know that. But I'm just the mother-in-law-to-be."

ADELE SPENT THE REST OF THE RIDE BACK TO THE bookstore trying to explain why she didn't know what Eric's favorite show was. I didn't say anything, but I certainly knew it was one that Mason watched whenever the series was on. It wasn't my cup of tea, but Mason was enthralled with the exploits of the low-life detective with family problems.

LATER WHEN MASON AND I MET UP, HE WANTED to hear all about it. "You were actually there? I didn't realize it was a real place. That's the spot Jack Hunter was supposed to meet up with Lucky Louie," Mason said, all excited.

"Was supposed to?" I asked.

"It was in the middle of Lucky Louie's cousin's wedding. The Kenter brothers came in the door just as they were rolling out the cake." Mason shook his head, reliving the moment. "Blood spatter everywhere."

I remembered what Tony had said about *shooting* having a double meaning. Now I got it.

"That would have been an interesting place for Adele's wedding," he said. "Or at least Eric would have thought so." Then Mason took in our surroundings. "This is ridiculous, Sunshine," he said. "Here we are again, outsiders in our own places. Relegated to hanging out in a restaurant." We'd gone to a new open-air mall that had a lot of places to eat and a nice place to take an after-dinner stroll. We'd picked a so-called casual dining eatery. It was a wait-on-yourself kind of place, but the food was prepared to order.

My mother was having another rehearsal at my house, and the energy around it was becoming more and more frantic as the actual event approached, making my place off-limits. Jaimee had a date, and Mason didn't want anything to stand in the way of its success, so when she mentioned she'd invited the man over for drinks before they went out for the evening, he wanted her to have the place to herself. Luckily, Brooklyn was studying with some friends. "I'll have to hide out in my room when I go home," he said. "In case they come back for a nightcap."

But then it was as if he'd just heard what he'd said, and he shook his head at the absurdity of it. "I hope her date is a big success and she and this guy ride off into the sunset."

We had taken an outside table next to a heat lamp. The days had gotten warmer, but nighttime still had an edge. Mason pushed around a piece of his braised short ribs.

"Maybe we need to change our relationship status." He said it in a casual way, and I wasn't sure what he meant. I also didn't necessarily want to know. As far as I was concerned, why mess up a good thing? So I did the only thing I could do—I changed the subject.

"Your mention of blood spatter reminded me of the mystery at Cheyenne's."

Mason chuckled and pushed away the meat. "Such lovely dinner conversation. And I know what you just did. I get it, you don't want to talk about it. So, tell me, where you are in the investigation?" He leaned on his hand and looked ready to listen. Then he put his hand up. "Wait, let me get us a French press pot of coffee."

I organized my thoughts while he was gone. He came back with the glass pot and pushed down the plunger before pouring us each a cup. "This is the best way to drink coffee," he said, holding up his cup in a toast. "Okay, ready to listen."

"Let me see, what developments have you missed in the mystery at Cheyenne's?" I stopped to chuckle. "*Mystery at Cheyenne's*—that sounds like the title of a Nancy Drew novel." I started with the quarrel between Matt Meadowbrook and his wife, which had made it sound like he had a wandering eye. Then there was his visit to Cheyenne's the night the nanny left to search for Mr. Snuggles. "I talked to the kids, and the spokesperson of the two said she hadn't seen him. Which means he must have gone there when they were asleep—which was when whatever happened, happened."

"That sounds suspicious. What about Garrett and Cheyenne?" Mason asked.

"They were at the taping of her show. He said they did back-to-back tapings. He did say he had to go home to pick up something for Cheyenne."

"Oh, another possible suspect," Mason said with sudden interest.

"No, I don't think so. It was before anything happened. The kids were still awake and the nanny was there," I said. "I hate to sound like a broken record, but I know there was a body in the yard. The only thing that makes sense is that it was Jennifer. But everybody believes she's still alive. I also know there can't be a murder without a body. So I need to find her body to prove that she isn't alive, and then figure out who killed her."

"I think we need dessert," Mason said. "How about the citrus olive oil cake?" When he returned with a small loaf of the yellow cake, he brought up something else. "You seem to be going around in circles. Why not focus on who had a motive to get rid of Jennifer and what it was?"

"What would I do without you?" I said as he cut the cake into small slices. "Of course you're right." Then I slumped. "Maybe that gets me out of going in circles, but it puts me back to square one."

"I trust you will come up with something," he said, touching my arm. "Could you tell me more about your trip to the Parisian Banquet Hall? That guy you talked to sounds like he could have been a character in the show." It was my turn to chuckle at his obsession with the TV show.

When we finally went back to our cars, we hugged for a long time.

"Think about what I said before," he said as he kissed me good-bye.

CHAPTER 21

I HAD SHELVED WHAT MASON AND I TALKED about regarding the Mystery at Cheyenne's. As much as I wanted to solve it, for now I needed to focus on what was going on at the bookstore. On Friday, almost all of the tickets had been handed out and Mr. Royal had made more improvements to the Sight and Sound department. He'd created a photo display on one of the walls with the candid shots of Cheyenne and Lauren in the bookstore. There were also some pictures of the group from their rehearsal. He asked me if I could get one of Ilona and some candid shots of the She La Las to finish it off.

He showed me the boxes and boxes of CDs and vinyl records we'd gotten in and suggested that we have a run-through of our own to practice moving the bookcases back and doing the whole setup of the area.

I left notes for myself on the information desk and pre-pared to change gears for the Tunisian class. Though, with all my responsibilities, it was hardly a relaxing diversion. Lauren had arrived early again, and she was sitting at the table working with a regular crochet hook and some purple yarn. The babysitter with her kids passed me as I walked to the yarn department.

"You did the trade-off again," I said to Lauren, indicating the group going out the door. She let out a sigh of relief.

"Yes. Thank heavens my ex is going to have them for part of next week, so there won't be any problem for the gig." I pulled out a chair and checked the table for stray yarn and tools before bringing out my Tunisian hook with the beginnings of the scarf on it. I hadn't had any time to work on it other than in the class, and I'd just moved into a third color of yarn.

"It must be much harder for you than for your sisters, since they don't have to worry about someone taking care of their kids when they have to do something," I said.

"They have their own problems," she said cryptically. I know I'd told myself that I wasn't going to spend any time thinking about the Mystery at Cheyenne's, but I couldn't help myself.

"You mean with their nannies?" I said. "Like the one who left so suddenly?"

"They're not all as professional as the one Cheyenne has now. A lot of them are looking for a way into our business. Or maybe for a husband."

I mentioned it being almost a cliché, and she nodded.

"That's because it's true."

"It sounds like you know about it firsthand," I said, hoping she'd keep talking.

"Why do you think Ilona has a manny now?" she said. "Don't you think some aspiring singer or actor wouldn't like Matt's help in greasing their way into the business? And if he ended up going off with her, all the better."

"Has that actually happened?" Now I was just curious.

"My sister seems to think so. But she knows how to take care of things before they go too far."

I was just about to turn the conversation to Jennifer when the group began to arrive. Adele took her spot at the head of the table. Elise, Rhoda and Dinah came in together. Melody and Terri were taking their time, talking as they came across the bookstore. Susan came up behind them and rushed them along. Franny wheeled Oscar up in the dog stroller and parked it next to the table. CeeCee came in at the end.

When they were all seated, Susan looked toward the empty chairs. "Where's your sister?" she said to Lauren in an accusing voice.

"I'm not my sister's keeper," Lauren said, pursing her lips. Susan turned to me, and then to Adele.

"We're not going to wait for her, are we? I didn't sign up for celebrity crocheting," she said, still in the snippy voice.

"Celebrity crocheting?" CeeCee said, glancing around at the group. "What a concept." She turned to Lauren. "Maybe I should talk to my agent," she said.

"Forget what I said," Susan said impatiently. A burst of noise came from the front of the store, and we all turned as Cheyenne, Garrett, the two girls and Ursula all came in.

I didn't dare look at Susan when the group reached the table. It was as if energy somehow swirled around us as Cheyenne made her entrance and made a big production of apologizing for being late. She seemed a little frantic, and I noticed that her sweater was buttoned wrong, so that one side of the hem hung lower than the other.

Cheyenne deferred to her husband. Garrett smiled at the group. "One of you taught the girls to crochet and said to come in if they needed help."

"That would be me," I said, feeling the stares of the class. I realized I was caught. I had probably said something like *Come in anytime*.

I could hear Susan making angry noises as the two girls and Ursula squeezed in.

"Can we finally begin?" Susan said with a pound on the table.

Adele waved to me and pulled me aside. "Pink, you made this mess—you deal with it."

She went back to her spot and started the class by showing off some more advanced stitches and instructed everyone to make a swatch.

I was left to crouch next to the two girls. Garrett came up behind his wife and whispered something and I saw her correct the buttoning of her sweater. Then he backed away, and while he tried to be unobtrusive, I saw that he was using his phone to tape the event. Everything seemed to be fodder for social media.

Susan gave me a sharp look. "You're disturbing the class. Can't you move the children somewhere else?" Adele seemed upset that she'd lost control of the class to Susan and said she was just going to suggest the same thing. I figured Garrett would edit that moment out.

I took the girls and the nanny out into the bookstore and pulled some chairs around a small table we had set up for customers to use for their drinks. Ursula showed me her hat, which was coming along just fine, and I saw her looking toward the café.

"You can go get a drink if you'd like. I'll help the girls." Ursula flashed me a thank-you smile and told the girls she'd bring them something, too.

Merci emptied the tote bag on the small table. Her younger sister followed her lead. They both had a string of chain stitches hanging off their hooks, and it was clear they didn't know what to do next. I showed them how to crochet the first row.

Merci looked back at the yarn department, and her face appeared concerned. "Mommy had one of her moments," the older girl said. I asked her what she meant. "You know. She gets all crazy. She says crochet makes her okay." It was true; even from here I could see that Cheyenne's face had lost its franticness as she moved her hook through the yarn.

Ursula was on her way back, carrying a holder with drinks. Judging by the way her eyebrows were furrowed, Merci seemed to still have something on her mind. "She should not drink our pink juice."

After that, there was no more talking about anything but crochet. Ursula had brought drinks for all of us. She handed the strawberry lemonades to the girls and a covered cup to me. "I didn't know what you like, so I got you a coffee." She offered to get me sugar and cream, but I thanked her and told her I drank it black. She took a few sips of her coffee and set down the cup while she watched me help the girls.

By the time the Tunisian class broke up, both girls had completed a few rows of their purses, and Ursula had learned enough that she would be able to help them. They were going to come back when they finished the two pieces, and I said I would help them put them together and add a strap.

"That was something," Dinah said when I went back to the main table. Only she and Elise were still there. I was thinking about how to respond to Dinah's comment when Mrs. Shedd came in to see how it had gone. No way would I repeat anything Merci had said and discuss what it meant now. I glossed over it and asked Dinah how the wedding plans were going.

Dinah seemed surprised, but I think she figured out what I was doing. "It's not the wedding that's a problem, but afterward." Elise and Mrs. Shedd both gave her a puzzled look.

My friend crocheted a few more stitches. "His house, my house. Where we should live."

Mrs. Shedd jumped right in. "If it was me, marrying someone, I'd opt for a new place. No old memories to get in the way of the new ones you're making." She stopped and smiled. "I sound like a greeting card, don't I?" She sighed, and I saw her glance toward the front of the store, where Mr. Royal was carrying something into the music department. "If it ever happens, that's what I'll do."

Elise cleared her throat. "You do remember that Logan is in real estate. You could talk to him, and he could at least tell you what's out there." Even with the class done, she had continued working on her scarf. Unlike regular crochet, where it didn't matter where you stopped, Tunisian crochet was more like knitting in that you needed to finish a row before stopping. Our vampire lover waved her hand toward the café. "You can talk to him now. You know Logan, always setting up shop in a café."

She waited for us to make a move, and there didn't seem to be a graceful way not to follow through. As Elise had said, Logan was sitting at a corner table with his computer out and papers spread around it.

Dinah stopped me before we reached him. "I'm not so sure about this. I think I should talk to Commander first."

"We'll just ask him some general questions about real estate," I said.

Logan glanced up from the computer screen as we reached him. "Is Elise ready to go?" he said.

"She's finishing up, but she suggested we talk to you about real estate," I said. I was trying very hard not to concentrate on his hair, but every time I saw him I had the same thought—his hairline was so odd, it looked like he was wearing some kind of cap. He was waiting for me to say more. "We just wondered how it's moving in Tarzana?" I said.

He seemed puzzled by the question. "Could you be more specific?"

And then I remembered what Elise had said. I'd ask him about Cheyenne's house. "I was wondering if you knew about that big house that went up behind mine."

He eyes lit with interest. "There's a story about that place," he said. He began by talking about the developer, and I smiled, nodded and didn't really listen until he mentioned Garrett's name. "He went directly to the developer and talked him into leasing the house to them at a low price while they finished it. The yard was just piles of dirt. It needed everything. A pool, retaining walls, extensive landscaping, and a patio along the back. And of course fencing and outdoor lighting." He stopped to see if he'd mentioned everything. I got the general idea and nodded, hoping it would get him to move on.

"I'm gathering they couldn't really afford the house now, but supposedly Mackenzie convinced the developer that they expected a jump in their cash flow in a couple of months and then they would just buy the house," Logan said.

I was pretty sure the jump in cash flow had to do with the release of their next album, which they all seemed to be hanging so many hopes on. It made me nervous to think about what would happen if the album turned out like their last one. I thanked him for the information, and Dinah and I went back into the bookstore.

Dinah shook her head. "That's a lot of pressure. No wonder Cheyenne seems a little frantic."

CHAPTER 22

IT WAS DARK AND LATE WHEN I WALKED ACROSS my yard. The full moon was so bright that I almost forgot about the pair of floodlights that didn't work. I could see the foliage of the orange trees in the blue light, and the air smelled sweet with the purple hyacinths that showed up every April.

I glanced toward Cheyenne's. It had become automatic now whenever I went into the yard, though this time I had a different perspective. It had never occurred to me that they were living on the edge financially.

Felix and Cosmo were waiting by the kitchen door, with the two cats close behind. I understood why Blondie wasn't with them when I opened the door and heard the noise. The terrier mix was no doubt hiding out in my room. My mother and the girls were obviously having yet another rehearsal. Samuel came into the kitchen and seemed surprised to see me.

"Did you hear the news? Liza and the girls got a gig at that nostalgia club that opened up in Toluca Lake. They're going to sing 'My Guy Bill' and other songs from that era." He seemed particularly happy.

"You're calling her Liza now?"

"I'm going to be their musical director. I'm not calling her Grandma," he said. He grabbed a thermal pitcher off the counter. "Hot water and lemon for their throats."

I let the dogs have a run in the yard and checked the cats' bowl before going into the living room. They were apparently taking a break and were sitting on the couches that had been moved across the room. I walked in on a conversation about one of their contemporaries—someone named Billy Kendricks, who had it made because he had written a song called "Keepin' the Edge." I was surprised the song had been written by someone from their era, since it had been featured in a recent movie and had become an anthem of sorts about not becoming complacent.

"The big bucks go to the songwriters," Samuel said.

"I'm glad you're here," I said, coming into the room. I told them about Mr. Royal sprucing up the music department and my mother put her hands together in amazement.

"Who would have thought vinyl records would make a comeback?" she said. I explained the gallery of photos he was putting up and told her he wanted one of the She La Las to add to it. I don't think the last word was out of my mouth before my mother told Samuel to get his camera and then began posing the group.

The great thing about digital cameras is that you can see what you get right away. It only took a few tries before we got some winners of the three women. They were all holding microphones and looking at one another. It captured their friendship and their joy of entertaining. Samuel went off to print up a copy for me to take into the bookstore.

"I suppose ChIlLa is getting him photographs, too," my mother said. I didn't mean to, but it slipped out that Mr. Royal had used some from their rehearsal at the bookstore. My mother seemed crushed that they'd been left out and I had to do damage control. Finally I resorted to changing the subject.

"I hear we have reason to celebrate," I said. When she didn't instantly respond, I told her that Samuel had told me all about their regular gig at the nostalgia club.

The reminder of the good news perked her right up, and I was relieved to see her eyes dance with excitement.

"Isn't it wonderful? We're going to be regulars there once a week. Unless we're on tour." Her bracelets jangled as she put her cup down on the coffee table. "Maybe it isn't so bad that we weren't part of that rehearsal at the bookstore. We might have just gone through our number once. But we've been working night after night here. You should have seen us, honey. We were so smooth when we auditioned," my mother said, doing a little of their choreography.

"Well, girls, shall we do another run-through," my mother said, "or should we call it a night?"

I certainly could get behind that last part and was surprised when the other two She La Las jumped off the couches and went right into dance mode, anxious to do the number again. My mother tried again to get me to stay and play the tambourine, but I begged off, grateful to get to the peace of my room.

I feel asleep surrounded by the two dogs and two cats, while Blondie watched us all from her chair.

* * *

I HALF EXPECTED TO FIND THE SHE LA LAS PASSED
out on the couch when I walked across the house in the
morning, but the living room was empty. Samuel's door
was shut, and I guessed he didn't have the early shift at the
coffee place.

I got Blondie to come across the house and to go outside
with the other two dogs. I even let the cats out, but I kept
them under my supervision. I hung around near the chain-
link fence so I could stop them if it looked like they were
going to climb over.

There was enough ivy on my side that I didn't have a
clear view into Cheyenne's yard unless I got right up to the
fence and looked over the top. If I could see in, then it
seemed they might be able to see me if someone happened
to look out the window.

I could hear that the workmen were back, and my curiosity got the better of me, so I moved next to a tree to shield
me from view and peeked over the fence. The spot for the
pool had been marked off, and a small Bobcat was moving
back and forth, unloading dirt. They seemed to have finished the patio that went under the second-floor balcony. I
couldn't figure out the rest of what they were doing; I could
just tell that it looked like they had a long way to go.

I grabbed the cats and brought them inside. The dogs
naturally followed me in. As I shut the door, I looked back
at what I could see of the house between the trees in my
yard. The white siding and the chimney complete with a
lattice design on top looked so innocent, but more and more
I was sure the house was full of secrets.

On a whim, I called Jennifer's number again. I had left
her a message days ago pretending to be her replacement

and asking where to send her things. There had been no call back. As expected, I got her voice mail, the slightly Southern-sounding voice asking for a number and promising a call back. It was her, but it couldn't be her. I left my cell number, since it didn't identify me, and left the same message about sending on her things, though I didn't really expect her to call back. Whoever I had talked to had probably figured out that I wasn't the replacement nanny.

I had begun to wonder if I would ever find out what was going on. Had somebody figured out how to commit the perfect crime? So perfect that nobody but me even thought there had been a crime? No one was looking for Jennifer because she didn't seem to be missing.

I remembered that Mason had suggested that if I figured out the motive I might be able to unravel the whole thing. *Good luck on that one,* I thought.

It was a relief to stop thinking about it and to get ready for work. I had an early day, and it felt more comfortable to go in when my day and the bookstore's were both starting at the same time. Bob had just brewed the day's first pot of coffee when I stopped in to pick up a red eye. I delivered the photographs to Mr. Royal. "Great," he said, admiring the shots of the She La Las. "I'll have a couple framed and on the wall this morning. Now, if you can just get something of Ilona. It should be something that goes along with the rest of these. You know, more casual than a head shot." As an afterthought, he suggested I get a photo of her husband as well. "He's really the biggest star of the bunch."

I went to the information booth to check over the day's calendar, making a mental note that I'd have to get in touch with Ilona. But for once, coincidence was in my favor, and an hour later she came looking for me in the yarn department as I was crocheting a swatch of a new fingering weight yarn we'd just gotten in. It always struck me how different she looked than her sisters. She was taller, with a slighter build. The others both had long dark hair, and she had blond hair in a short, straggly cut. All of their personalities were so different, too. Cheyenne seemed to stir the air around her. Lauren blended in with the background. Ilona had a confidence that made it seem like she owned her surroundings. I was sure the little girl with her was her daughter, since they had the same body shape and were dressed like twins in jeans, sweaters and blue sheepskin boots.

"Cher saw that her cousins were making purses, and she wants to make one, too. I understand you're the one who can make it happen," Ilona said.

"Of course," I said, getting up from my chair. I offered to give her a lesson right then and provide her with the same kit I'd given her cousins. "And the same offer that she can come in if she needs help down the line."

"Maybe you could show me, too," Ilona said. "I feel like the odd man out, since both my sisters know how."

"I'll turn you both into hookers in no time," I said. She smiled at the joke, and we all sat down at the table. I handed Cher a big plastic hook that worked well with little hands and a small ball of yarn. Ilona got a basic size J hook and her own ball of yarn. I smiled to myself, thinking this was my chance to find out about her. I started off by complimenting her on how well the three sisters seemed to get along. "And your families as well. All the children are around the same age and seem close."

I showed them both how to make a slip knot and then a length of chain stitches. "It's a challenge," she said. "All of it. My sisters and I are in different places, as you've probably noticed. Cheyenne and I both try to help Lauren." Both the mother and daughter held up what they'd done with pride. I demonstrated going back over the chain stitches with a row of single crochets. They both tried to do the same. Cher was fearless and went across the row with glee. Ilona was more careful, but as she neared the end of the row seemed to realize she'd picked up how to do it.

"It must be difficult for you, since both you and your husband are famous," I said. I saw by the way she drew in her lips that I had hit a sensitive spot. She glanced at her daughter as if she was considering what to say. Cher wasn't paying any attention. I'd shown her how to make a chain stitch at the end of the row and turn her work. She'd already started making the second row before I even told her what to do.

"It's not easy having to share your husband with his adoring fans," she said finally. "Particularly when he charms everyone and doesn't always consider the consequences." She had gotten into a rhythm of making the stitches, and I noticed that her shoulders had relaxed.

"I saw how he was with the kids at Cheyenne's the other day," I said, trying to steer the conversation. "I'm sure they were having more fun with him than they do with their nannies. Particularly Cheyenne's new one. I suppose they all like the one who left better." I said it in an offhand manner as I watched Ilona move to the next row.

She didn't seem to notice my awkward transition, and her expression momentarily darkened. Then she smiled. "His charm hit a brick wall with the new one. At least I don't have to worry about her." She stopped moving her hook, as if she was thinking about something.

"Then you had a problem with the one who had the emergency?" I said, continuing to try to sound casual.

Ilona glanced at her daughter again. I guessed she was considering what to say in front of her. "It's not a problem anymore, but she was always auditioning for him." She put extra emphasis on the word *auditioning* and said it with distaste. She looked up from the swatch of stitches she'd made with a surprised expression. "It's just like Cheyenne said. Doing something with yarn seems to get you talking like it's some kind of therapy session. I wouldn't want to leave you with the wrong impression. Matt is a great guy, and we're a happy family."

It wasn't until after they'd left that I realized she had spoken about Jennifer as if she was gone for good.

CHAPTER 23

THE NEXT TIME THE HOOKERS GOT TOGETHER FOR happy hour, it was a small gathering of just me, Rhoda, Sheila, and Adele. I really wished Dinah were there so I could tell her about Ilona. It helped make sense of things when I had a sounding board, and she was so good at playing Doctor Watson. Adele spent the whole time moaning about the place Mother Humphries had dragged her to.

"You're going to have to make a decision soon or you'll have to send out change-the-date cards or cancel-the-date cards." Poor Adele let out a wail as Rhoda mentioned the last option.

I tried to change the subject back to crocheting, but Adele continued on.

"This is such a disaster. I have everything for the wedding. I even crocheted my bouquet and that bow tie for Cutchykins. He has his tux picked out and his best man and groomsmen lined up." She turned to me. "Pink, I didn't tell you this before because I thought it might upset you, but Eric asked Barry to be one of the groomsmen, so he'll probably be right there in front with you." The wail started again as Adele said, "But in front of where?"

I think we were all relieved when happy hour ended, as it had hardly lived up to its name. I cleared up the yarn department and then headed home. I'm not sure what I was expecting, but certainly not what I found. I walked into a kitchen fragrant with the smells of Chinese food. White containers littered the counter. The She La Las had kicked things up. Not only were they rehearsing in the living room, but my father and the other husbands were there, plus some people I didn't know, all acting as an audience. When I went through my living room, my son was playing the keyboard with gusto and my mother and the other She La Las were dancing around, clapping their hands and urging their audience to join in.

I found all the animals huddled in my room. Blondie observed the others from her chair, no doubt unhappy with the company. I hadn't heard from Mason all day, but I was sure his house was more peaceful than mine. I slipped back across the house, and I didn't think anyone noticed that I had left, or even that I'd been there.

The streets had grown quiet, and it took less than ten minutes to get to Mason's. It was the first time I'd ever just come over unannounced. I even planned to let myself in. His house always seemed a little mysterious at night. The dark wood of the huge ranch-style exterior made it blend in with surroundings. I got the key out as I approached the door.

I expected Spike to come running toward the door barking when I opened it, but it was quiet. I considered calling out hello as I came in, but I figured that would send Spike into a barking frenzy for sure. The real center of Mason's house was the den, which looked out on the backyard, and I headed down the hall toward it. As I got closer I heard voices and recognized Mason's and Jaimee's. I stopped to listen, concerned about what I might be walking into.

"So the other night went well for you?" Mason said.

"James was very nice," she began. "He's about your age and a lawyer—a litigator. He even looked a little like you, though he could use some help with his style."

I was about to walk in, but what she said next made me stop in my tracks. "He was a lot like you, and when I saw how nice it was, it made me think, why settle for almost when I could have the real thing?" She laughed awkwardly, as if she was very nervous. "We did have some good times. I thought maybe we could give us another try."

There was no way I was walking into the middle of that. I barely waited until she finished before starting to back down the hall. Just when I got to the door, the toy fox terrier figured out there was an invader and came charging down the hall, barking at full tilt.

I speed walked to my car, anxious to disappear before anyone knew I'd been there. I was in shock. Jaimee wanted Mason back?

When I got back to my place, I grabbed some of the Chinese food and went across the house to the master area. With the door to the den shut, I could barely hear the She La Las doing the audience-participation version of "My Guy Bill." I drowned out the last of it by turning on the TV. How awkward. I didn't want to tell Mason that I'd been eavesdropping, but I was curious as to how he'd reacted. He must have figured out some diplomatic way to tell her *no way*.

I thought about calling him, and even started to dial a

few times, but decided I should wait and let him call me
and tell me about it. I longed for some distraction and
checked to see what was on TV, and then I remembered
Peter had set up to tape Cheyenne's show tune program.
The program list showed that two episodes had been
recorded.

The animals were clustered at my feet, hoping I'd be
clumsy with my chopsticks. I hit play and the first episode
began. My eyes were looking at the screen, but I was having a hard time concentrating. When Cheyenne was on the
screen, I focused momentarily. The other two judges
seemed to slip into the background compared with her.
But I zoned out again when the contestants started doing
their renditions of songs from musicals. There was a big
production at the end where all the contests and the judges
got together and started singing "There's No Business Like
Show Business" and the public was urged to vote for their
favorite contestant. I hit end. The list came up and I moved
on to the next episode. I was getting a lot of hungry looks
from the animals at my feet and decided we all needed
another plate of food.

Nobody noticed when I came through the living room
followed by a parade of cats and dogs. Nor did they notice
when I went the other way, carrying a plate of food with
the same escorts.

I settled in my room and hit play. Felix and Cosmo
wanted to make sure I knew they were there and each gave
my leg a swipe with their paws. The cats were more aggres-
sive and jumped onto the arms of the chair. Only Blondie
stayed put. She didn't like people food. When they'd all
had a hunk of chicken, I finally looked at the TV screen.
It took a moment for it to register, but when I saw Cheyenne
on the screen, I realized I must have set it up to play the

same episode again. I'd seen enough to get the idea of the show anyway and just shut it off. I checked the phones for messages, but the sounds from the living room had gotten louder, and I figured there was no way to escape it so I might as well join them. My mother's face lit up when she saw me join the impromptu audience and she grabbed the tambourine, gave it a shake and held it out. Why not? I took it and joined them.

THE PHONE RANG EARLY THE NEXT MORNING, AND I grabbed it when I saw it was Mason. I'd barely gotten out a hello when he started talking.

I could tell by the sound that he was in his car. "Sorry for calling so early. There was an emergency with the same client and I'm heading to New York."

"Oh, okay," I said, sitting up and trying to get my bearings. "I suppose Jaimee and Brooklyn will take care of Spike."

"Well, actually, I had to get a dog sitter, because they're coming with me." He said it in a matter-of-fact voice, and I got that he couldn't say more because they were in the car with him.

I knew that my voice was on speaker, so all I did was wish him safe travels. "We'll talk later," he said just before he signed off. I waited for his usual "love you," but there was only dead air. He'd already gone.

I was sure all would be explained eventually. Mason didn't know what I'd overheard, so he wouldn't realize how upsetting it was that it seemed like they were going on a family trip. I just wanted to talk to Dinah. This was the time when I really needed a best friend. But I knew she was tied up all day giving exams to her students.

We didn't meet up until the happy hour gathering. We had some drop-ins, along with Sheila, Elise, Eduardo, CeeCee, Adele, Dinah and me. Lauren came with her daughter Justine, who wanted to make a purse like her cousins. I was expecting Adele to make another scene about her wedding, but she was strangely quiet. She offered Justine a crochet lesson, and I made up a kit for her.

"You seemed to have gotten over your wedding blues," I said to Adele when the hour had ended and it was just Dinah, Adele and me.

"Pink, I'm a professional teacher. I would never let my personal life interfere." She gave her head a haughty shake and said she had to prepare for the next story time. She was going to read a book called *The Sleeping Garden* and dress as a sunflower.

When it was just Dinah and me, I mentioned having a lot to tell her. You never knew who was listening at the bookstore, so I suggested my house. Samuel had told me that now that it was getting close to the performance at the bookstore, the group wanted to rest their voices and would be taking the evening off, so I knew my house would be peaceful.

All the animals except for Blondie were waiting by the door when we got to my place. Dinah was impatient to hear my news, but Samuel had also told me that he wouldn't be able to feed the menagerie, and I had to take care of them first. Actually, my first act had been to check my landline to see if Mason had called. He hadn't. Nor had he called my cell during the day.

When the dogs and cats were fed and had had their run in the yard, Dinah and I heated up some of the leftover Chinese food and took it in the dining room. She laughed when she saw the detective kit and Peter's microscope at the end of the table.

"Well," she said, holding her chopsticks in midair, "any mystery updates?"

I started out telling her about Ilona and the weird stuff she'd said about not having a problem with Jennifer anymore. I was going to go into what she'd implied about Matt, but I just lost it and started to talk about Mason.

"The other night, he suggested we think about upgrading our relationship."

Dinah seemed surprised. "Interesting, after hearing that all he wanted was something causal, no strings." She looked into my face. "How do you feel about that and what do you think he meant?"

"When he said it I was a little shocked, and I'm not sure what he had in mind. The idea did start to grow on me, but it might be irrelevant anyway." I told her what I'd overheard and how Jaimee and Brooklyn had gone on his emergency trip with him.

"Oh, dear," she said, putting her hand on my arm in a reassuring manner. "That's the trouble when people have exes hanging around—and children. It's too bad that things didn't work out with Barry. His exes are totally out of the picture, and Jeffrey worships you."

"You have a point." We went back to talking about Mason and both agreed it was foolish for me to jump to conclusions. "Enough about relationships," I said, shrugging my shoulders like I was dropping a heavy cape. "Let's talk about my neighbors." I brought up again that Ilona had talked about Jennifer as if she knew the nanny was never coming back. "Maybe that's because she knows Jennifer is dead. She had a motive for wanting her out of the way. She was pretty clear that Jennifer made a move on her husband."

"Ahem," a voice behind us said. "Excuse the theatrical throat clearing, but I didn't want to scare you," Barry said. He held up Jeffrey's key. "Jeffrey had a rehearsal tonight, and he wanted me to cover for him." He held up a bag of dog treats. The dogs had figured it out and Felix and Cosmo were gathered at his feet.

"By the way, I couldn't help but overhear you talking about motive. Remember what I said: no body, no murder." He saw the microscope next to the detective set. "What's that for?"

"Nothing," I said.

"No one can say you aren't persistent," he said, seeing right through me. The dogs both put their paws up on his leg, and he leaned down to give each of their ears a ruffle.

"Well, haven't you become the conscientious pet owner," Dinah said.

"I'm trying to make up for the past," he said. "It's never too late to make things right." I felt his eyes on me and purposely looked away. "What's going on around here? I noticed your living room looks a little torn up." I explained the She La Las were using it again. "No Mason tonight?"

I answered with a shrug and he finally went off to pour the bag of treats he'd brought into the jar on the counter. The dogs followed him outside, and he played fetch with them while Dinah and I watched through the French doors.

"Do you think he heard what we said?" I toyed with my chopstick. She nodded.

"You didn't see how he looked at you when he thought no one was looking," she said. "There was practically steam coming off his eyes."

We heard the kitchen door open, and we stopped talking. Barry came back into the room a moment later. "I see the floodlights are still out. I can take care of them if you like. Remember, I said I'd do the repair of your choice as a birthday present."

"No, that's okay," I said, a little too quickly. "Everything is under control here."

CHAPTER 24

MASON DID FINALLY CALL THAT NIGHT. I WAS standing outside looking up at the night sky as the dogs had their final time in the yard when the phone rang. The midnight blue was crystal clear, and it was surprising how many stars I could see. It was late here, but much later where he was. The mechanical voice on my phone merely said it was coming from a private caller, but I knew it was Mason. So now all would be revealed.

"Sunshine, I'm sorry I couldn't talk this morning. I'm sure you realized you were on speaker and Brooklyn and Jaimee were in the car." He sounded exhausted. I went inside and the dogs followed, and I had to cradle the phone with my shoulder while I doled out some of the fresh treats Barry had brought.

I had been relaxing into that mode of being ready to fall asleep, but the sound of his voice made me instantly wide awake, and my heartbeat kicked up. It was so odd, because I usually felt so comfortable talking to Mason, but then he wasn't usually telling me how he, his ex-wife and his daughter had flown off to New York.

"I'm sure you're wondering why the two of them came along," he said. Was there a little unease in his voice? I made a sound to show I was listening, and he continued. "The client I went back there for last week messed everything up, and I had to do damage control. I thought it would be good experience for Brooklyn to see how I handle things. The *Housewives* show wasn't taping this week, and Jaimee pouted." He let out a sigh. "I'm embarrassed to admit this, and I keep thinking I'm immune to it, but she knows my buttons."

I waited to see if he was going to say more, like bring up what I'd overheard, but he didn't. I wasn't sure how to feel. I finally settled on upset that he was keeping something from me and concerned about what else he might not be saying.

I was wondering how all this affected what he'd said the other night, but I was hesitant to bring it up. And then he did. "Have you had a chance to think over what I said?"

"I started to, but I think we need to deal with it face-to-face," I said. "We can talk when you get back."

"That sounds ominous," he said. "Don't make any rash decisions. We can work this out." We both agreed that he needed some sleep and that we should end the call.

"Love you," he said.

I swallowed hard before I responded, "Me, too."

I THOUGHT IT WOULD ALL SEEM BETTER IN THE morning, but it didn't. Any way I looked at it, he had lied to me by omission, and yet I kind of understood. It was possible he hadn't mentioned it because he thought hearing about Jaimee's desire to get back together would upset me. And it would certainly put her accompanying him in a different light. If he'd turned her down, he could think there was no reason to bring it up. But what if it was different? What if this was really a tryout of their being together and he was keeping me hanging until he saw how it worked out?

I didn't really let on, but I had been thinking about what he'd said about changing our status. Though he hadn't said the words, I figured he meant some kind of commitment, like us living together, or maybe even getting engaged. I had thought having that conversation sounded like a good idea. Now I wasn't so sure. But for now, I pushed it to the back of my mind.

Before I'd left for the bookstore I had already heard from my father. He was worried the She La Las had over-rehearsed and was concerned about their voices. I laughed when he told me he'd seen my mother's feet doing their dance moves in her sleep. We came up with a plan for their final rehearsal.

By now I was too occupied thinking about Mason and the event the next night to notice what the workmen were doing in Cheyenne's yard as I left for work. I think I had begun to feel hopeless about settling the Mystery at Cheyenne's anyway. Maybe it was time to throw in the towel.

When I got to the bookstore, there were so many loose ends to tie up. We had to move everything around and arrange for a backstage area. Adele put on story time regardless, and Ursula caught up with me while the girls were in the children's department.

"I just wanted to give you a heads-up. I understand the Mackenzies have arranged for a new nanny, so this will

probably be my last time here. I want to thank you for all
your help." She glanced toward the children's department,
and I knew she meant with Adele. Then she asked if I would
keep an eye on the girls when they came with the new
nanny and help them with their crochet if they needed it.

Just for a moment I wondered what that meant about
Jennifer Clarkson. But then I pushed it out of my mind.

Mr. Royal spent the afternoon rearranging the bookcases so there was a big open space in front of our updated
department. Then he arranged stanchions around the area
set aside for the crowd. He planned to attach the rope the
next day. We'd brought in curtained panels to close off the
yarn department and create a backstage area. Any book
shoppers had their work cut out for them with everything
moved around. Yarn shoppers were simply out of luck.

In the afternoon we had a meeting to discuss how the
event would go. It was basically up to Mr. Royal, Mrs.
Shedd, Adele and me to pull it off.

WITH EVERYTHING MOVED AROUND AT THE BOOK-
store, I suggested the Hookers meet somewhere else for
happy hour. I would have suggested canceling it all
together, but if ever there was a time I needed it, it was
that day.

CeeCee was glad to provide the location if I was willing
to bring some treats. Our actress Hooker's sweet tooth was
legendary among the group, with a special emphasis on
chocolate. I had whipped up a batch of my version of Bob's
double chocolate cookie bars to take over.

I was glad to leave the chaos at the bookstore and avoid
the chaos at my house. The She La Las were gathering
there for their last rehearsal. My father and I had come up

with the idea that they should save their voices and just lip-synch and go through the dance steps. But it was up to him to see that they did it.

I let out a sigh of relief at the quiet as I got out of my car in front of CeeCee's. Her house reminded me of something out of a fairy tale. The stone cottage was set back from the street in the midst of a small forest of trees. Tall bushes lined the inside of the fence and completely blocked the outside world from view. I noticed the bushes with new interest as I walked up the pathway to her house. They were just what I needed to go between the trees in my backyard to shut out most of the view of Cheyenne's.

Rhoda, Elise, Sheila, Eduardo, Adele and Dinah were already sitting in CeeCee's dining room, and the long dark wood trestle table was littered with hooks and balls of yarn. The mural she'd had done on one wall of herself as the character from *Caught by a Kiss* barely registered, though it did seem like Anthony's eyes followed me around the room.

CeeCee's housekeeper was off for the evening, so I made the coffee while she watched, insisting she needed to know how to do it for an upcoming role. When we were all settled with cookie bars, drinks and our projects, CeeCee smiled affectionately as she gazed over the group.

"It's so nice having the regular group without any outsiders." There was an edge on the last word. In case we had any doubts who she was talking about, she elaborated. "People in the pop music world are so different from us actors." She searched for words to finish her thought. "Cheyenne seems to steal the moment." Someone mentioned that Lauren didn't seem the same, but CeeCee ignored the comment.

"I don't think Cheyenne is always like that." I mentioned what her daughter had said about her having what sounded like a meltdown, but CeeCee seemed unmoved in her opinion. I sensed she was really upset because Cheyenne had gotten so much attention from Mrs. Shedd and Mr. Royal.

"That Susan just kept stirring the pot," Rhoda said. "She's certainly hostile to Cheyenne. You'd think she knew her from somewhere else."

Not everyone knew who Susan was. Adele zoomed in and explained she was one of her Tunisian crochet students and was very demanding. CeeCee took back the floor and turned to me. "Molly, dear, I have the feeling you've been keeping something from us." I saw Dinah's eyes go skyward. "Didn't you think you saw something like a dead body in Cheyenne's yard? Did you ever get that resolved?"

The whole group turned to me while Rhoda said, "Didn't you decide it was an inflatable doll?"

"Well," I said. Now that Cheyenne and Lauren weren't at the table and there was no chance Mrs. Shedd would suddenly appear, why not tell them the whole thing? Hooks stopped in midstitch as they gave me all of their attention. I tried to make the story orderly, but it came out as a hodgepodge of facts. The blood residue I'd found under the cushion, which wouldn't come from a plastic doll. The sudden departure of the nanny with nothing more than her phone and wallet.

"It's crazy, but I think the body was hers," I said.

Their eyes all opened wider, but their expressions changed to confusion as I reeled off that Barry had talked to her after I'd seen the person on the ground and Mason had found proof that she'd gone to San Francisco.

"I talked to her on the phone," I said, shaking my head

as if it would make all the pieces come together so they made sense. They all started talking, but I put my hands up to stop them. "It doesn't matter anymore. The only proof that there was a body is maybe some blood residue on the chaise cushion at Cheyenne's. I've used up all my chances with Barry. There's no way he would check it out, or could. And as he keeps reminding me, if there's no body, there's no murder. So, I have officially given up. Now all I want to do is plant some of the same kind of bushes CeeCee has, so I can't even see into the yard."

Dinah didn't know the part about me giving up, and she seemed surprised. Really, I hadn't known, either, until I said it.

"I'm so sorry," CeeCee said. "We all know what a crack detective you are." She sounded disappointed in me. There was no use defending myself, because bottom line, I was disappointed in me, too.

When the hour ended, CeeCee suggested we all stay, saying we could order pizza, watch TV and hang out. Elise, Eduardo, Rhoda and Sheila had to go, but Adele, Dinah and I stayed.

"We can watch that show of Cheyenne's," CeeCee said. The pizzas had come. We'd thrown diets to the wind and ordered a large Alfredo pizza, and a large cheese and tomato pizza as well.

CeeCee hit the button on the remote, and *Show Me Your Show Tune* began to play. It was the same episode I'd seen, so I put most of my attention on the rich, creamy pizza, and I only looked up when CeeCee began talking about what a low-budget show it must be.

"How can you tell?" I said, looking at the screen.

"It's obvious they don't have someone doing wardrobe. It's very bad form in reality shows to wear the same outfit

in more than one episode." I studied the image of Cheyenne on the screen for a moment.

"That's why I thought my machine made a mistake," I
said. Adele said she was going into the kitchen to get more
ice for the soda we'd gotten with the pizza.

"One show of that is enough," CeeCee said, bringing
up the list of shows she'd recorded. "You have to watch
this," she said. "Some people say it's the best show on
television. It's about a scummy detective who's stuck taking care of his father. The acting is amazing." She hit play,
and the program began with a bunch of shots and narration
meant to bring you up to speed. It was just registering that
it was the program Mason loved so much when a scene at
a banquet hall came on. There was no doubt where it had
been filmed, and I tried to wrestle the remote from CeeCee
to end it before Adele returned. Instead, it slipped out of
both of our hands and landed on the ground just as Adele
walked in. She stooped down to pick it up, but when she
straightened, she saw the screen and began to wail about
her wedding.

I thought about our trip there and the nonsense about
the shootings and the guy's nephew who was an Elvis
impersonator/songwriter. For a second it reminded me of
something else, but I couldn't put my finger on it and let it
go. In retrospect, the whole thing seemed pretty funny.

Adele's wailing about her wedding brought an abrupt
end to the evening, and CeeCee showed us to the door,
saying she was sure we all had someplace we needed to be.

Adele rushed out and drove away in her Matrix, but
Dinah and I took our time. "Can you blame CeeCee for
basically getting rid of us?" Dinah asked. "Who wants to
hear about Adele's wedding problem again?" We both
laughed at Adele's dramatics, but then Dinah looked

serious. "Did you really mean it? You're really not going to get to the bottom of what happened in Cheyenne's yard?"

I shrugged hopelessly. "I hit a dead end. I don't know how to stop somebody from getting away with the perfect crime." As I opened the door of the greenmobile, I added, "And for now, all I can think about is getting through tomorrow."

CHAPTER 25

THE NEXT MORNING, MASON'S CALL WAS MY alarm clock. "Hey, Sunshine," he said in a bright voice. I mumbled a sleepy hello before he continued. "I wanted to wish you good luck on your event."

"Thanks," I said, stretching as I got up. I think he was waiting for me to say something more, because there was a pause before he spoke.

"I have just about wound things up here and I'm coming home tomorrow. Let's do something special on the weekend. Any thoughts of what you'd like to do?"

"We can talk about it when you're home," I said.

"Sure, if that's what you want." He sounded like his usual fun-loving, affectionate self, but I still held back. I'm sure he noticed, and when he didn't question it, it made me more uneasy. True, he didn't know what I'd overheard, but he knew what was going on in his relationship with his ex-wife, and maybe he felt guilty.

I blew all thoughts of it from my mind. Today was D-day—or really M-day, for music. We'd never done anything like this before, and there was so much riding on it. Mrs. Shedd wanted it to be a success for Mr. Royal. Mr. Royal wanted it to be a success because he wanted it to start something new. I wanted it to be a success because if it flopped I was sure to get the blame.

My living room was still in chaos, but I figured I would worry about it later. The animals sensed there was something up and followed me as I went back and forth across the house, getting ready. When I left, Samuel was still asleep, resting up for the big evening ahead.

I tried to avoid looking toward Cheyenne's yard as I walked across mine to get to the driveway. I heard voices and something clanging. I couldn't help it—my eyes turned toward the activity. I couldn't see much other than that the workmen seemed to be working on something in the middle of the yard.

We did our best to try to keep it to business as usual at Shedd & Royal, but really we were just anxious to get through the day. I went home in the late afternoon to change, and then it was back to the bookstore and showtime.

When I came back to the bookstore, I had to thread through the crowd in front of the entrance. Mr. Royal was just coming out, holding a handful of wristbands. He began to take tickets and give out the wristbands in exchange.

I heard him urging people who wanted either ChIlLa's or the She La Las' album to buy them first, as there was just a limited supply. He let them know that after the performance there would be a chance to get them signed.

Mrs. Shedd was standing at the opening of the roped-off area, checking wristbands and letting people in. She seemed overwhelmed, and when she saw me, she waved me over.

"Here, you take over," she said in a nervous voice. "There are so many people. We've never had a crowd like this."

I think she was relieved to help a confused-looking book shopper and get away from the crowd. I had no problem with the job. I recognized some of our regular customers, and everyone seemed to be in an upbeat mood.

Adele had said she would be the talent liaison—she'd come up with the title. She had escorted the two groups and their entourages in through the emergency exit and brought them into the backstage area. I caught a glimpse of her as she looked out through an opening in the screens covering the yarn department. She was throwing her head around in her usual self-important manner.

The people with wristbands filled the area directly in front of the Sight and Sound department, but then I noticed people gathering behind the roped-off area, farther back in the bookstore. Dinah and Commander waved at me from that space. I offered to slip them into the enclosed area, and they chose to stand in the back.

And then it was time to begin. With author events, I always did the introductions, but this was Mr. Royal's baby, so he went to the front. I'd never realized what a natural he was at being in front of a group, but then he was like the world's most interesting man. He got the audience revved up and he gave the signal. Adele led the She La Las to the front.

I was used to seeing them in their rehearsal clothes and my son dressed in his jeans and graphic T-shirts, so I did more than a double take as they approached the performance area. The She La Las were all wearing bouffant wigs, hot pink short shifts, and go-go boots. I wasn't even sure which one was my mother until she waved at me. My son wore a dark suit, white shirt and thin black tie. He went to the keyboard, and they got in position.

I saw my father standing on the sidelines. It was sweet how my mother was always a star to him. The music began, and I let out sigh of relief. So far, so good.

I suppose the disaster in my living room was worth it. The She La Las had the choreography down perfectly, and their voices sounded great. I could see how much all three of them loved being on the stage. I was pretty proud of Samuel, too. I knew that moments like this made up for all the hours he spent hanging around an espresso machine in his job as a barista.

They did a long version of "My Guy Bill," and the crowd seemed to still want more after Samuel made the music crescendo into a finale. Everyone applauded. Mr. Royal returned to the front as the She La Las headed back to the yarn department backstage area.

Once Mr. Royal had announced them, Adele led ChIlLa through the crowd to the front. It was interesting to see the transformation from the three women I'd seen in the bookstore into performers. Cheyenne was in a long black dress with her long hair loose. Her lips were painted a dark wine color, and she had on a ton of eye makeup. Lauren wore chunky heels with thigh-high hose, a very short skirt, and a halter top covered with a sparkly silver sweater that went almost to her ankles. Her makeup was similar to her sisters', but her dark brown hair was hidden under a wig. The wig's black hair was cut into a mullet. In contrast, Ilona was wearing a long, filmy, pale blue dress. She had on sandals that almost made her look barefoot and a crown of daisies in her short blond hair.

I hadn't realized that Samuel was going to play for them as well. Cheyenne spoke to the crowd and said how happy they were to be there in what was now her neighborhood. She waved to Samuel, and he began the intro. They were pros and also maybe because they were sisters, their voices were in perfect harmony. Since they were there to promote their current album, even though it had been out for a year, they did a couple of songs from it. The biggest response came when they did the superstar hit from their first album. It had become a classic, and I saw some of the audience singing along.

The small group sounded much bigger as they clapped, whistled, stomped and shouted for more.

"We thought you might say that," Cheyenne said, flirting with the audience. "So we decided to give you a sneak peek of a song from our upcoming album." She started to step back with her sisters and then added, "I should tell you it's called 'Another Day, Another Chance' and was written by my sister Lauren, of the capital L small A in our name. The album is available for preorder," she added with a smile. Lauren had taken out a guitar, and Cheyenne glanced back while continuing to talk to the group. "Thank you, little sister, for writing a song that's sure to be number one on the pop charts."

The crowd hushed as Lauren began to play the intro. By the time they had sung,

> Don't give up on your dreams,
> Though they have been slammed and creamed.

I had the feeling that Cheyenne was right. The tune had a stirring emotional sound, and the lyrics were inspiring.

> Floating out on an ocean of despair,
> Where it seems the world is giving you the cold
>   shoulder,
> And nobody cares.
> You're down, but not out.
> Be unstoppable,
> Put your arm in the air and shout,

I believe in myself. I have the spark.
It might just be a tiny light,
But it can illuminate the dark.
I will blow on it until it burns into a bright flame.
To inspire the world, so they will have faith to do the
     same.
Another day, another chance to show the world who
     you are,
Another day, another chance to reach out and hook
     on a star.

The audience had begun to sway in time to the music. ChIlLa sang the chorus and then upped the emotion as they repeated the whole song. And I congratulated myself on how well everything was going.

Why did I always tempt fate? I saw that Eric Humphries had come in. It was impossible to miss him. He was well over six feet, with a barrel chest, and he was wearing his motor officer uniform, right down to the boots. He stopped a good distance behind the roped-off area. He watched the performance for only a moment, and then I noticed a troubled look come over his angular face. He looked from the crowd, and then at the wall near the front. I saw him walk over near the entrance and examine something on the wall. When he returned, I could tell he was counting.

How could we have missed the obvious? None of us had considered what the allowed capacity was for the space when we'd decided how many tickets to give out and to let extras stand in the back. I was sure we had too many people, but even if there was just one too many, Eric was a real rule-follower, and he would blow the whistle. He'd make everybody leave right in the middle of the song.

I couldn't let that happen now. Luckily, I had a little

time. Eric was an exacting type, so he counted slowly, and I was sure he would do it more than once. Adele was hanging by the edge of the performance area, doing what she could to make it look like she was part of what was going on. By the way she was acting, I didn't think she even realized her fiancé was there.

I edged toward her and pulled her away. "You have to get Eric out of here," I said quickly.

"He's here? Cutchykins really did stop by," she said, looking around the bookstore until she saw him. He was too busy counting to notice her. She was about to wave to get his attention when I stopped her.

"He's going to ruin everything. He's counting." I pointed to the capacity sign in the front. "And Mrs. Shedd and Mr. Royal will know who did it. Your fiancé."

Adele looked stricken. She wanted more than anything to be Mrs. Humphries, but she also viewed herself as a career woman. "I'm on it," she said. I wanted to ask what she had planned, but she was gone before I could ask her.

I turned back to where Eric was doing his counting. I thought Adele would pop up next to him, but she seemed to have disappeared completely. Then she showed up next to me, breathless, with a smile on her face. She touched her ear and pointed toward the outside.

I strained to listen and could just make out a car alarm going off. "Watch," she said, her eyes flickering in Eric's direction. He abruptly stopped the counting and cocked his head. Then he was out the door, his radio in hand. Adele gave a naughty laugh as she told me she'd pretended she was me and had hit the panic button for the Matrix.

When the song ended, the crowd kept clapping and asking for more. Everybody seemed at a loss as to what to do, but then I saw Cheyenne whisper something to Mr. Royal.

With all that was going on, I hadn't noticed that the She La Las were hanging out of sight next to a bookcase.

"You asked for more, you'll get it," Mr. Royal said. "C'mon back up, She La Las, and all of you can do an encore of 'My Guy Bill.'"

The She La Las were on their way back before he'd finished talking. My mother grabbed me as she passed and shoved a tambourine in my hand. Samuel was already playing the song when we got to the front. Cheyenne pulled Mr. Royal, who conveniently had a harmonica in his shirt pocket, into the group. He played, and the two girl groups began to sing. Then the audience joined them. I hit the tambourine for all it was worth and actually began to enjoy the whole thing. Pretty soon everyone seemed to be dancing. In the midst of it all I got jostled to the side of the Sight and Sound department and banged right into the photographs Mr. Royal had so carefully hung. And now they were all cockeyed. I stopped my tambourine playing long enough to straighten them, and as I did, I looked at them. Funny—I hadn't realized that Jennifer Clarkson and the kids were in the background of the photograph of Cheyenne. I stared at the nanny for a moment, and then I had a weird thought. But there was no time to pursue it. My mother danced up to me and nudged the tambourine, and I went back to shaking it. And pretty soon I was dancing, too.

I glanced out and saw that Barry and Jeffrey were standing outside the roped-off area. Jeffrey was ready to join the dancing, but Barry was clearly staying an observer rather than a participant.

Somehow they managed to make "My Guy Bill" go on for fifteen minutes. I was relieved when it finally ended and I could put down my tambourine.

Afterward we set both groups up at tables and they signed

CDs and albums. For the first time, I noticed Garrett and his video camera. Mr. Royal came up next to me. "The brave new world," Mr. Royal said. "I thought we should get the local news to cover this, but Garrett said he would tape something, do a quick edit job, and then upload it to the TV station's Facebook page, and of course to ChIlLa's Facebook page and website."

Mr. Royal wanted to end the evening with a wine toast. The signing had ended, and both groups had retreated to the backstage area. Mrs. Shedd, Mr. Royal and I headed to the closed-off yarn department to join them. Adele had gone off with Eric to try to help him figure out why her car alarm had gone off.

The She La Las and their spouses were hanging around the table, still high from the night's performance. My mother noticed me looking around. "Samuel left. You know him—he's meeting up with some friends," she said. "He said to congratulate you on your tambourine playing." She gave my arm a squeeze. "Music is in your genes."

"What about ChIlLa?" I asked.

"They left, too." My mother went on about someone going to a hotel overnight. "I can't blame Cheyenne for wanting to avoid it." My mother punctuated the comment with a shrug. "You'll probably hear the noise. Their pool is being poured, or whatever the term is, in the morning." She reached out as Mr. Royal handed her a glass of red wine. "Personally, I want to make this evening last as long as possible."

CHAPTER 26

MR. ROYAL WAS BUZZED FROM THE SUCCESS OF the evening. He sent me home and said he'd take care of putting things back in order. When I left he, and Mrs. Shedd were drinking the last of the wine and seemed deep in a happy conversation.

"Why don't you come with us?" my mother said as the She La Las got ready to leave. They were back in their everyday clothes, but still floating from their performance. They were all going out to a late dinner to celebrate. I begged off. I just wanted to go home and relax.

Of course, when I got home, I was too wired to relax. I wandered around the house, trying to come down from the event. Crochet usually worked, so I went looking for the bag with the Tunisian project. I found it in the dining room, and as I went to pick it up, I looked at the detective set. It was just a reminder of my failure to solve the Mystery at Cheyenne's.

"Nancy Drew would have done a better job," I said to Felix, who seemed hopeful that since I was in the dining room, food might be involved.

There was no reason to leave the set out anymore. I started to put everything back in the box. The Blood Detector was still in the plastic bag and didn't fit properly in its slot. I went to extract it and toss the plastic bag, but light caught on something in the bag. When I held it up, I saw what looked like some fine hair. I was trying to think how it had ended up in the plastic bag, and then I remembered that when I had planned to use the Blood Detector on the chaise cushion at Cheyenne's I had run my hand over the underside of the cushion. "It must have been on the cushion," I said to myself. As long as I had everything out there, I looked at the mass of fibers under the microscope. Something about them seemed familiar. I looked through the evidence containers I'd collected until I found something that looked similar. I'm sure it wasn't certain enough of an exact match to stand up in court, but it was enough to convince me.

How had the pink fibers from Adele's bargain yarn ended up on the cushion on Cheyenne's balcony? I found that crocheting helped me think at times like this and took out the scarf I'd started to make in the class. I was still getting used to using a hook with a long cable attached, and it seemed a little unwieldy as I tried to figure out where I'd left off.

I let my mind wander as I finished the row with the loops and began to take them off the hook, and random facts floated in. I had a cornucopia of images. The first Tunisian class, the nanny's room, tonight at the bookstore, Cheyenne on the show tune program, even the banquet hall and more things. On a hunch I took out my cell phone and listened to a voice mail, glad for once that I was in the habit of not deleting things. And then, as if by magic, everything sorted itself out and made sense.

I knew what had happened and how I was going to get proof of at least part of it. But who knew how long it was going to take? I stuffed the ball of yarn and Tunisian crochet project in the pocket of my hoodie. I looked at the detective set and wished it included a night vision scope.

All was quiet outside except for the chirping of some night birds as I crossed my yard and found the old gate in the chain-link fence. The warmth of the day was long gone, and there was a bite to the air. I was glad that I had changed into sweatpants and brought along an old beach towel.

My heart rate kicked up as I crossed into Cheyenne's yard, though there was no reason for it. The yard was empty and the house was dark. I was sure their spending the night at a hotel was part of the plan.

The floodlights from my house threw some dim light into the yard. The ground was still uneven, so I moved slowly toward the dug-out area. The rectangular space for the pool seemed like a black hole. I was sure the pool was where the action was going to take place—more particularly, I was sure it would be at the deep end of the pool. I found a spot in a shadow that was close to the end and put the towel down. My plan was to sit up until I heard something and then lie down and blend with the ground. And then, once I knew Jennifer was being buried in the bottom of the pool, I'd find a way to get the cops there.

When I was situated, I tried crocheting, but it was hopeless in the dark. Too bad they didn't make lighted Tunisian hooks. How long is this going to take? I wondered, feeling the coldness of the dirt coming through the flimsy towel. And then I heard the sound of a door closing and I assumed a prone position.

Someone was coming across the yard, and there was the squeak of a wheel as they pushed something. I knew who it was and figured they were pushing the wheelbarrow I'd seen in the yard before. As for the contents, I didn't want to think about it.

My heart rate kicked up now for good reason, and I tried to breathe as quietly as possible. The point was for me not to be discovered. The figure reached the big opening in the ground, just a few feet from where I was hidden. I couldn't see their face in the darkness, but I knew who it was. The wheelbarrow was upended, and I heard a thud as the body hit the ground. The figure walked down to the other end and climbed into the hole. It seemed like the coast was clear, and I sat up, planning to wait until it seemed like the digging had begun before slipping away.

I leaned toward the dug-out area, listening. I never would have thought she would be the killer. She seemed so nice, but then wasn't that what they always said? I knew it was Lauren who'd dumped the body in the hole.

How long should I wait before sneaking away and calling the cops? The seconds seemed like hours. Finally, I was sure she must have started digging and wouldn't hear me if I got up. I stood quietly and started to back away, but my foot caught on something, and I fell backward.

"What are you doing here?" an angry voice demanded. The sound startled me, and I looked up. I should have figured that she wasn't alone in it. Garrett was standing over me, holding a shovel. "So you're the nosy neighbor who has been causing all the trouble." He'd already started to raise the shovel, and I knew I had to get out of there. I tried to get up, but my foot had caught on a big root.

Below, Lauren had heard voices, and she was asking him what was going on.

"You'll have to dig a hole big enough for two," he said in an angry voice. The shovel was over his head now, and I knew what was coming.

I tried pulling my foot free again, but I was trapped. And then it was as if time slowed down, and I had an idea—I'd use the only weapon I had. I wrapped the hook and cable around Garrett's ankle and then pulled.

Garrett yelped in surprise as he lost his balance and fell backward into the big hole. I gave myself a thumbs-up for ingenuity. I pulled hard, and my foot finally came free. But tripping him turned out to be just a temporary fix. He was already out of the hole and coming after me with the shovel.

It was hard to run on the uneven dirt as I aimed for my yard. Before I could reach it, I fell over something, and Garrett caught up with me. I tried to crawl away, but he was next to me, swatting with the shovel. It was hopeless to escape, and I tried to cover my head as I prepared for pain.

And then, out of nowhere, we were bathed in bright light, and a moment later a voice yelled out, "Freeze! I have a gun."

We all became like statues as Barry came closer. "Where did you come from?" I said as I struggled to get up.

CHAPTER 27

"OKAY, HOW ABOUT TELLING ME EVERYTHING YOU know?" Barry said to me. We were sitting on the towel along with Lauren and Garrett. Barry had already placed them under arrest for suspicion of murder and read them their rights. He was still in his work clothes and conveniently had a bunch of those plastic ties cops use as handcuffs. He had bound their hands and their feet. We were all just waiting for his backup to come. He'd already tried asking Lauren why she was in a dug-out pool with a body in a plastic bag, but before she'd even opened her mouth, Garrett had told her not to say anything. Barry'd produced a flashlight that worked as a lantern, illuminating the area around us.

"First, you tell me how you happened to be here," I said. Barry cracked a smile.

"Still answering questions with questions?" he said.

I shrugged innocently. "I learned it from you."

"Too bad I was such a good teacher," he shot back, not missing a beat. "I came over to deliver your birthday present. Remember I said I'd do a repair of your choice?" He glanced at the pair to make sure they weren't moving. "No matter what you said about putting in new bulbs yourself, I knew the fixture on the garage was too high for you to reach comfortably. And you refuse to ask anybody for help. I also knew you left the ladder in your yard, and I figured I could change those two bulbs without even disturbing you. It was a pretty good present." He looked directly at me. "I think it might have just saved your life—or at least it certainly saved you from a bad headache." He shook his head and gave me a stern look. "You shouldn't have been here in the first place."

"I had no choice. Would you have come if I'd called and told you there was going to be a body buried in the yard? When I heard about the pool being poured, I figured it out." I couldn't help it—my eyes flashed with defiance.

"I might have given you a rough time, but I would have come. I'll always come if you need me." He seemed to realize that it was getting too personal, and he put his cop face back on. "These two won't talk. So why don't you tell me what you think happened?" He seemed to be preparing for me to answer with another question, but I gave him a break and just started to talk.

"It was all about hairstyles and outlines of people," I said. I told him about Logan Belmont and his hair that looked like a hat. "I don't have to look at his face. I just see that hair and know it's him." Barry was trying to keep his cop face, but I saw his dark eyes look skyward with frustration.

"How about starting from the beginning," he said.

"Remember you said you talked to Jennifer at the house

after I called?" I said. "That wasn't Jennifer. It was her," I said, pointing at Lauren. "She was wearing a wig and mimicking a Southern accent." I told him how I'd seen what a good mimic Lauren was at the crochet class, when she'd made fun of Susan. "She has the same build as the nanny, and with the long blond wig had the same outline. I bet the kids would have noticed, but they were sound asleep, thanks to the allergy medicine they'd been given."

"I didn't drug them," Lauren said in a shocked voice. "That was all Jennifer. It turned out she had a whole supply of allergy medicine and gave it to Merci and Venus all the time before sitting them down in front of a video."

Barry seemed confused. "What about before I went over there?" he said, urging me with a nod. "The real beginning. What do you think happened?" he asked me again.

"I think that Lauren went over to talk to Jennifer. The kids were asleep, like I said, and Cheyenne and Garrett were at the taping. There was some kind of an argument, and Lauren pushed the nanny over the railing. I'm just guessing, but she probably landed badly. There was so much stuff lying around out there."

"It was an accident," Lauren said frantically. "We were just talking. Well, maybe it was sort of arguing. She was being so unreasonable. When I pushed her, I didn't realize she would fall over the railing."

"You should have called us then," Barry said. "And maybe none of us would be sitting here now."

"That's where he comes in," I said. Garrett pulled at his restraints angrily.

"That's nonsense. I did come home, but the girls were awake and Jennifer was reading them a story. I was back at the taping when the police called to check on things."

"That was me you spoke to," Barry said.

"And you were on a cell phone, so we know you could have been anywhere," I said. "You certainly weren't back at the studio."

"Prove it," Garrett said in a belligerent voice.

I turned to Barry. "He said he went home to pick up Cheyenne's outfit for the second show. It's all there on the recording device on my TV. She was clearly wearing the same clothes as she was in the first show because Garrett didn't get back in time."

"So you think he helped with the cover-up?" Barry asked, and I nodded. Garrett seemed to be struggling to keep himself from talking.

"It's obvious now the plan was to stash the body. I heard there was a freezer in the garage. No wonder Garrett didn't want the girls going out there and helping themselves to ice cream treats." I glanced at Garrett, and he was looking at the ground.

"He must have been worried about blood. That part of the story is true, only it wasn't the girls who threw the cushion off the balcony to mark the spot—it was Lauren." I mentioned my visit there later that night. "Now maybe you'll acknowledge that the Blood Detector really does work." He shook his head with a smile and he muttered something about confiscating the whole detective set.

"The next part was very clever," I said. "Lauren created a reason for Jennifer to disappear."

"Oh, please, she never would have come up with that. Lauren's not that smart," Garrett said.

"That's a terrible thing to say," Lauren retorted. "I knew how to sound like Jennifer and how to arrange the hair on the blond wig so it fell forward to cover a lot of my face."

"But who got you the wig?" Garrett said. "I knew

Cheyenne still had all of them from the Alice in Wonderland shoot." He suddenly realized what he'd said and stopped talking.

"Remember, you said the nanny seemed upset when you went over there that night," I said to Barry. "I bet that wasn't acting at all." I spoke to Lauren. "You'd just killed somebody, and suddenly the cops were at the door."

I noticed that Barry seemed uncomfortable as he realized the mistakes he'd made, basically because he hadn't believed what I said.

"Lauren must have called the nanny service and said she had an emergency and had to leave so they would send over a replacement. She ordered the shuttle to pick her up and paid with Jennifer's credit card. She did the same with the plane ticket and traveled as Jennifer, using the dead nanny's driver's license to check in and get through security. They probably just looked at the honey blond hair and eye color that matched the license and didn't check her features that carefully, so they let her through. After she got to San Francisco, she probably ditched the wig and flew back as herself."

"You're right, that was very clever." Barry nodded toward Lauren.

"You don't really think she could have come up with all of that on her own—that is, if any of it's true," Garrett said. "What proof do you have, anyway?"

"You're wondering about proof? You just dumped a body down there," I said.

Garrett tried to pick up his hands, but they were held together. "I didn't dump anything down there."

"Maybe not, but you told me to do it," Lauren said.

"Back to what I figured out," I said. I told Barry with a certain amount of pride how when I'd listened again to the messages that were supposedly from Jennifer in San Francisco, I'd noticed something I'd missed the first time. "I could hear the television. It was the weather report. Not only did it say *Los Angeles* but I recognized the distinctive voice of the guy who does it on Channel 3."

Barry started to say something, but I stopped him. "There's more. How do you think I figured out it was Lauren?"

Barry sighed, but there was a sparkle in his eyes. "I haven't the foggiest. Why don't you fill me in."

When I brought up the detective set again, Barry chuckled. "I hope I don't have to go to the district attorney and tell her our case is based on a kids' set."

I told him about Adele's bargain yarn and the fibers floating all over the place and how I'd taken samples of the pink fibers off my jacket. "Everybody at the first Tunisian class left with some of them sticking to their clothes." I spared him the details of exactly how I'd come to examine the cushion after it had been replaced on the balcony and went right to the big reveal. "I found a tuft of the same fibers stuck to it," I said. "The only way they could have gotten there was if someone who'd been there when Adele was working with that yarn had carried some away on their jacket and transferred it to the cushion when they held it against themselves." I stopped. "Whew, that was a mouthful." To further explain, I told him that Lauren had been wearing a fuzzy gray hoodie at the class and that Barry had mentioned the nanny wearing a hooded sweatshirt jacket when he saw her. "It was the same hoodie, and the fibers had stuck to it."

"Good work." Barry gave me a pat on my shoulder. "But do I get some of the credit?" he said in a flirty way. "I'm assuming you learned some of your skills from me. You've told me that you learned answering a question with a question from me."

"Actually, I learned that from *The Average Joe's Guide to Criminal Investigation*." He feigned a wounded look.

"Shall I finish this up?" he asked, not taking his eyes off me. I put my hands up and gave him the floor.

"She or they would bury Jennifer, the pool would be poured and a body would never be found. There'd probably be a final phone call from 'Jennifer' quitting her job. If her family or friends came looking for her, Garrett would just say she'd gone to San Francisco and never come back. No body, no murder."

"It would have been a perfect crime," I said. I left off the part where I deserved the credit for it *not* becoming the perfect crime, but I could tell Barry knew what I was thinking.

"I'll never doubt you again," he said in a melodramatic voice.

"Yes, you will," I said.

"Okay, maybe I will," he teased. "But if you say there's a body somewhere I'll definitely come and check it out." I heard Garrett groan.

"It's Nick and Nora Charles," he said. "At least the flirting part—they had snappier dialogue."

Barry ignored the comment and continued to speak to me. "I suppose you have the motive all figured out, too."

I nodded my head with a smile. "I think it was all about a song. That song they played tonight." Barry bobbed his head in recognition, and I continued. "If you noticed, Cheyenne said that Lauren wrote it. I think Jennifer really wrote it." I mentioned seeing her playing guitar with the kids and the CDs and forms in her room. Barry laughed when he heard that I'd realized they were to register the lyrics and a sound performance of the song through our trip to the Parisian Banquet Hall. It turned out he was a fan of *Jack Hunter*, too, and knew all about the place.

"I saw the CDs and the forms in the nanny's room, but I have a feeling they aren't there anymore." I told him Ursula had complained to me that someone had gone through her room.

"So this was all about stealing a song," he said.

Lauren snorted in annoyance. "I did not steal the song. It was all a mistake. I had this song in my head and I started playing it on the guitar. The lyrics just seemed to come to me. There is no way I realized it was in my head because I heard Jennifer playing it. Cheyenne heard me playing and encouraged me to finish it. She said it was the hit we needed for the next album."

"Shut up," Garrett said. "Why are you telling them anything?"

Lauren ignored him and went on, saying there hadn't been a problem until the nanny heard Cheyenne singing it and raving over how Lauren had written it and it was going to be on their next album. "She said she wanted all the credit for the song," Lauren said. "I thought we could make a deal. That's what we were arguing about."

She turned to Garrett. "He talked me into covering it all up. She'd already copyrighted the whole thing. The stuff in her room was just copies. With her gone there would be no one to bring it up, and no one would dispute that I wrote it. All the money is in the publishing, and he manages all of us, which means he would get a big cut of the money I made." She slumped forward. "It was going to be my chance to shine. I'm tired of being the poor sister."

"You took your time showing up," Barry said as a bunch of uniforms came through the yard. Two of them helped

Garrett and Lauren up and escorted them to the street. Barry talked to someone in charge and pointed toward the bottom of the pool. I looked away, not even wanting to think about Jennifer's body probably beginning to thaw.

Barry came back to me, seeming very chipper. "That worked well," he said with a pleased smile. "And they said they weren't going to talk."

"That was a setup?" I said. He nodded and showed me a device that had gotten it all on tape.

He offered to walk me back to my yard, but I said I'd be fine. "Well, then, I guess it's good night." He started to walk away, and then turned. "We make a good team."

It was a relief to get back in my yard, and as I opened my door, the phone was ringing.

I was surprised it was Mason. "What time is it where you are?"

"It's getting-up time here. I'm catching an early flight. I just wanted to say I saw the L.A. news on my phone. I had no idea you were such an accomplished tambourine player." He punctuated it with a chuckle. He sounded upbeat and cheerful, despite the hour. "It looks like it was quite an evening. Did anything else happen?"

I let out a tired laugh. "More than you can imagine. It's too much to tell you on the phone. We'll talk about everything when you get back."

Wasn't that the truth.

CHAPTER 28

I WAS SURPRISED TO SEE CHEYENNE AND HER girls at the yarn table when I came in the next morning. I wasn't sure what kind of reception I was going to get now that she must know that I was not only the nosy neighbor from before but also the person who was responsible for her husband and sister being arrested.

When I got closer, I saw there was a franticness to the way she was moving her hook. Merci and Venus seemed confused. "Just do what Mommy is doing," Cheyenne said to them.

"I'm sorry," I said.

She looked up and saw me. First there was anger in her eyes, but then her expression collapsed in helplessness. "I didn't know where else to go. What am I going to do?" I sat down with her, and she continued to crochet. "I'm trying to keep it together for them." She looked to the two girls, who were clumsily moving their hooks through a row of stitches. "This is the only thing that helps." And then she told me that she'd been in rehab for pretty much every problem, from undereating to overeating to drugs and alcohol. "The only thing I never did was cut myself. And rehab's where I learned how to crochet. It saved my life. The rehab stays have been a big secret," she said. "I've been clean, sober and eating right for almost a year." She sighed. "And I made it through last night and today without anything but a crochet hook."

She looked at me, seeming to need to talk. Her big personality seemed deflated at the moment. "Never again," she muttered. "I was so overwrought with trying to get everything together, and then when Ilona started on me, saying she was sure Jennifer had something going with Matt—" She let out a big breath. "I should never have let her talk me into going through Jennifer's room on her day off for evidence that they were having an affair. My sister is paranoid when it comes to her husband. There was nothing—but that's when I found the allergy meds. I just needed something to let me relax for a while." She looked over at her girls and had a fierce look. "If I hadn't been so desperate myself, I would have killed her for drugging them. Instead I just drank half the bottle." She hung her head, and her long hair fell forward. "It wasn't a dance number that night. I'd lost it, and Garrett was trying to get me back inside before I fell off the balcony. I had to pull myself together when the police showed up."

"So then you didn't know anything about who really wrote the song?" I said.

"No," she said regretfully. "I absolutely believed my sister wrote it." She looked at her daughters. "They don't have to worry. I'll never fall off the wagon again. I have to be strong for them."

I left to get a cup of coffee, and when I came back the three of them were gone. Justice might have been served, but it still made me sad at how everything had turned out.

The mood changed abruptly. With the success of the previous evening, Mr. Royal wanted to make musical performances a regular event. My mother came by when the crochet group gathered. Now that she was going to be living in the area, she thought she might join us.

LAUREN WAS EVENTUALLY CHARGED WITH MANslaughter, fraud, false impersonation and a bunch of lesser charges. Garrett was charged with being an accessory after the fact and withholding evidence, which in this case meant hiding a body. Both of them faced a long time in prison.

The album came out a month later, and with the whole story connected with "Another Day, Another Chance," it went platinum. Jennifer's family got all the money from the publishing. Cheyenne moved out of the house, and the developer was left to try to sell it. Logan Belmont got the listing, but since they had to disclose that a murder had taken place there, it languished on the market, though in the meantime the yard had been finished and a tall white fence was put up, making my gate useless.

Mrs. Shedd realized that between music nights and crochet classes, she'd held just about everything else at the bookstore, and she offered to host a double wedding for Adele and Dinah, since the place had meaning for both of them. And when it was time for the actual event, what everybody said about things coming in threes had proved true.

Adele came down the aisle created in the event area

first. She was wearing a silk dress with a crocheted overlay and beamed with happiness. After a moment's pause, Dinah followed her, wearing the elegant dress we'd picked out. She smiled, though she still seemed nervous. She reached the front and the music played on. I swallowed hard as it came time for the third bride to walk down the aisle and join them.

Adele's Tunisian Crochet Scarf

Easy to make.

Supplies
5 skeins Lion Brand Vanna's Choice,
medium weight, 100% acrylic (170 yd,
156 m, 3.5 oz, 100 g) in different colors
Size K-10½ (6.5mm) crochet hook with
4" cable and stopper
Tapestry needle
Dimensions: Approximately 8½ inches by
72 inches before fringe
Technique: Tunisian crochet
Abbreviations: ch (chain), yo (yarn over)

Tunisian Stitches

Foundation: Starting with 2nd ch from hook, *insert hook under horizontal bar at back of the ch, yo and draw up loop. Repeat from *for remaining chs, keeping the loops on the hook. When done, there will be same number of loops on hook as chs.

Afghan Stitch

Part 1 (return pass): Yo and draw through 1st loop on hook, *yo and draw through 2 loops on hook. Repeat from * until there is only 1 loop remaining on hook.

Part 2 (forward pass): Starting with 2nd vertical bar on hook, *insert hook under vertical bar in the previous row, yo and pull through bar, keeping loop on the hook. Continuing to keep loops on the hook, repeat from * across for each vertical bar in the previous row up to the last vertical bar at the edge of the scarf. Insert hook through both vertical strands at edge, yo and pull through both strands. There will be same number of loops on hook as in foundation row.

Note: Change colors of yarn at end of part 1 (return pass) when there are 2 loops on hook. Varying the numbers of rows in each color creates an interesting pattern.

Bind Off: Starting with 2nd vertical bar from hook, *insert hook under vertical bar in the previous row, yo and pull through the bar and the loop on hook. (There will be only 1 loop on the hook.) Repeat from * across for each vertical bar in previous row up to last vertical bar at edge of the scarf. Insert hook through both vertical strands at edge, yo and pull through both strands and loop on hook. Fasten off.

Ch 30 with color A
   Make foundation row. 30 loops on hook.

Work afghan stitch (parts 1 and 2) until ready to change color. To make a clean transition between colors, change colors at end of part 1 (return pass) by drawing the new color through the last 2 loops on the hook. When the scarf is approximately 72 inches long, bind off after completing a part 1 (return pass) row. Fasten off and weave in ends. Add fringe.

Liza's Granola

3 cups old-fashioned rolled oats
1 cup raw almonds
⅓ cup pure maple syrup
½ cup melted coconut oil
½ teaspoon salt
1 cup sunflower seeds
2 teaspoons cinnamon
1 cup dried cherries

Mix ingredients in bowl and spread on baking sheet lined with parchment. Bake at 300 degrees for approximately 50 minutes or until toasty in color. Cool in pan and store in airtight container. Makes 8 cups.

Molly's Double Chocolate Cookie Bars

2¼ cups all-purpose unbleached flour
1 teaspoon baking soda
1 teaspoon salt
1 cup butter, softened
½ cup unsweetened cocoa powder
¾ cup granulated sugar
¾ cup dark-brown sugar, packed
2 teaspoons vanilla extract
2 large eggs
4.5-ounce dark chocolate bar broken into small pieces
1 cup coarsely chopped walnuts

Combine flour, baking soda, and salt in a small bowl. Combine sugars and cocoa powder in a small bowl. Using electric mixer, cream butter, gradually add the sugar and cocoa mixture. Add vanilla extract. Beat until blended. Add eggs one at a time, beating well after each addition. Gradually beat in flour mixture. Stir in chocolate pieces and nuts.

Preheat oven to 375°F. Line 15 x 10-inch jelly roll pan with parchment paper. Spread batter in pan and bake for approximately 20 to 25 minutes. Cool in pan on wire rack. Cut into bars. Makes 48 cookie bars.

Turn the page for a preview of
Betty Hechtman's first Yarn Retreat Mystery,

YARN TO GO

Available now from Berkley Prime Crime.

I WAS IN THE MIDDLE OF LAYING OUT THE INGRE-dients for my carrot muffins when the call came. It's lucky I hadn't started mixing them, because you can't just run off and abandon muffin batter for an hour and expect it to be okay. I didn't even understand who it was at first. All I heard was something about no refund on a credit card bill, the word *retreat* and that I "better do something about it."

"Who is this?" I said when the caller finally took a breath.

"Casey, this is Tag Thornkill," an exasperated voice responded. He could have left off the last name. I mean, it's not like I know a bunch of Tags. Immediately my demeanor changed from irritated at the interruption to concerned. Tag is my current employer, or half of the pair, anyway. He and his wife, Lucinda, own the Blue Door restaurant, which is where I presently work. I'm the dessert chef. Tag doesn't know it, but I also bake muffins for some coffee spots in town using the Blue Door's kitchen. Lucinda had given her okay and saw no problem with the arrangement as long as I brought in my own ingredients.

So every night when the restaurant closes and everyone has left, I come in and bake the restaurant's desserts for the next day, along with batches of muffins for the next day's coffee drinkers.

Let me be clear from the start: I'm not one of those fancy cooking school graduates who does French pastry. I had never even thought of baking as being a career. It was just something I started doing when I was a kid. It might have been a reaction to having a mother who was a cardiologist and thought cookies only came in white boxes from the bakery.

My first experience as a dessert chef happened at a friend's bistro. He didn't care that I didn't have any formal training. The truth was in the cake. He loved what I baked and hired me. Unfortunately, he sold the bistro after six months and it became a hot dog stand that didn't offer dessert.

After that I tried law school, but by the end of the first semester, I knew it wasn't for me. Nor was being a substitute teacher at a private school. Then I tested out a lot of other professions. In other words, I worked as a temp. I did things like handing out samples of chewing gum on street corners, spritzing perfume on anyone I could get to slow down at a department store, some office work and my favorite, working at a detective agency.

My poor mother was beside herself. If I'd heard it once, I'd heard it a zillion times. "Casey, when I was your age, I was already a doctor and a mother. And you're what . . . ?" Talk about knowing how to make me feel like more of a flop. My father wasn't all that happy, either. He was a doctor, too—a pediatrician. When I broke up with Dr. Sammy Glickner, things really hit the fan. He was my parents' dream come true: Jewish, not just a doctor, but a specialist in urology and nice. They said nice; I said bland. Well, not totally bland. He was very funny in a goofy sort of way.

But I needed a fresh start. And who better to help me with it than my father's sister, Joan Stone. Let's just say we both had the black sheep thing going. Her main advantage was she actually had a profession—actress. She wasn't an A-list star like Meryl Streep or Julia Roberts. Most of her parts were playing somebody's aunt Trudy or the noisy neighbor down the street. Her one claim to fame was she'd been the Tidy Soft toilet paper lady long enough to build up a nice nest egg before she left L.A., moved up north and started a new career.

But now back to the call.

With a nice tone, I asked Tag to repeat what he'd said.

"I was checking Lucinda's credit card receipts. There is a charge for Yarn2Go. My dear wife explained that was your aunt's business and the charge was for some kind of yarn trip." He paused as if he expected me to say something, and when I didn't, he continued. "I checked all of her later bills and there was no mention of a refund. What do you have to say about that?"

The "oh no" was purely in my head. Barely three months after I'd left Chicago and relocated to my aunt Joan's guesthouse in the northern California town of Cadbury by the Sea, my aunt had been killed in a hit-and-run accident. It was horrible. There were no witnesses, and the cops still had the case open, though it didn't look like they were going to find the driver. I didn't care that the cops, my parents and all of my aunt's friends insisted it was just an unfortunate, random accident. I didn't buy it.

Here are the basic facts. It was six thirty on a Sunday morning. My aunt never got up before eight. No one could explain, at least to my satisfaction, why she would have been out walking by the water at that hour. It was barely even light. I simply didn't buy the cops' explanation that maybe she'd taken up an exercise program and not mentioned it to me.

I mean, I was living in her guesthouse, which was just across the driveway from her house. True, we'd agreed to stay out of each other's lives, but still . . .

My aunt had left everything to me, and when I'd met with the lawyer, he'd brought up her retreat business. While Joan had still done occasional acting gigs, her real passion had become putting on these retreats that she called "vacations with a purpose." Basically all I knew about them was that they had to do with making things with yarn and she used the hotel and conference center across the street to host them. Joan had tried to explain more to me, but she got totally frustrated when I kept mixing up crocheting and knitting. I knew that you needed two things for one of them and one for the other, but not which for which. Needles, hooks, not my thing. All my creative endeavors had to do with baking.

I had told the lawyer I had no interest in continuing the business for obvious reasons. He'd looked through the papers I'd brought in and said they appeared to be for her taxes, so for all intents and purposes, the business was over.

"So what are you going to do about it?" Tag repeated, pulling me back to the here and now. I said something about checking into it when I got home, but that wasn't good enough. I could practically hear him pacing. Tag was one of those people who went around straightening pictures on the walls at other people's houses. He couldn't deal with things being out of order or unsettled. He said he wouldn't be able to sleep until it was straightened out. I glanced at my watch and saw that it was ten o'clock. I really wanted to continue making the muffins, but I knew Tag would be frantic until he had an answer, and he was sort of my boss. So I decided to run home and check. I'd finish the muffins when I returned.

Even though the restaurant was in downtown Cadbury and my place was on the edge of town, the route was direct, and a little over five minutes later I pulled my yellow Mini Cooper into the driveway. When I doused the headlights, the yard became invisible. I was still getting used to so much darkness at night. In Chicago, wherever you were, there was some light coming from somewhere. Here, on the edge of a small town that didn't allow streetlights, it really was pitch-dark.

There's something else I haven't mentioned. I had inherited my aunt's house, but after we'd cleaned out the refrigerator and I'd returned the packet of papers I'd shown the lawyer, I hadn't been able to bring myself to go back inside, let alone move into it. The space would have been wonderful. The guesthouse was basically one room. But in my mind the house still belonged to my aunt, and in some wishful corner of my heart, I thought she still might come back.

I fumbled with the keys as I headed toward her back door. A noise in the yard startled me as I pulled out the small flashlight I always carried. It was like my own personal headlight. I aimed the light around the yard and caught a deer nibbling on the petunias in one of the flower boxes. The delicate-looking creature blinked at the light but didn't seem concerned by my presence. Not really a big surprise. Deer wandered around the seaside town at will, helping themselves to gardens and flowers. They really loved the small cemetery and were always lounging between the gravestones.

"No more stalling," I said out loud. In one swift move, I put the key in the lock, turned it and pushed open the door. The air inside seemed warm and a little stale. Was it my imagination or was there still a trace of my aunt's signature scent, Penhaligon's Elisabethan Rose? I couldn't help it; my eyes filled with tears at the thought of her. I flipped on the light quickly. Everything was just as it had been. She could have walked in and felt right at home. The bunch of lavender flowers she'd been drying was still hanging upside down. Her coffee mug was rinsed out and sitting on the counter.

I felt a real tug when I saw the shopping bag that the hospital had given me with the clothes she'd been wearing that morning. It had been sitting there since November, untouched since I brought it in.

"I'm sorry," a female voice said. I turned in time to see Lucinda come through the door. A quick glance at her face made it clear she'd overheard Tag talking to me on the phone about the yarn retreat charge. Her frilly pink nightgown showed through the opening in her Burberry trench coat. Only Lucinda would have thought to add a silk scarf and lipstick. "I tried to reason with him, but you know Tag. It's exasperating how exacting he is." Though the pair were in their fifties, they'd only been married a short time. They'd reconnected at their thirty-fifth high school reunion. Tag had been her high school crush. But years later she was divorced, he was widowed and they picked up as if no time had passed. Almost, anyway. Lucinda's favorite saying was "be careful what you wish for." Two seventeen-years-olds was one thing, but two people who have had years and years to develop habits and their own definitions of the way things should be—was something else entirely.

"If it was up to me, I wouldn't care," Lucinda said, closing the door and standing in the middle of the room with me. "I was so upset about Joan, I forgot all about it."

"It's got to be some kind of mistake." I hung my head. "It's my fault. I shouldn't have been such a baby. I should have come in here a long time ago."

Lucinda put her arm around my shoulder. "We'll deal with it together."

From the first time I'd met Lucinda, I'd liked her. Like my aunt Joan, she had a sense of fun, and our age difference didn't seem to matter. We were all on the same page, though visually we made an odd pair. Lucinda was smaller and lively looking with neatly styled black hair that softened her square-shaped face. She always looked put together, even in a trench coat over her nightie. I was a little rougher around the edges. Jeans, a long sleeve T-shirt and a fleece jacket was my usual attire. I had shoulder-length hair that resisted any style. It wasn't straight and it wasn't curly but went its own way. I tried to remember to put on some makeup, but it wasn't my top priority. Besides, all that sea air gave me a lot of color.

And when Joan had Lucinda taste my pound cake, she had gotten the idea of having me bake the desserts for the restaurant. I hadn't known Tag then or I would have been more flattered that he approved the idea.

Having Lucinda with me now made it easier to go through the house. We passed by Joan's bedroom quickly. The door was shut, but I knew everything was still as she had left it that fateful morning. Her toothbrush was still in the bathroom, and tufts of her black hair were still caught in the comb. I turned on the lights in the living room. Examples of my aunt's handicraft were everywhere. A colorful afghan was folded over the end of the couch. Purple irises graced a needlepoint pillow, and a soft fog gray shawl hung across a wing chair in front of the fireplace. It must have fallen off her shoulders the last time she sat there.

"All the papers are in her office," I said. We walked down the short hall. In an effort to make it seem like I was comfortable being in there, I pulled open a closet door. Yarn of every color tumbled out and bounced off my head.

"What the . . . ?" I said, picking up a ball of cotton candy pink yarn that had hit my foot and rolled off.

"It's your aunt's stash." Lucinda noticed my confusion. "That's what it's called—stash. Joan told me everybody who gets into yarn has a stash. I'd probably have one, too, at least a little one, except for Tag. He's a sweet guy in a lot of ways, but he's nuts when it comes to details. He saw I had one extra skein of yarn and made such a fuss, I said I wouldn't buy any more until I used that one."

"Skeins?" I said.

"Sorry, that's what they call these," she said, picking up a ball of yarn. "It's really a silly term. It's not like there is a universal size of a skein." To demonstrate, she pointed out a large peanut-shaped one of forest green yarn and a small fuzzy baby blue one in the mess on the floor. "Both of these would be called skeins. Go figure."

She helped me stuff everything back in the closet and shut the door before it could fall back out again.

Joan had taken the smallest of the three bedrooms and made it into an office. An adorable lion was guarding the desk. Lucinda explained it was crocheted. There was a basket of half-made things in the corner. "Those are WIPs," Lucinda said.

"Huh?" I said, picking up a forest green tube that looked like it might be on its way to becoming a sock.

"Works in progress," Lucinda said. "Don't get the idea I'm some kind of expert. Your aunt told me all of this."

As I held the tube of yarn, four silver needles slipped out and hit the floor with a pinging sound. I picked them up, examining the sharp double points. "These look like they could do some real damage." I tried to put them back the way they'd been but finally just stuck them into the yarn and put it on top of the stuff in the basket. "I have to stop getting sidetracked."

The padded envelope with the papers I'd taken to the attorney was on the desk where I'd left it. I was about to dump out the papers when I noticed a box covered in red bandanna print fabric. I lifted the top and looked inside, surprised to find that it was a file box. I'd started to push through the hanging dividers when I heard something hit the bottom with a clunk. "I wonder what this is," I said, fishing out a small black flash drive. Lucinda pointed to the computer on my aunt's desk and suggested I put it in and see what was on it.

We both watched the screen and I kept clicking on things until I got the flash drive to open and then opened a file. "What's that?" I said, looking at what had come up on the screen. It said *RIB* across the top, then *Test*. Lucinda shrugged and said it didn't mean anything to her. "We're not getting anywhere." I turned off the computer and pulled out the flash drive, dropping it back in the box.

I had a sinking feeling when I saw the tabs on the hanging dividers. They all said something about retreats. I pushed through them until I came to one that said *Upcoming*.

Inside there were several files all marked *Petit Retreat*. I opened the last one and there were several printed sheets with a bunch of questions.

"That's the information sheet I filled out when your aunt talked me into signing up." Lucinda leaned over my shoulder and looked at the page. "That's what she called it." Lucinda pointed to the heading that read *Petit Retreat*. "She said of all the retreats she put on, this was the most special. I told her I barely knew how to knit, but she said I would have a great time. Frankly, the idea of spending some time away from Tag and the restaurant sounded appealing. I love him, but our styles are just different. If he would just relax a little."

The more we looked through the papers, the more upset I felt. There were seven other people besides Lucinda who had sent in the money for the retreat. From the pile of receipts it was obvious my aunt had already paid all the expenses. "What am I going to do?"

"You can try to cancel the weekend, but you'll have to give everyone a refund. Not me, of course. I'll deal with Tag."

"With what money? Nothing personal, but I'm not exactly getting rich from baking. The house is paid off—maybe I could get a loan." I sagged. "But that would take a while." I looked at the date. "The retreat is in two weeks."

"You could go to Vista Del Mar," she said, referring to the hotel and conference center where the retreat was being held. "And Cadbury by the Sea Yarn and Supplies, and see if they would return the money."

"What am I going to say? 'Sorry, folks, for the last-minute notice but I didn't follow through with things, which my mother will be happy to tell you is my habit.'" I rocked my head with dismay. I barely knew Kevin St. John, who ran Vista Del Mar, or the mother and daughter who owned the yarn store. How could I ask them to refund the money? "There has to be another option."

"Well, you could go ahead with the retreat. Everything is paid for and arranged. All you would have to do is take your aunt's place."

"I have no idea what these retreats are. I know zero about yarn things except for what you've just told me. I don't think knowing that *skein* is really a meaningless term is enough. Joan was a master at arranging things, taking care of problems. I'm afraid my expertise is in making them—problems, that is."

Lucinda extracted one of the invoices from the file and waved the yellow sheet in front of me. "Joan hired a master teacher. Her name is Kris Garland, and your aunt raved about her. You don't have to know anything. You would just have to greet everybody and hang around for the weekend. I'd be there to help you. And Vista Del Mar is right across the street from here." She pointed to the wall of trees outside the window. When I still hesitated, Lucinda brought up the obvious. "You don't really have a choice, do you?"

I took the fabric box to the guesthouse, promising to think about putting on the retreat, before walking Lucinda back to her car. I held the flashlight as she pulled out her keys.

A red Ford 150 pickup truck slowed as it neared us and stopped next to Lucinda's white Lexus. I knew the color and make even in the dark because I knew who it belonged to. The driver's window opened and a man stuck his head out. I shined my flashlight in his face and he squinted in response.

"Hey, anything wrong?" he asked.

"No, everything is just fine," I said in a curt voice.

"Just being neighborly," he said with a smile. "I'm just down the street if you need a cup of sugar." Lucinda stared at him for a moment. I knew she was trying to process who he was. She was used to seeing him in uniform and driving a police car.

"The Cadbury police officer," she said with a friendly smile, and he nodded.

"Well, somebody's glad to see me. Night, ladies," he said and pulled his head back inside before driving off.

"I think he likes you," Lucinda said.

I threw my arms up in a hopeless manner. "I don't think he even knows my name. Not that I care anyway. Do you have any idea what goes on at his house?" Ahead we watched his taillights disappear as he pulled into a driveway. "It seems like every night there's a bunch of cars parked outside. There's loud music that seems to be coming from the garage. He never parks in it and I think it's some kind of party room. I know they say cops have to blow off steam, but he's ridiculous. Well, he can just party hardy without me."

I waited until Lucinda left, then I locked up and went back to the restaurant to finish my baking. By the time I took out the last batch of carrot muffins, I had made my decision. Lucinda was right. I had no choice but to go ahead with the retreat. She had promised to be my wingman. What could go wrong?